# ENOUGH ROPE

C STREET MYSTERY
BOOK 2

## RICK ROTHERMEL

ROUGH
EDGES
PRESS

**Enough Rope**
Paperback Edition
Copyright © 2023 Rick Rothermel

Rough Edges Press
An Imprint of Wolfpack Publishing
9850 S. Maryland Parkway, Suite A-5 #323
Las Vegas, Nevada 89183

roughedgespress.com

Paperback ISBN 978-1-68549-233-5
eBook ISBN 978-1-68549-232-8
LCCN 2023939900

*This book is dedicated to the memory of Author Robert B. Parker.*
*Spenser led me to Street.*

# ENOUGH ROPE

ENOUGH ROPE

# PROLOGUE

*August 30, 2010*

A low-slung pearl blue 1969 Pontiac GTO coasted to a stop in the median of northbound Sunset Boulevard, the turn signal winking as opposing traffic passed. When the traffic cleared, the driver continued onto the uphill side street. Inside the car, Sarah Tolliver, a black woman in her mid-thirties, looked across toward the driver.

"So, Street, just admit it. I kicked your butt! Mister *I majored in pool in college* just got his ass handed to him!"

Street responded, "Okay, you beat me. Three straight games. That never happens! I do need some practice", he looked over at her, "or maybe just a less vindictive opponent." He smiled. "Which street is yours? I came in the other way."

She pointed. "Third left, second house on the right. Home sweet home, thirteen years."

"I like this area of Hollywood. It has some class but less pretense than farther north. Is this the street? Blakely?"

She nodded. "That's the one."

The driver turned the corner and stopped in front of the modest frame house. Street looked at Sarah. "So even though you brutally pummeled me, I had a great time. What shift are you working this week?"

"I start nights tomorrow. Come in and do a ride-along one night this week, so you can remember what you gave up."

"It's been five years since my last day on duty in Jersey. I don't miss it at all. Once in a while, I do like to sit in the passenger's seat, though."

"Well, call me, and I'll set it up. Have a good night!"

"I will. You, too." Street slipped the car into gear as Sarah exited and walked the short stone walkway to her front door. When he saw lights from the inside of the house, he drove away, passing a few cars parked at the curb.

Five minutes later, as he left a 7-11 on Sunset Boulevard, his cell phone rang. He looked at the screen and smiled as he tapped the screen and spoke to the phone. "Sarah! Let me guess. You grabbed my jacket instead of yours?"

"You did indeed!"

"I need that for a meeting tomorrow night. Mind if I swing back by and snag it?"

"No sweat. I have to take the trash barrel to the street for tomorrow morning. I'll bring the jacket with me."

"Done. I'll see you in three."

Street drove from the 7-11 parking lot and made his way back to the side street leading back to Sarah's house. As he made the turn onto the uphill side street off Sunset, he had to brake to avoid a dark-colored late-model Chrysler 300 with tall custom rims as it slid tail-wide across his path. Regaining his route, he drove the short uphill street to the proper turn and flipped to his high-beams to illuminate the dimly lit tree-lined residential street.

Past the first house, he spied an odd scene. The green trash barrel lay on its side next to the fence at the front of the property, debris scattered onto the street from the open container. Past the barrel lay a startling scene. He set the e-brake on the GTO, flipped the switch for the fog lights, and sprang from the car, phone in hand. "Sarah!" he called as he ran to the prone body. He knelt beside her and assessed her condition as he tapped the screen of the phone. He took his red satin jacket from under the trash container and used it to apply pressure to her most visible wounds.

As he worked, he listened to the phone's speaker. Momentarily the operator's deep male voice announced, "Los Angeles 9-1-1. What is your emergency?"

"Operator! My name is Street. I am a licensed private investigator. I am in front of the house at 2212 Blakely in East Hollywood. I have a gunshot victim, a thirty-five-year-old black female. Looks like two wounds, lower left abdomen and lower extremities. Victim is conscious. Need a heavy bus at this location ASAP! Also need an LAPD shooting team and a Gang Task Force Supervisor! Victim is an LAPD Gang Task Force officer! Advise the responders to enter from the north."

"Very well, Mister Street. Stay on the line with me. Help is on its way."

Within seconds he heard multiple approaching sirens in the distance. "I'm applying pressure, feels like a shotgun wound, mid-calf. It's a big one. Second wound, left lower quadrant abdomen, smaller caliber, maybe handgun, through and through."

"You're doing fine, Mister Street. Thank you. Keep the pressure on the wound. Do you see any other wounds?"

"Negative. Worst of the two is the lower calf. The left knee and femur above it are practically powder."

"I hear you, Mister Street. Keep the pressure directly on the wound. Your help should be there in seconds."

"They just turned onto the street. Thanks for the assist."

———

Two hours later, the big trucks had departed, and the Crown Vics of the LAPD detective bureau and the van filled with Crime Scene techs had taken their place. As the questioning continued, the lead officer, Captain Adam Fair, Sarah's immediate supervisor, was equally friendly and concerned. "She's lucky you were here, Street.

We appreciate your help. Good descriptions. Were you ever on the job?" The took his red jacket from under the

"Five years, Atlantic City P.D. I left five years ago, came out here, and turned private ticket. I gave you my card; if there's any help I can give, just let me know. Sarah's a good friend."

"To you and to us, too, Street. She's a good cop. Thanks for your help." He turned to walk to his car.

A second officer disconnected his phone and told the others, "That was the escort officer. Sarah's at that new hospital in Westwood. They have a world-class trauma unit there." He turned to Street. "We're going out if you want to follow."

"I'll get out there later." He gestured at his bloodstained khakis and shirt. The jacket he'd returned for had been disposed of earlier into the now-uprighted trash barrel. "I need to change clothes and get a shower. Captain Fair has my number. Please keep me posted as you can."

# 1

*October 10, 2010—Los Angeles, California*

It had been a slow few weeks since the end of my previous involvement, the resolution of the long-unsolved double murders of Ron and Annie Connors. I had spent days doing paperwork, wrapping up the multi-state, many-jurisdictional procedural clot that came from said resolution. After that one ended, loose ends had to be tied up, some legally and some out of pure caution since I had skirted a local or state law or six in my pursuit of the culprits. There were bureaucrats to be consulted, legalities to be determined, reports to be filed, and in a couple of cases, excuses to be dreamed up. All part of the gig.

I hate doing paperwork, but every so often, bureaucracy raises its ugly, hair-plugged, chemically-colored head. Permit renewals and licensing fees come up with an end-of-quarter due date and a fifteen-day grace period, and that year I'd let everything slide longer than usual. Car registration renewals and updates time out. In California, the procedures for all that are practically a religion—a lucrative one—for the ever-bloated rosters of state and municipal employees. Finally, that Tuesday, I had accumulated an all-inclusive stack of mail and, simultaneously, the time to dispense with it all. I opened each in succession, checking for pesky errors and unattractive pictures. The driver's license had come first. Name, C. A. Street. Age, 35, birthdate July 6, every year. Weight, 190 (or so); height, 6' 2"; eyes, blue; Hair still light brown, though I knew I would need a Just for Men I.V. feed within the coming decade. The *dashing and heroic* part was apparently lost in the editing process. So far so good.

My PI license was next, a pricey devil, but everything looked okay on it. It fit in the frame on the wall of my combined den/office at my home, as had the five that preceded it. I'd bought the place shortly after I arrived in L.A. in mid-2005. I had money then, winnings from a weekend vacation binge that I'd taken with my then-fiancée. I had started that *off* weekend in Atlantic City employed, engaged and soon to be married, and set for a predictable future. I'd left A.C. a few weeks later, single and jobless with the remnants of two million bucks, the *net* fruits of a freakish serial-jackpot-win at a city-wide weekend Casino slot tourney. The winnings and the ensuing events indirectly cost me my job as a cop and eventually my fiancée. I came away with a nifty cross-country trip in my old GTO, traveling to a new life I'd only imagined, in the place I'd dreamed of since I was a kid.

I inserted the new license into its frame and hung it behind my desk, level with the other frame holding the pricey diploma for my Masters degree in Criminology from that big school in Jersey. I'd completed my Masters at night school while I was a cop. That all seemed so far away now, and not just in miles.

I tossed the eleven chunks of junk mail, including a homemakers' magazine I didn't remember subscribing to, then got to the property tax bill. Yikes! The State of California really tries to lay away people who own stuff. My carefully-manicured corner lot with the 56-year-old, remodeled 3300 square foot brick ranch and the separate garage/apartment at the rear edge of the property garnered me a mid-four figure bill due annually. What the hell, I was grateful I had the resources. I wrote another check, along with my quarterly franchise tax payment, lessened somewhat by some careful money management in Nevada, where financial concerns are a bit less panicky and the state personal income tax rate is *zero*. I dearly love California, especially the scenery and the weather, but it can be really irritating and intensely expensive to live here.

Last step, registration renewal for my GTO. All the boxes held the right info—1969, Pontiac, color blue, license STREETC because some of my TV heroes from my kid-hood had cool cars and unique personalized plates. What the paperwork didn't mention was that this was the same car that my dad had owned when he was in college, and the same one that carried me home from the hospital after I was born. My folks had forsaken it for a minivan when I was two, then over two decades later, when I was a cop in A.C., I had found the stripped and gutted body behind a barn after a chop shop raid. I'd bought those same bones at the forfeiture auction a little later and put the car back on the road myself to use as a daily driver. After I moved to L.A., I had it rebuilt at immense expense by a renowned hot rod shop down in Orange County. There wasn't room for the whole story on the reg form.

A couple of car magazines had arrived as well, and I tossed them over the back of my recliner for study later.

With the two hours of funds extraction complete, I went to the garage to get my car for the trip to the hospital to visit Sarah. It had been a rough go for her. My go-to for billiards competition, my athletic onyx-skinned friend had suffered greatly from the attack that evening. After a week, she had finally lost her right leg, above the knee. Six long, complex surgeries completed, she was now due for release from her torturous five-week ordeal.

I was to play a part in her continued care, utilizing a plan brought to fruition with the help of her LAPD Gang Unit supervisor. Captain Adam Fair and I had gotten to know one another fairly well during Sarah's hospitalization, and I respected him more than I did some in his charge. He greeted me as the elevator door opened to the hospital's fifth floor.

The atmosphere in the wide hallway was *restful*, with muted colors and modern upscale appointments, typical for this part of west L.A. Adam Fair walked toward me, all six foot six of him, and I guessed this was his day off because his usual crisp uniform had been supplanted by khakis, white leather running shoes, and a bright red polo shirt. We shook hands and walked toward Sarah's room, fifty feet down the hall to the left.

Fair motioned toward a couch in an offset from the hallway and said, "Let's give them a few minutes. The nurse is in with her."

"What's the latest?" I asked as we sank into the grey suede-covered overstuffed sofa.

Quietly he explained, "Street, our *outside* team says there's still a contract out on Sarah. It's been confirmed. They obviously knew where she lived, and they seem to know that she survived the attack. We are trying to get a thread, but it seems like it's a combo deal, a street gang protecting their meth trafficking system. We're also hearing rumors of a static operation from somewhere in the valley. We have intel developing there. Sheriff's department in San Berdoo is going strong chasing a similar operation out there. What we need right now is time. Absolute secrecy as to her whereabouts for maybe six to eight weeks would be of value. She'll be doing rehab after she's out of here, and the final adjustments to her prosthetic start as of the day after tomorrow. Are you still open to what we talked about last weekend?"

"Tell me what you need, Adam. My place is hers as long as she needs it. I have security measures, and I can set up a comms system that is as good as what you guys use."

"Well, we'll reimburse you for whatever costs you incur on a per diem basis, and with your centralized residence location, we can have bodies on site at a moment's notice any time it's needed."

"I appreciate that. I am still working on another matter, and I have a Vegas trip coming up. I'll be working there for the next three days. How about we set up a private comm system, just you, Sarah, and myself? I want as few heads as possible involved in this. Maybe a set of three dedicated burner phones? I can pick some up from my gadget guy this afternoon, and you can get one of them when you drop her off. When will that happen?"

"I'll bring her in my own van at, let's say, eight tonight. We don't know what resources the contract holders have at hand, so let's keep 'em guessing. It's just me and you." He took his cell from his jacket pocket and tapped the face until a picture of a late-model Dodge high-top van became visible. I looked at it and smiled.

"Looks good! How many kids?"

"Five. Two each from my wife and me and one we share. Two-and-a-half to thirteen years. It's just a private riot every day." He opened the phone to another picture of a smiling light-skinned black family.

"And you love every minute."

He smiled. "Yeah, Street, I do. If anything, it makes my work more relatable. I get more madness at home than from the street gangs some days. Each one keeps me on my toes for the other. I was an only child, and my dad was LAPD, killed in action in '68. I followed in his footsteps, hung with it, and I have the career he should've had. I think he'd be proud."

I was impressed. "I'm sure he would be. Second-gen LAPD?"

He lifted his brow. "Third, actually. My grandfather was a traffic officer in south central, died of a heart attack at age 36. Dad followed him, killed in the line of duty. I follow in the footfalls of both of them."

"And you oversee anti-gang efforts city-wide? I'm impressed."

He grinned thinly. "Thank you. It's been a long road. I put a lot into it over the years. Did nothing other than cop stuff for eighteen years. I finally married one of our dispatchers. We didn't start a family 'til I was almost 40."

I offered, "Sarah speaks very highly of you. I can tell you're really devoted to your career. You are the embodiment of the LAPD I imagined when I was a kid. Sarah is exceptional as well."

He commented quietly, "Thanks. Sarah is good people. She brings a lot to the table. I have to tell you that the Policy Board is reviewing her status for a decision in a few weeks, and I fully expect they will pension her out. Bureaucrats love kicking officers off the job. There's a chance she'd get full salary at her current rank. She's a fighter, but that leg of hers is past tense, and it's going to take months for her to get well from the attack and to get used to the prosthetic."

"Okay, I'll keep that in mind. My place is her place for as long as she needs it. You guys catch the villains here and make us all proud."

"Thanks for that, Street. We owe you." He offered a fist-bump as we looked toward the most recent movement in the hallway. "There's the nurse. Let's see how she's doing." We rose from the sofa and walked toward Sarah's room.

I spent the rest of the afternoon and early evening running errands and waiting in traffic on the various freeways around Hollywood before hitting a series of surface streets, landing at home an hour before the appointed meeting time. It was a warm, cloudless afternoon in L.A. (when isn't it?), and the sun was merging slowly toward the western horizon as I arrived home.

As agreed, the light beige high-top Dodge van approached my driveway at 7:56 that evening. After the hospital, I had gone to visit my pal Zig for the synched phones we needed, then to downtown Burbank shopping to get new bed linens for my guest bedroom— down the hallway past the living room, third door on the left, with its own bath suite that I'd designed myself during the remodel. Sarah looked tired and had lost a few pounds, as I had expected. Adam delivered her to my back door, picked up his phone, thanked me, and rushed home.

I had sent out for some food that evening from the more dependable of the area delis, so the table next to the kitchen island offered a variety of eats, all quite good. The aroma alone made it an easy sell. "Nice place, Street," she commented as she re-entered the den/office combo on her crutches after I had shown her my *turf*. She stood beside the lounge chair, turned, and looked at me. "Here's the deal. Do not try to *walk* me. Do not try to help me get around. I am not helpless. I am still royally pissed about this shit.

I'll get back to form in a little while. Give me time, and give me space!"

"Are you done?" I asked after she finished. "Here's what I'll do. I'll help you if you ask for it, and I'll stay out of your way. You help me with meals, try not to leave a bigger debris field than I do, and we'll get along fine. I'll do the same. This isn't a pity party. I don't work that way, I never have, and I never will, but I am here to help if you need me. You cool with that?"

Sarah closed her eyes as she nodded. She stood next to the overstuffed chair and exhaled. "Yeah. Sorry if I laid it on too thick." She looked around the room. "Can we start over?"

"Sure." I stood up and shook her hand. "Welcome to my home. I feel a little responsible for you. This is your space for as long as you need it. You can help me with my work if you feel like it, and we'll keep an eye out for one another. Your rehab team can work with you here as well. I'll clue you in on the security system in the morning. Make yourself at home. Can I fix you a sandwich and some of that deli chicken soup? It is epic!"

"Street, that sounds great. I am absolutely beat from the drill they put me through with that damn leg this afternoon. Hurts like a bitch, and I have *nerve memory* of my real leg and foot that makes every move pure hell. You know how I hate pain meds, but I am gonna do some tonight so I can sleep for the first night in the last week." She looked around the combined kitchen/den. "This place is nice and quiet and totally unlike the hospital." She walked to the table, opened the soup container, and poured some of it into a different bowl after she crushed some oyster crackers into the bottom of the bowl. She looked across the table and snagged a set of silverware. "You got one of those Sam Adams with my name on it?"

As I stacked paper-thin Black Forest ham onto the Provolone-topped old-fashioned rye for my own sandwich, added the baby Swiss cheese, the garlic dill pickles, and brown mustard, I said, "Sure. I'll get you a glass. Get a chair in the den, and I'll bring it in to you." I assembled my sandwich on a square plate, grabbed it from the table, and snagged a pair of beers from the door shelf of the fridge. I joined her in the den. She ate quickly and retired within a half-hour.

I stayed up late that night and fired up the DVD for one of the best TV detective series ever, the fifth season of Mannix. That put it at 1971-72, starting almost a half-decade prior to my own birth. Re-runs of the series and others on indie stations on cable in Jersey and New York had influenced my earliest fondness of law enforcement and the snoop business and, in my adult years, I had become a collector of the better of the old shows on DVD. Mannix was and had always been my favorite. I loved the old L.A. vibe, the cars were cool though he let them get too beat up, and most of the stories were bearable. I knew early on though, that the boy needed some serious security upgrades—definitely locks for his car hood, better security for his condo, and a little better judgment when selecting his clients. I made it a point to watch, learn, and apply the education.

Since my big payday, I'd made some material improvements at my house. Early in Sarah's second day in residence, one of the last phases arrived. I had a two-story garage and apartment structure in the rear corner of the lot on which my house sat. Think of the place the Fonz lived. In my five years there, I had slowly re-modeled the fifty-year-old structure, and the last project had been the new concrete surface for the high-ceilinged three-stall garage. Today the new four-post garage lift had arrived in big, heavy wooden crates.

The remodeling contractor arrived and drilled holes in the fresh concrete floor for the guide bolts, then a forklift guided the corner posts into place. With the verticals bolted down and squared, the horizontal beams were added, then, finally, the lift arms attached themselves to the tracks. An electrician joined the party an hour later, hooking up the 220-volt power source. After the techs were paid, I lowered the rack and drove my beloved '69 Pontiac GTO onto the tracks. After I put the car cover on the Goat, I stood beside the rack and hit the switch. The car raised six feet with a variety of hums and metallic *clunks*. Cool! That put the car, which had first been a part of my life when I was two days old, into a secure, out-of-the-way storage place. An hour later, my friend Zig drove my newest acquisition into the driveway.

I had made an impulse buy a week before...a new 2011 Mustang GT coupe. A six-speed, five-liter, metallic burgundy number that spoke to me when I saw it being offloaded from the convoy truck as I waited at a traffic light on Lankershim in North Hollywood. The GTO, my dad's college car when new, the car that I'd had rebuilt at great expense, had started collecting rock chips and scratches in daily use since I got rid of my old TrailBlazer, so I'd convinced myself that a substitute would make sense. Zig had commandeered the 'Stang for two days, installing a small gun vault in the corner of the trunk, advisable for travel through firearms-restricted areas. He'd had the windows tinted and upgraded the factory lighting and sound system as well. After that, he'd broomed the emblems from the exterior and had it compounded and buffed to within an inch of its life. I can't leave my cars alone.

Zig rolled into my driveway after the sun went down that evening. It looked *handsome*, all lit up as it idled in the driveway. I took the driver's seat, and Zig took shotgun for the return trip to his shop in the western section of Burbank. We talked about many things as we traveled through the Hollywood Hills on Cahuenga Boulevard on as many surface streets as possible. "Cool little car, Street! You gonna miss the GTO?"

"I'm not getting rid of it, Zig, just getting it off the road for a year or so. I don't want it to get beat up, and I also don't want to become recognizable for only one car, especially a unique one that can make me a target. That one makes me very easy to spot. I may even change the color next time."

"Sounds like fun, almost. How's Sarah doing?"

"She's doing well. The *fake leg*, as she calls it, is still a struggle for her, and I know she'll be glad to be mobile again. Sitting does not suit that woman."

"How are you and the hottie doing?"

I smiled. "Dierdre? She, too, is great. We're in the growth stage of whatever it turns out we have started. She's the best I've found in a few years. I want it to work this time. She's a keeper, and I hope she feels the same way about me."

"Street, you get a smile on your face every time you talk about her. First time since I've known you that you've been visually happy! You're an intense cat—you and I both know that. That won't ever change. This woman makes you happy, you hang onto her, whatever it takes, y'hear?" There was more. "Course, she's fun to look at, too!"

I smiled as he took the father stance with me. "Gotcha, Pop!" I had not been close to my own overworked dad, and Zig's U.S. Marine son had lost his life in Iraq almost a decade before, so this did both of us good. I let him out at the rear door of his store on Magnolia Boulevard in Burbank after we thanked one another and shook hands. Friends are good.

————

The next morning, I sat at my office desk at 9:45 doing some accounting and billing when the phone rang. The caller I.D. showed a Riverside number of friend and operative Catherine Gadsden. "Lady lawyer! How are you?"

"Doing well, Street. How's business?"

"Getting by. I'm still wrapping up the last of the Connors stuff and looking at new gigs. You?"

"Divorce crap. I hate it! People need to learn how to get along, y'know? But listen; I did hear from my pal in Carson City, the one in the Nevada Secretary of State's office. Remember her? She had some interesting news."

"You're dying to tell me. I can hear it in your voice."

Catherine sounded enthused. "You know me well. Get this: one of Grant Carty's corporations is back up and running. About two months ago, it opened a subsidiary based in an office in Studio City, purposed with doing property redevelopment. I know you said he's in a rest home or whatever it is in Las Vegas, and Vinnie Bongelli's sequestered in the care of the FBI, so it's not either of them doing the filing. Name on the paper is an attorney's office near Vineland and Ventura in the valley. Maps show a small building on a busy corner. I tried their number, talked to a clerk and a receptionist, got nowhere."

"Interesting," I said. "Who's the resident agent?"

"New name. Female, and I've never heard of the firm."

"Ah. Send me the info. I'll go to Studio City and check it out."

"I knew you would. Keep me posted."

**2**

*A month earlier...*

Trey Thomas, a slim twenty-year-old kid with long black hair and dark eyes, walked past his mom's office in the Studio City condo that they shared, and she called to him.

"Trey! Come here for a second."

"Yeah, Mom, what's up?

"You are to leave that Chrysler where it is for a while. Nobody drives it till I say so."

"What's wrong, Mom?"

Trey knew that his mom was a force not to be trifled with. The sturdy thirty-seven-year-old single mom had raised him after she had become pregnant in her junior year in high school, courtesy of one Grant Carty. She was now an attorney in their new hometown of Studio City after they had left Riverside and her ex-husband just a few months before. Roberta Thomas-Schwinn did not mince words when she was *ticked*.

"What's wrong is that the inside of that car smells like the inside of a bong. My eyes watered when I walked past it, and all its windows were closed! If you're in a fender-bender or stopped at a

DUI and license check, they'll bust your skinny ass and take you to jail, no questions asked. Just leave it where it is. And you find a detailer to come in, clean it up, and deodorize it, too. Your mess, your money. Give me your keys!"

Trey's speech impediment only showed up when he was stressed. "M-ma, don't do that! I'll be c-careful with it. I have never once been p-pulled over in that car!"

Using her *mom* voice, she laid down the law. "Yes, son, and that's how it will stay for a few weeks. There is a BOLO from the LAPD giving the description for a similar car wanted in a police officer shooting a couple of weeks ago. I know that's not you, but it's close enough to accurate to justify an automatic street contact by LAPD. That would create an issue. It stays parked for now. Got it?"

Trey exhaled heavily, abandoning the discussion. "Yeah, ma. It s-stays parked."

"You can use my car if it's really something important. Joyriding and smoking your body weight in pot does not qualify. I have some work for you as well, so just chill." She looked straight at him and put her hand out. "Keys!"

Trey grudgingly dug into his left-front pocket, bringing the key fob with him. "You want me to clean it up myself? I'm not d-doing much this week."

She took the key fob and smiled a cautionary face. "Mmmm, no. Just get a pro to come do it right. You're going to be busy this week."

———

After Catherine and I disconnected, I opened the double doors to the patio. I didn't recognize the blue Chevy Colorado pickup in the rear driveway. I walked to the patio and saw Sarah off to one side under the pergola canopy toiling away with her physical therapist. Sarah was working hard enough that sweat was pouring off her face and had soaked her warm-up suit, but she seemed to have good balance as she clomped along on the portable treadmill the PT tech had brought.

Surveying the scene, I walked back into the kitchen and snagged an eight-pack of bottled water from the door shelf of the fridge. I put it in a round Pyrex tub, dumped a couple of trays of ice cubes into the tub, and took it to the redwood table on the patio. As I opened the door, both Sarah and the PT guy looked over at me.

I walked out and put the tub on the patio table. "Hi! I'm Street. Thanks for taking care of this one. Thought you might like a little hydration." Sarah looked at the water bottles with genuine lust.

The PT tech extended his hand, and we shook. "Carl Waddley, Mister Street. Glad to put a face to a name. Sarah has mentioned you several times." He motioned toward the water. "One of those have my name on it?" I nodded and watched as Waddley snagged one of the waters. He was a large unit indeed, six-feet five-inches tall, Caucasian, well-tanned, maybe 245 pounds, and almost solid muscle. His sizable biceps showed a USMC insignia. His head was shaved, but his thick eyebrows and his salt-and-pepper beard made up for the dearth of hair atop his head. He moved with the physical clarity of a lifelong athlete.

"Absolutely! Help yourself." I looked at Sarah, who had toweled off and had taken a seat on one of the wide patio chairs. She twisted the cap off her water bottle and took a long sip. She looked tired; understandable since this was the end of her two-hour workout. She looked up at me and smiled.

I asked, "So who's winning, Sarah, you or the treadmill?"

Sarah said, "Street, I think I'm coming up third. The treadmill, the sun, and then me."

"There's a nearly-empty three-car garage about fifty feet away. Why don't you set up there? It has AC and a shower. I can arrange whatever else you need to get the job done. Take a peek at it. If it makes the cut, fine. If not, make me a list, tell me what you need." I looked at both of them as Sarah looked at Carl.

Carl spoke first. "Let's see what you have, Street." We walked toward the rear of the property, and I opened the front door. The garage was a high-ceiling three-car unit beside a one-bedroom *Fonzie apartment* above the workshop that opened into the garage space. I kept my Craftsman tool chest and a few shop tools that I never had time to use next to the walls and cabinets in the space, but the rest was empty. The other half of the garage space was occupied by car-guy garage stuff—a Craftsman rolling toolbox, a compressor, a generator, and the shiny new four-post lift with full-length tracks. My GTO was perched covered above the new Mustang, itself a handsome thing, in the stacked space. My black Tahoe was parked outside, baking in the sun.

Sarah looked at the surroundings as Carl asked about the floor strength. Under the fresh engine-turned vinyl tile surface lay a half-century-old, eight-inch thick concrete slab, so strength was not an issue. Carl spoke up first. "I think this will work out great! I can have it arranged by tomorrow morning. Sarah? Fewer sweat stains on the spandex?" Sarah gave a tired smile in return.

I was happy to hear that the new, marginally-protected turf would pass muster. Working out on the patio had potential health issues from sun exposure. Though I love it, the L.A. sun is an authentic bitch. Also, while the L.A. atmosphere was far cleaner than it used to be, the city still had its *bad air days* during the stiff Santa Ana winds or the stagnant air inversions that somehow always seemed to accompany the seasonal wildfires. I also wanted her sheltered most of the time because, as her boss had mentioned, there was a contract out for her murder. She and I had agreed that she would stay armed or would be within easy reach of a weapon at all times. We knew she was safer here, but she was also a far more skilled shooter than I was, so I was fairly confident of her safety while she was in residence.

After a short hour with Sarah and Carl, I returned to the house to wrap up an hour of office work before I left for a lunch date with my emerging lady love, the fair Dierdre King. I opened the computer and its Gmail file to find Catherine Gadsden's send describing the newly energized corporate entity she had mentioned. I printed the page, looked at it, then I folded it and put it in my briefcase to deal with later.

Lunch with Dierdre King was always an adventure. She and I had been an item for a couple of months, and there was considerable progress being made for each of us. We had first met when I was in the middle of the Connors' matter. Her father, a private investigator like me, had been murdered by Carty eight years prior with no solution in all that time. She had lost both parents within a few months and had worked her way through college from that point on, concluding with a great job with the news division of a television network based in deepest Hollywood. We had done a fast start a week after I had wrapped the Connors matter, and each of us seemed blissed out. It didn't hurt at all that she was just about perfect in my eyes and receptive to my attentions. She said I was kinda cool, too.

Dierdre was a student of Hollywood, almost as much as I was a student of old TV cop shows and detective series. She was also the one and only female of interest in my history who didn't take that hobby of mine as a sign of potential mental illness. She had actually sat one evening the previous week and watched two hours of the classic Harry O series from the mid-70s, coming away with a distinct fondness for David Janssen. In my amazement, I had gifted her with a DVD set for his Fugitive series from the sixties. She'd loved it.

She was also a *car guy* like me, though her preference ran to newer iron. She had decided on a new Dodge Challenger SRT8 a few weeks earlier, and it was set to be delivered by the next Saturday morning. It would be her first new car, and she was anxious for its arrival. It would replace the tired Mazda 3 she'd driven since college.

Dierdre met me at Huston's, a tiny hole-in-the-wall barbecue spot on Cahuenga, a half-block south of Hollywood Boulevard, just down the block from the best sidewalk newsstand in town. We sat at the distinctly down-market formica table and ate simple but tasty fare, and she talked. That was usually how it went with us. She was excited about her new acquisition.

I chimed in, "Okay, it sounds great. Were you able to get the color you wanted?"

"Didn't I tell you? Plum Crazy purple! It's the only six-speed 2011 model in the L.A. Zone so far. They're doing a dealer trade for it. Anyway, what I need to ask you is, can I bring it to your house on Saturday? I want to detail it...my way...like I did when I was in school. Clay bar, sealer, wax, glaze, the whole course! You want to help me with it? We could make it a weekend."

A weekend with Dierdre King is not something I would ever pass up. "Of course! Sounds like fun. I'm always doing that stuff to the Goat, and the Mustang could use it as well. It'll have a layer of I-15 grime all over it any day now."

"Is Sarah still at your place?"

"She is, but her PT keeps her wiped out. She'll be in bed by nine every night. She says 'hi', by the way. She likes you a lot. How's your food?"

"Excellent, as usual. You know all the cool little spots! I'm taking notes. And I'll have you know, I turned down an executive staff lunch at Musso & Frank's to have lunch with you here today."

"Well, geez, D-girl, that's not much of a sacrifice, is it? I mean, c'mon, what does Musso & Frank's have that Huston's doesn't? Besides a wine list, inch-thick sirloins cooked to perfection, garlic-butter basted baked potatoes, broccoli au gratin, white linen table-cloths, candles, waiters slavishly awaiting your every whim, and fresh warm German Chocolate cake for dessert?"

She reached across the table, touched my hand, and said, "You."

I looked at her and smiled. "Ooooh! Good answer."

"I have to get on your good side. You introduced me to David Janssen and all, so I owe you." She smiled her sly smile.

"You and ol' Dave getting along pretty well, huh?"

"I think he's hot. In a subtle, sensitive way."

"He was that. Y'know, according to Hollywood lore, his major flame for a while in the sixties was Suzanne Pleshette. She was in some early Fugitive episodes. And a young Suzanne Pleshette was a major babe, much like yourself." Conspiratorially, I lowered my voice, "I even heard that when the Fugitive producers gave him a new motor home to use as his dressing room on location shoots, she was part of the presentation. Inside the motor home. Au naturale."

"Interesting. I would've done that, no problem."

"You would?"

"Oh, I would. In a heartbeat." Her faint mischievous smile and lifted right eyebrow hinted at her sense of humor, worthy of a response.

I cleared my throat and spoke softly. "Well, tell you what. When you come to the house Saturday, bring the DVD set. Wow...I may have to dye my hair jet black and start practicing my facial tic. And maybe get a motor home." I flexed my cheeks for her. She smiled. That was always a good thing.

We wrapped our lunch and walked back to the sidewalk newsstand nearer to Hollywood Boulevard on the east side of Cahuenga. Faced with hundreds of covers and titles, Dierdre shopped carefully, thumbed through a few, and finally dropped a twenty on a couple of east coast showbiz trade papers and a pair of women's magazines. I picked up a copy of Hemmings, an Auto Trader, a Pontiac title that I had missed, and a new Sue Grafton paperback. We held hands as I walked her to her car, parked back down Cahuenga. She kissed me goodbye, and I left, anxious for the weekend.

# 3

*August 28, 2010—Las Vegas, Nevada*

By the start of Carty's fifth week at Casa Arroyo Convalescent Center, he had regained much of the mental strength that he had lost during his five-year cold storage at the secluded house in the stark Nevada desert. Television had helped a little with that, as did a controlled diet, massage therapy for his numbed limbs, and massive loads of vitamins. Carty had never been a news junkie and, in his narcotized haze, had avoided media for a half-decade before his injury. Now he found current local and national events marginally interesting. Some black dude was president? Cool.

His facial features hadn't changed at all. His extensive burn tissue was a big issue. For all intents, the left half of his face and much of the front surface of his body had been severely burned in the meth lab explosion that had very nearly killed him. The resulting scar tissue was now dark reddish-brown and rough-textured. The consulting cosmetic surgeon at the facility had told him a few days ago that with new technologies, his features could be corrected to his wishes within a three-year period, probably

including a half-dozen or more surgeries with plenty of recupera-
tion time between sessions. Carty was encouraged by that, but he
knew that *his way* would take nowhere near as long. Now he spent
some time concentrating on his plans, post-departure.

Before he could take his leave, though, he had to be able to
walk. His pain med regimen had been moderated somewhat, but
he was still mentally tethered to his bed. That had to change. He
had been using a bedpan since a week after his arrival, and he was
tired of that too. The condom catheter he'd been subjected to at the
house in the desert had been removed weeks ago, and those physical limitations were a thing of the past. Now it was time for a
challenge.

That night, a little after 8 pm, he detached his wire leads from
the adhesive pads that connected to his chest, and he waited. When
no one came running into his room, assuming his sudden demise,
he swung his feet off the side of the bed and slid off the mattress
until he could feel the cold linoleum on the bottoms of his bare
feet. He tried to wiggle his toes, rewarded by an odd tingling—
almost a burning sensation. A cramped left calf muscle was
immensely painful, quite odd in its feeling as the blood flowed into
his legs with the assistance of gravity. New, yeah, and not pleasant,
but almost welcome to him.

It took him five long minutes, resting on the edge of his bed,
sweating from the very exertion of rising and sitting upright, to
make his next move; standing upright on his own two feet. He held
on tight to the tall rolling bedside table, hoping that it wouldn't
scoot out from under him. He steadied himself again and finally
began to shuffle awkwardly a foot at a time across the six feet
between his bed and the bathroom. His legs shuddered with every
tiny step.

At some point in his prolonged shuffle-and-shake expedition,
Carty gained an unseen observer. The north wing's night attendant,
a squat Hispanic woman, Lupe Oswego, watched from the shadows
just outside Carty's open suite door, ready to help him if he stum-

bled. She tensed when he faltered and smiled thinly when he made progress.

Finally, sweaty, slouched, and tired, Carty shuffled his way around his rolling table to grab the cast aluminum handle to the bathroom door. He pulled it open, sidestepping a little late as the door swung wide across the tops of his feet. The lower edge of the heavy, metal-clad wooden door nicked skin off the top of three of his toes of his left foot as he opened it. He could feel the blood trickle down onto the floor as he walked, leaving a smeary trail of toe-shaped blood spots. The sensation was not an unwelcome one.

Finally in the bathroom, he braced himself against the tile wall with one arm, dropped his pajama bottoms down his legs, and peed into the bowl. The use of that organ from an upright position for the first time in a half-decade was an awkward sensation. Pins and needles flowed through his lower trunk, and his right knee buckled once. He moaned and cringed simultaneously to the point that he was light-headed. Dammit! He had to get over this! This stuff had to come back to him! He closed his eyes as the flow quelled, then nearly collapsed as his bowels released, a foul-smelling surge of dark semi-solids flowing down his legs, onto his feet, saturating his pajama bottoms before pooling around his feet.

He tried to clench his abdominal muscles, breathing hard, his pulse racing, again unsteady on his feet, then he turned around and plopped hard onto the seat above the bowl. The motion and the function made him dizzy and gave him a headache. He strained and released again, a huge flow in one spasm, then another that made him groan. The process left the room with a heavy medicinal odor, and Carty, bent forward at the waist, nearly passed out in its wake. As he sat, wobbly and breathing heavily, trying to concentrate, breathing deeply to avoid fainting and inhaling the stench from the floor, he had a vision of Elvis Presley expiring on his toilet while taking a dump. Whatever.

As his vision finally cleared, he looked to his right, noting the heavy grey vinyl shower curtain around the industrial-spec shower stall. He felt behind his back for the flush lever for the toilet, felt and heard its powerful action, then turned and looked past the thick drape for the first chrome lever, which started the water flowing in the shower. Soon he reached back in and twisted the lever to its limit. He felt the hot spray as it splashed over the top of the vinyl partition and saw the steam fill the small room. Finished on the bowl, he grabbed the thick metal assist bars, slowly lifted himself to standing, and shakily stepped from his pool of sludge past the tiled rim of the stall into the scalding mist of the shower.

Reveling in the sensations as he clenched the assist bars in the stall, Carty tempered the heat after a few minutes. He used the thick green liquid soap, cleaning his own body for the first time in memory. His damaged form felt like a stranger's. When a pair of *ripe* sebaceous cysts on his lower back erupted, he pressed their contents into the stream of hot water, happy to feel the sting and see the residual blood on his fingertips. He explored the scarred areas of his chest and abdomen. He knew he was thin, but he was unprepared to feel the texture of his own ribs under his skin. The sensor pads from the hospital monitors fell from his body into the water on the textured shower floor. After two minutes of standing, he sat on the fold-out seat at the rear of the shower stall and let the hot water flow over him.

After 25 minutes—he had no sense of time tonight—he grasped the assist bar on the shower wall, stood up shakily, yawned, shuddered, and hit the lever to cut the water. He reached past the shower curtain for the thick towel from the rack above the toilet, dried off in the shower, then wrapped the towel around his waist.

He opened the curtain to see that the floor in front of the bowl had been cleaned and the seat lowered. A clean set of pajamas lay on the top of the toilet tank. Enthused and smiling, he stepped out of the shower, dressed shakily, and soon shuffled back across the room to his now-freshened bed. The return trip took half the time of the original. He smiled and moaned quietly as he lay back down on the fresh, cool, crisp cotton sheets. How long had it been since he'd even taken a dump by himself, let alone a hot shower? His lower body still ached sharply from the new exertion of long-dormant organs and muscles, but he knew he would sleep soundly that night.

From the shadows in the hallway, his clandestine caretaker smiled and raised her fist in silent victory.

**4**

Before the weekend, there was work to do.

I went home, handled some mail and paperwork, checked on Sarah, and packed the Mustang for three days in Vegas. Proper break-in of new machinery is best accomplished with varying altitudes and engine speeds, so instead of the cruise-controlled, more-direct I-10/I-15 route, I drove north on the Five to State Highway 14 and east through the high desert, along the charmingly-titled but otherwise bland Pear Blossom Highway. This route usually added an hour to the trip because of local speed limits and a few extra stoplights along the way, but when I paused in Baker for my usual gas stop and fried zucchini snack, I was a bit less tense than my normal freeway route left me. The area around the freeway access in Victorville had built up heavily since my last trip through, and the slow traffic there was an annoyance. The freeways would remain my *normal* route for future Sin City journeys.

I arrived in Vegas early in the afternoon and drove the loop freeway toward the eastern part of the valley along the Boulder Highway to get to my most recent favorite lodging, the East Side Cannery. I spent most of the afternoon on the phone setting up appointments with the subjects I'd visit the next day. Those completed, I took a nap on the king-size bed, then spent some time on the laptop. I didn't have a client for this effort, so I could slouch off with considerable energy but zero guilt.

Tourists need to go to the Strip when they visit Las Vegas. Walk the walk and do the casino thing, then go see a show! Eat 'til you explode, drink a bit too much, and then pay a cab driver to sit at a day-long traffic light! Help the local economy any way you can, but then go drive the Red Rock National Monument to see some *miracles of nature*. Go see Boulder Dam to see a stunning man-made miracle, and take in the Neon Museum for a *local history* lesson. I had done all that already. I had seen a lot and learned a lot though most of my time in town had been work-related. This trip was no different. I had people to talk to, places to visit, and, as it would turn out, opinions to change.

———

For my second day in Las Vegas, I made an appointment with peripheral elements of the Grant Carty legal case. I met the one that showed up for lunch at a good barbecue place opposite the main gate of Nellis Air Force Base. Marshall Quince, a Sheriff's deputy with authority over his agency's case against Carty, seemed somewhat baffled with what he was facing. He was officious and not overly friendly. I was fine with that. We'd met in the front foyer and had been shown to a booth halfway back to the north side of the room. He took the visibility seat with a view of the front door. He'd been to the restaurant many times and had recommended it as our meeting location.

"What do you know about this guy, Street? They just plopped this case onto my desk last week. I understand this Carty cat is bad news, but I need to know what is in it for the Sheriff's department."

I looked at him. "You're kidding, right? Did you read the material I provided your office? It covered the whole ordeal. Carty is good for multiple murders right out there on that ranch, in your jurisdiction, under your purview. That same facility was a major drug transport and manufacturing site. It's all there in black and white. What else do you need?"

He stared blankly at me. "Well then, I'll make it a point to study the material. You wanna give me the short strokes?"

Bureaucracy ticks me off a lot, but I was used to the drill, so I played along. "Yeah, I guess I have to. Carty was your basic mid-level drug trafficker in SoCal since he was a kid. He was discovered, coached, and managed by a crooked attorney who had an amazing system. Carty became upwardly mobile and, by his mid-twenties, was a mid-level player in the Southern Nevada and California drug trade. He was also highly possessive of his territory. At one point, Carty and his stepbrother abducted a rich kid, a minor rival drug dealer wannabe, and dropped him out of an airplane. The kid didn't bounce. The victim's celebrity uncle hired a P.I. to find the killer. Soon the stepbrother, a slacker named Arnie Sutton, took the fall for the murder. Carty was never mentioned in the prosecution though he was the instigator and the pilot of the plane from which the kid was dropped. Sutton bought 25 to life, thanks to the defense efforts by the very same weak lawyer I mentioned earlier. The victim's uncle, a living legend in L.A. and well-known around the world for decades, testified in the murder trial, as did the PI he had retained. Their testimony resulted in a quick and easy conviction."

I took a sip of my iced tea. "The uncle and his wife were murdered in their driveway a short time later. The sole suspect in the uncle's murder was a business rival who had indeed threatened Connors with certain death. Connors' sister, mother of the dead kid and spokesperson for the solution to her brothers' murder, refused to look at anyone other than the former business partner as a suspect, but there was no direct evidence, so a slam-dunk conviction never happened. I talked to the presumed doer, and he was only hostile because he kept running his mouth. Got me so far?"

"I think so."

"Thirteen long years passed with no solution to the double murder of Ronnie Connors and his wife. Connors' sister, a very wealthy businesswoman in her own right, hired PI after PI with no result because everyone just looked at the disgruntled former business partner and nowhere else. She appeared on America's Most Wanted a whopping twenty times in thirteen years, calling each time for the arrest of just that one suspect! My attorney friend got a call from her one day, and I got the next nod. I uncovered a link between circumstantial 2nd material evidence regarding the kid dropped from the plane and the Connors' murder. I took that to the client and got the go-ahead to follow up on the whole deal. I eventually located Carty. He had been severely burned in a meth lab explosion at his ranch out in the desert sometime before. The same attorney/racketeer was in the mix the whole time, along with a few additional players. Rest assured, by the time this cat was in his position at the convalescent hospital, lots of water had flowed under the blood-soaked bridge."

"Okay."

"So Grant Carty, the guy in the bed at the sorta hospital, is responsible for maybe a dozen murders. He killed the actual shooters, the two men he hired to kill the Connors, the same double murder that he had, in fact, commissioned. There was also a kid from San Bernardino who apparently just stumbled into the drug processing facility at the ranch, and the husband of the Sutton trial prosecutor, as well as another L.A.-area P.I., a half-dozen meth lab workers who bought it in or shortly after the meth lab explosion, and at least three unidentified victims.

"The Feds, if they ever get off their butts, can share Carty with the State for dozens of counts, including numerous capital crimes. For now, the State has him. When Carty was rescued from the ranch, the State took custody of him. The ambulance took him to the big hospital in North Vegas, where he was examined. Their diagnosis was for continued care at the convalescent facility where he is now. They want your department to guarantee his safe storage until he's up and around and healthy enough for a trial."

"How long will that be?"

"You'll have to ask the doctors."

"Who's going to pay for the protection service?"

"I don't know. I would assume the Feds will pick up the tab. I understand they pay eventually. They have the crooked attorney under wraps out in Thousand Oaks, and that end is apparently making some progress."

"I don't know. This new batch in DC is in the process of getting the national credit rating dropped, so it might be a while. The new president screwed the local economy with one damn speech! This town is a fucking mess!" He paused. "How's your food?"

"The barbecue's excellent, but the slaw is a bit vinegary for my taste."

"Yeah, that isn't my favorite either. I like the potato salad better. You were a cop?"

"Yeah. Five years, Atlantic City. Won some money, pulled up stakes, and moved to L.A. You?" I took a bite of corn on the cob.

He lifted his eyebrows and smiled. "I'm Las Vegas born and raised. I've seen lots of changes, and more are overdue. And I do love being in the department here. Good duty."

"Good for you," I answered. "I have heard it's a decent place to work. How long did you work the jail?"

He smiled. "Oh, I lucked out! I got the courthouse instead. Lawyers don't throw their shit at you or spit at you as often as inmates."

"Good point. Married? Kids?" He wore no rings.

He grinned. "Divorcing, and two, a ten-year-old boy and a five-year-old girl. We split up last year, and the kids split their time between us. I'll re-marry when it gets finalized next month. My girl-friend's on the job."

"May be easier that way." I took a sip of iced tea.

"You?"

"Single and shopping. I have a prospect in the wings."

"Good luck with that."

"And to you."

The waiter arrived with new drinks and the bill. I paid. The meal dispensed with, I asked, "Shall we go see Mister Carty?"

"Sure. Follow me in your car."

———

Twenty minutes later, we were in the manager's office at the convalescent facility, a sprawling single-story processed-block affair on the western edge of the Vegas Valley. The founder and manager, Tom Leggitt, was an enthusiastic, genial gentleman in his late-60s. White hair, a bit thin, clung to the back and sides of his head. A thick fluffy ivory mustache and bushy eyebrows topped a thin face and a tall physique. He wore running shoes with his midnight blue suit trousers and a bright red logo golf shirt. He shook our hands and invited us to follow him to the south wing of his facility. Minutes later, we stopped at the appointed room, a darkened single suite that was a big improvement over Carty's former desert storage facility. I could see a pajama-clad Carty asleep in the hospital bed.

Leggitt took the clipboard from the rack outside the open door, looked at it, and spoke to us. "The patient is showing considerable improvement in the weeks he's been here. Our therapists are world-class for a facility this size. We're pleased with his progress."

I asked, "You're aware of the charges against him, correct? All the murders, the drug manufacturing and trafficking, the kidnappings he's responsible for? He's a dangerous guy."

Adamant, Leggitt responded, "That remains to be seen, Mister Street. The formal charges have neither been officially established nor filed."

"True enough, but we do know what he did. For the safety of your staff and the general public, he needs to be restrained."

"Handcuffs? Restraints? Never in my facility, sir. The young man who brought him here said the same thing. We will not acquiesce to that at this time. Bring me formal charges, then we can talk." A short, plump Latino duty nurse walked between us as the manager spoke.

I looked at Deputy Quince for support, but there was none. He shrugged and said, "Our department has no prison hospital life support facilities, Street. This is as close as we can come, and the management here calls the shots here.'

I looked back at the facility manager. "Then it's on you, Mister Leggitt, if he escapes. His escape would create some real trouble. You might end up with some serious legal liabilities as well. Are you ready for that?"

Leggitt scoffed. "Come now, Mr. Street. I look at that man in there, and I see someone who is very badly damaged. He is lucky to be alive. He was warehoused for what, five years? He has a long way to go before he can threaten anyone! You see many more problems with him than I do."

I looked at him and gave up. His turf, his rules. I'd learned when I was a cop that *turf* always has its privileges. "Okay, whatever. Would you at least keep me posted on his condition? God knows how long it'll take the government agencies to get their asses in gear, and I need to know what's going on with him."

The administrator seemed amenable now. "I'd be happy to, Mister Street. I saw your e-mail address on your card. I'll advise you if there are significant changes."

I replied, "Better yet, how about a phone conference weekly, say Tuesday mornings at ten am? You call me. You have my number."

"Tuesdays at ten. Yes, sir. That'll work. I'll write that down on my office schedule and have my secretary remind me."

We shook hands, and I left, fully realizing that the government types were not going to be my only problem.

———

Despite my recent months being absorbed in the Connors' murder investigation, I had other business to contend with, including consultancies to attorneys on their cases. That day in Vegas, I had to spend time at an attorney's office in discussion with the staff, hoping to formulate a timeline for use in the defense case for their corporate client. After I arrived and got my head around the matter they were trying to deal with, it was a relatively easy assignment. I made a series of suggestions for their investigator, made a good contact for any consulting work they would have in Southern California, had a great early dinner at Ruth's Chris Steak House with some pleasant people—for lawyers—and collected a nice check for my time and trouble.

Between my appointment and dinner that afternoon, I traveled to a strip center off of Spring Mountain Road to check out the status of the Las Vegas location of the former law practice of Bongelli and Associates. Vinnie Bongelli had been the ringleader and creator of the operation that caused all the issues around Carty and the Connors' murders. After a bit of Vegas-style embellishment —I dropped my tie and unbuttoned my shirt a bit—and some sleight of hand regarding my identity, the attractive receptionist answered my *easy* questions, verifying that Bongelli had liquidated the holdings of the Nevada practice and that Bongelli's former associates were now the rein-holders. Manniford Law was now the handler of the former Bongelli accounts in Nevada, including his unique prisoner management system. Good to know down the road.

I collected a few business cards for the practice associates while the receptionist was out of the room, intent on doing some research on them later. The former Bongelli staffers seemed to be carrying on admirably, but they deserved added scrutiny soon enough due to their proximity to the slime trail that Bongelli had left behind.

Calling the vast Las Vegas Metro Detention Center, I also learned that Vance Boyd, the Bongelli operative with whom I had played chase for the better part of a month, the poor sap who I had eventually lured into a confrontation with the side of an LVMPD cruiser, still had three months left on his term in Clark County Jail. Good place for him.

## 5

The next evening when Lupe Oswego's shift began, she made her rounds in the facility wing for which she was responsible, leaving Carty's room for the last stop on her route. She knocked softly on his door, paused a few seconds, then strode into his room. "Well, hello, Mister Grant! How are we feeling this evening?"

People in the hospital didn't often talk to Carty. He looked at her and smiled a bit, then quietly said, "Fine, I guess. How're you?"

"I am great! I was so pleased to see you making your way to the bathroom last night. I hope you don't mind that I just let you do it on your own. That is how you regain your strength."

"Yes, you did that. I appreciate that. The new pajamas were great. I dearly love that shower! Thanks."

Softly, she said, "I also brought you these." She had a trio of energy bars in her right hand. Carty looked at them and took them, laying them on the bedside table.

Carty looked up at her now, hitting the *off* button on the remote for the TV. "Thank you. I've never had those. Are they good?"

"They are. My son has them all the time. He loves them."

"Well then, thank you."

"If you really need any help getting around, let me know, but I know you want to get out of here on your own before long. You keep working like I saw you do last night, you'll be back up and running around in no time."

"Well, I sure hope so. Not too sure about that *running around* part." He looked at her and smiled. "That'll take a while."

Lupe smiled as she moved farther into the room and approached Carty. She touched his arm and spoke in a conspiratorial tone. "You know, I saw those men who came here to check on you. They said you have some really serious legal issues to answer for when you get better. Mister Leggitt, the owner here, really stepped up for you. Those men wanted you restrained in your bed, and Tom told them he wouldn't do that."

Now Carty paid a little more attention. In his own low, raspy tone, he asked, "You heard them talking about me?"

"Oh, certainly! People who don't work here don't ever pay attention to the *hired help*. I can come and go as I please, and no one notices at all. They said you were suspected of some serious crimes, and they want you to stand trial as soon as you're better."

By now, Carty had turned and slid his legs off the side of the bed. He sat up straight. "Okay. What else did you hear them say?"

Lupe had her audience in hand now; she was a master at this, having raised three sons in her forty-eight years. "Well, one of the men said you were even responsible for some murders. I thought at the time, and I still do, 'Why, that nice Mister Grant could never have done anything like that. There is just no way. He's far too nice a man for that...and injured the way he is? No, there is simply no way at all.'" She paused for a few seconds, raised an eyebrow, and asked, "I am right, aren't I, Mister Grant?"

Suddenly considering new options, Carty frowned as he answered absently, "Sure." Then he looked at Lupe and finally *got* what she was talking about. "Can we stay in touch on this, Lupe? I may need some extra help as I get better."

"I understand, Mister Grant. We'll get you through this, honey. Just leave it to me." She took his hand as he sat at the edge of the bed and squeezed it, then she turned and left the room, grinning.

By the end of Carty's sixth week at the facility, he and Lupe had become friends of sorts. She was his evening attendant five days a week, a servant, and increasingly, a confidant. She had drawn him out quite a lot in their conversations. She had also read the transfer file from the Sheriff's department and had a good idea of the issues he faced should he be taken into custody for his crimes. He was a very bad dude, but he was vulnerable at this point. She had no fear for herself, nor for her son, who'd be doing the work and eventually cashing in for both of them.

In the evening of that next Friday, Lupe made her move. At the start of her first break, she went to her locker in the staff coffee room and snagged a small package. She then walked to Carty's room, entered, and closed the door. Carty was napping, his TV volume soft. Lupe hit the *off* button on the remote. With the sudden quiet, Carty stirred. As he opened his eyes, he saw Lupe standing at the foot of his bed, and he woke with a start.

Lupe smiled at Carty and quietly asked, "How are you, Mister Grant? Getting stronger?"

Carty gained his composure after he shook off his sleep. He propped himself up and answered, "Um, yeah. Been shuffling laps in the hallway." He looked embarrassed as he said, "I still get tired and fall asleep after."

"You look good, though. Your color is much better now." She looked toward the door furtively and approached him. "Mister Grant, can you keep a secret?" She put her hand in the pocket of her jacket.

"Um, sure. What's up?"

"I got you a present! You can't tell anyone, though. It's not something anyone else needs to know about." She withdrew the packaged cellphone from her pocket and handed it to him. "They package these things like they're wrapped in iron, so I opened it for you."

Carty looked at the phone and smiled excitedly. "Thank you,

Lupe! I really appreciate it! I've needed one of these! How did you know?"

"Oh, Grant, I just pay attention. You can learn a lot just doing that." She smiled.

"Well, thank you. I will pay you back as soon as I'm out of here. I have some money stashed away. Soon as I can get to it, I'll get ya handled."

"Oh, I trust you, Grant. Anything you need, let me know. Anything at all."

———

Another week had passed. It was Saturday, and the weekend crew at the convalescent hospital was on duty, so Carty was surprised to see Lupe Oswego in the hallway outside his room as he rounded the corner, walking behind his metal implement. He almost didn't need it anymore, but it was valuable when he got tired, so he dragged it along whenever he took his daily stroll.

Lupe, dressed in a white skirt and a red blouse, had been shopping. She carried two bags from a clothing store that Carty didn't recognize. A tall young Latino accompanied her. They greeted one another in the hallway and then hurriedly entered his room. Lupe closed the door. As Carty settled on his bed, Lupe spoke, still softly. "Grant, this is my son, Carlo. Carlo, this is the man I told you about."

The young man grunted in response and flipped a two-finger salute as he settled on the arm of the chair in the corner of the room. Lupe, in charge, with her son and her patient on her turf and with her initiative, addressed Carty specifically. "Mister Grant, I know you want to get out of here as quickly as possible. I was talking to my son, and he has an idea. He is without a job and has offered to be of assistance to you if you need it. He has a truck and can take you wherever you need to go as soon as you get out of here."

His voice was stronger now. "That sounds good, Lupe. I need

that. I can pay him as I get my bearings. I'll have money as soon as I can access it."

"That's good, Grant. Let's try to figure you a date for when you want to try to leave. There are some concerns in the short term, as I am sure you know. We'll talk again by Thursday, okay?"

"Sure, Lupe. Anytime you want." He shrugged and waved at his surroundings. "You know where to find me."

"Very well then. We will talk again. Oh! And I was shopping and found some things you will need now that you're mobile. I got you some clothes! I don't know your taste, so I tried to stay conservative." She shook out the bags onto the bed. Three pairs of tan 30w x 32l khakis, a brown knit-leather belt, some logo car-theme t-shirts, one red polo shirt, a cello-wrapped dozen pairs of 30" waist jockey shorts, two packages, five pairs each of knit socks, and a pair of net-styled off-brand tennis shoes. He was impressed. Carty looked at the clothing and smiled as he sorted it.

A receipt shook out of one of the bags. Carty, genuinely touched by the gesture, couldn't recall his last clothing purchase. "You spent hundred-eighty bucks? Lupe, you didn't have to do that. I don't know what to say!" He looked at the pile of clothes, then back at her. "Thank you!"

"Now, don't wear any of that in here. Just keep it in the drawer until you get ready to leave." She looked at her son and pointed absently. "Carlo, remind me to get Grant a satchel for when he leaves, okay? One of those soft-sided things we saw at Target?"

"Sure, ma." Carlo didn't talk a lot.

Lupe looked from her son to Carty. "So anyway, Grant, I will see you next week. You take care and build up your strength! You'll need it!"

———

Fifteen minutes later, Lupe and her son entered the southbound 15 freeway driving her silver 1999 Nissan Sentra sedan toward downtown Vegas. Carlo was working a weekend temp concessions job at the Convention Center there. She turned to him as she drove into the parking lot adjacent to the Aerial Tram stairway and asked Carlo, "So what did you think, son? Do you want to work with him?"

"Hey, why not? You say he's got money?"

"Pffft... Maybe a LOT. And I think there will be a reward for him once he escapes. If we keep an eye on him, we'll be in for a share of it, if not the whole amount. Give it some thought, and let's talk tomorrow."

"Will do, ma. See you soon."

———

It had been four days since Lupe had spoken to Carty about his pending departure. As she entered his room that evening, she found him sitting upright in the hard-cushioned chair next to the window. She smiled as she walked to the bed to start the drill to change the sheets. Carty looked at her and asked, "Lupe, when will your son be available for that thing we talked about?"

"When do you want him, Mister Grant?" Her pulse quickened. Maybe this was about to get real.

"I'm thinkin' maybe by the end of next week. How much notice does he need?"

"Maybe a couple of days to clear his calendar. What day are you thinking?"

"Let's try for Thursday next week. I'll need him for the first half of the first day, at least. I have some running around to do. I'll pay him day by day."

"He'll be driving you?"

"Yes, ma'am, and I'll need his help getting lodging for a few days. I have some old friends in town that I need to contact."

"Very well. I will speak to my son this evening, and I will get back to you soon." As they talked, she had stripped Carty's bed and replaced the linens with fresh sheets. Lupe was a *machine* with bed maintenance after twenty-one years on the job.

**6**

Carty had started paying attention to local TV as his days dwindled before his departure from the facility in the Vegas suburb. The room's set, one of those new flat-screen things, was on most of the time. The usually-dreadful afternoon fare of syndicated drivel from cable channels and local movie stations had acquainted him with jewelry stores, restaurants from drive-thru joints to fine dining overlooking the Strip, dating services, 1-900 *talk to a bimbo* lines, and car dealers from junk to luxury.

The car dealer patter caught his eye, as he had held a wholesale dealer's license for several years as part of the cover-business network the mouthpiece Bongelli had set up. Carty had used the dealer solely as a method with which to transport bulk quantities of illegal drugs. He hadn't cared about the business side of the operation, but a few names and faces still stuck in his mind, nestled between the blank spots.

Carty had noticed that an old friend was a talking head on one of the more boisterous spots. He found a pen among the detritus in the drawer of the adjoining bedside table and had taken down the number three days before. Now that he sensed some urgency regarding his eventual exit, he put his new cell phone to work, curious as to the result. With two days till his escape, he made a call.

A feminine voice answered the phone with a perky, "Nellis Specialty Motors, how may we assist you?" Carty recalled his friend's habit of staffing his business with prospective showgirls, dancers, and female *entertainers* of various stripes. This voice sounded like a looker.

"Afternoon, darlin'. Is Lloyd in?"

Her voice was smoky, and he envisioned her appearance and smiled. "I'll have to check, sir. He's real busy filming his commercials today. Who may I say is calling?" Carty guessed a southern accent, maybe Georgia. He'd been good at identifying voices when he was a kid. He grinned at being able to recall random items from his old life.

"Tell him it's Grant. I'm an old friend."

"I'll do just that, Grant. Give me a minute." The line clicked as it went to *hold*. A local oldies station provided the hold music. Jefferson Starship. It took almost two minutes before the gravelly voice came onto the line.

"This is Lloyd Ring. How may I help you?'

"Lloyd, this is Grant Carty."

There was another pause, then the voice said, "Please hold just a second, sir. I can't hear myself think." Seconds later, the background noise lowered, and the voice returned. "Sorry for that. Who's this again?"

"Grant Carty, Lloyd. Remember me?"

There was ten seconds of absolute silence. "Grant Carty? Holy shit, man. I thought you was dead! Where are you?"

"I'm in town. It's a long story for another time. We'll get to that. We still have some open business, don't we, Lloyd?"

That again. Ohhh shit. Lloyd had hoped that was long forgotten. Time to man up and face it...see what goes down. "Umm... yeah, Grant, I guess we do. After you stopped comin' around, I guess I forgot about it. I gotta tell ya, brother...I'm off all that shit. I'm straight as a board now! I got married and have a little boy and another one about to pop outta the old lady. My father-in-law helped me open this place. Hell, you and me ain't seen each other in what, eight years?"

Carty corrected him. "Six and change as I see it. I need some help from you, Lloyd. One thing, and then we're even."

Lloyd was nervous now, remembering one coke order that he still owed Carty for, probably six grand from when he was a slinger in North Las Vegas. Shit. He had been *scared straight* after a nasty bout with the North Vegas cops, missing a possession-for-sale arrest by the skin of his teeth. He hadn't even thought of that era of his life for a long time. He'd have to tap dance his ass off to get that much money out of the business with his father-in-law watching the till. Hesitatingly, he responded, "Grant, whataya need, brother?"

"I need a set of wheels, Lloyd, for about a week. I'll return it when I'm done."

Lloyd thought Carty's voice sounded weak, but he didn't want the grim details. "Grant, buddy, I don't know. The State DMV has cracked down on dealers here like you wouldn't believe. Last time the inspector came in, he had all of us spread out on the floor like we was fuckin' criminals! I can't do anything out of formula anymore, or they'll have my ass!" Lloyd silently hoped the dodge would be sufficient. All these years later, Carty made him really nervous.

Carty made the deal slightly better. Softly, calmly, he said, "Lloyd, my brother, I'll take you at your word. Tell ya what. One vehicle, one week, you get five large at the back end, and your account is square. I wouldn't ask if I didn't need the help."

Lloyd was silent for a few seconds, then he exhaled and said, "Carty, we haven't seen each other in years. I am not into your thing anymore! I am out! I'm straight now! I can't risk any of this crap!"

Carty responded, "Hell, Lloyd, I'm out of it, too! And I bet I'm a hell of a lot straighter than you are! I can't even take a friggin'

Tylenol! I got hurt real bad a while back. I'm in a hospital. I need wheels to go get a shitpot full of money I got stashed away. Don't have to be nothin' fancy. Four wheels and a license plate will do just fine. At the back end, you get paid nice and fat. C'mon, brother! Let's make it happen."

Softly, Lloyd said, "Goddammit, I need my head examined." He paused, looking for a vehicle on the dealer auction list that hadn't been processed into stock. "Okay, look. I'll handle it just this once. I got a black Dodge Durango. I just bought it, it's not stocked in yet. One week, right? Five large at the end?"

"Exactly, Lloyd. Count on it."

"Awright. Gimme the address. I'll send a driver to bring my guy back." He paused, listening to silence. "Don't make me regret this, Carty."

"Count on it, Lloyd. Thanks." Carty smiled to himself. Done deal. Phase one complete.

———

Lloyd Ring sat at his desk, opened the drawer, and shook a pair of Extra Strength Motrin gelcaps into his palm, then opened the Dr. Pepper he'd picked up a few minutes earlier from the corner convenience store two doors north on Nellis. He leaned back in the chair and closed his eyes as he considered his next move. His memory was clearer than he'd let on. Yeah, he owed Carty money, maybe $7500, for a quantity of prime nasal dosage he'd taken delivery of almost seven years ago. The coke, in realistic terms, had been great stuff, maybe even a bargain at that price, and he'd made serious bank passing it on, but in recent years he'd turned his life 180 degrees. He didn't want to go to jail, and he wasn't going to lose his new life, regardless of what he owed Carty. Maybe he could even turn the sumbitch in.

He slammed the Motrin, took a long swallow of Dr. Pepper, then pressed the intercom button and called his shop attendant/detailer, asking him to come to the office. Moments later, the office door opened, and the tall young black man entered the office. "Hey, boss. What's up?"

"David, I need you to deliver a car for me. Here's the address. Take that black Durango on the fence line, wash it, and fill up the tank. Have Pablo follow you and bring you back. Make sure the temp plate is on right, but take the dealer plate frame off of it and check the tracker. Make certain it works right." He pulled a fresh hundred from his pocket. "Here's some money to get lunch while you're out. Keep the change. This is a personal favor to me, off the books, okay? No one else knows about it, ever. You got that?"

David smiled as he took the bill. "Yeah, boss. Will do. Thanks!"

———

Carty had watched from his window as the black truck arrived that afternoon, and he smiled at the thought of an escape from whatever level of captivity he had been subjected to for years now.

"Lupe!" Carty called the next time he saw her in the hallway. The squat woman ambled into the room, and at Carty's suggestion, she let the door close. She stepped to his bed as he slid onto the sheets. He said, "There is a black Dodge Durango in the parking lot. I can see it from my window. Belongs to a friend of mine. He sent it over here for me. The keys are on the visor above the steering wheel. Next time you go outside, if you'd get me those keys and lock it up for me, I'd appreciate it."

"Okay, Grant. I'll bring them in to you. It'll be a little later, when I take my break. If you're asleep or out of the room, I'll put the keys in the drawer by the mirror. How are you doing with your walking?"

Carty shrugged. "Crankin' on, farther every day. I did a lap without the walker yesterday. Still kinda slow, and I had to stop a time or two and sit down to rest, but it's getting better."

Lupe beamed. "You are such a trooper, Grant! I am so proud of you! You keep that up, you'll be out of here in no time!"

Carty looked at Lupe and grinned on the *good* side of his face, then turned to look out the window toward the parking lot. "That is the goal."

Lupe left the room. Her next stop was the break room to call her son.

## 7

The chosen day had finally arrived. Early that morning, Carty had walked to the black Dodge Durango on the back row of the parking lot and back to his room, mostly to test the effectiveness and sensitivity of the surveillance camera system for the convalescent facility. He made the round trip and came back to his room with no ill effects, either from the length of the walk or the fact that he still wore his hospital pajamas and robe for the jaunt. He knew that Lupe had set a ten o'clock meet time for her son to arrive at the parking lot. Carty was to keep an eye out for the kid's arrival. He would then walk nonchalantly from the facility, get into the truck, drive away, and never look back.

It happened just that way. Dressed in his khakis and his red polo shirt, carrying his new grey satchel loaded with the clothes Lupe had provided him, he took the side exit door and hoofed it, as well as he could, toward the truck. The kid stood beside his mom's Sentra. Lupe was in the driver's seat of the little sedan. She let the car idle with the AC on full and ran the window down as Carty approached. She smiled at him cautiously.

In his most sincere voice, Carty said, "Thank you for this, Lupe.

I have a few days work for him, he'll be well-compensated for his time and trouble. There'll be some extra in the deal for you, too." He couldn't help smiling again, happy to finally be on the outside of the hospital, freer than he'd been in years. He realized how fast his heart was beating.

"Very well, Grant. Call me if you need anything at all, and bring my boy back safe, you hear me?"

Carty responded, exaggerating just a bit, "Lupe, he's in the arms of the angels. I'll take good care of him. Talk to you on Monday. Thank you again."

Lupe looked at her son once again, then at Carty, then she put the car in gear and drove out of the parking lot.

Carty looked at the young man and said, "You're drivin', my friend."

————

The first stop of the trip was the drive-through at the huge In & Out on Sahara on the west side of the freeway, a suggestion of Carlo. "How long since you had a double-double, Mister Grant?"

"Just call me Grant, man! Probably seven/eight years. A little different from the hospital food, too, huh?" he chuckled. "No green beans, no applesauce, no wrapped plastic fork. Thanks for buyin'."

The kid smiled past his french fries. "No problem, Grant. I figure you're good for it."

Fifteen minutes later, they tossed their debris into the trash barrel and left the parking lot to head north on the 15. Carty marveled at the changes that were still being made in the city skyline and the freeway system itself. "Whoa, man. I don't have any idea where shit is anymore. I used to be a man about town kinda guy, y'know?"

"Well, it's still almost the same except for the touristy stuff. North Las Vegas has gotten rougher lately. The drugs and gangs make it bad for everyone else. We live on the border of the two towns. There is gunfire at night, it makes my mom nervous for my brothers."

"Gang shit's bad, pard. Those sumbitches are mean 'n stupid. Stay away from drugs too. Shit'll kill you." He gave the kid directions for the Caraway turnoff and the route to the ranch. He was suddenly nervous as the truck followed the crowned roads leading to the ranch property. "We'll check it out first, then we'll need to hit a store for some supplies. I have some stuff here that I need to pick up. You just stay in the truck this time. I won't take long."

Carlo's mom had been stern with her son in preparation for what she had called *the Grant project*. "Don't ask him about his past or his business! He was a very bad man for years. He seems to have straightened out physically since he was burned, and he's no longer an addict, but I think he is still really dangerous. And do not argue with him! He has killed people! And carry a gun and a knife just in case something happens!"

"Ma! Stop! The guy can barely walk! I can take care of myself. It'll just be a couple of days, and then I'll be back. It's easy money! I'll call when I can."

The desert sun was high that noontime after a sudden, brief rainstorm an hour earlier. By the time the big black Durango pulled through a series of puddles at the side of the barn at the end of the 3/4-mile-long driveway, it wore a thick coat of desert grit. Carty directed the kid to park close to the side of the barn near the door. There were bright yellow ribbons of vinyl tape warning 'CRIME SCENE: DO NOT ENTER' laying on the ground around the perimeter of the barn and the nearby house. Carty stood next to the truck, trying to get his bearings. He frowned and wiped a bead of sweat from his forehead. He felt his heart racing. He hadn't seen the outside of the facility in almost six years. He choked up for a few seconds before he steeled himself and walked to the side door of the barn.

Inside the barn, the sun shone through the high windows onto the dusty floor, with wide shafts of light creating intermittent stretches of glare and shadows across the main room. Carty looked around the large space, trying to remember the layout. Again, almost six years had passed since his injury, but he'd realized that because of his addictions, he'd practically been semi-comatose for a long while before the burn injury. His binges had been legendary. His memories from back then were foggy and distant.

After a stationary moment, he shook it off and walked to the cabinets on the far side of the room. He lifted a lid on a nearby Craftsman rolling toolbox and picked up a long black-handled screwdriver. After he slid the cabinet door open, he used the screwdriver as a lever to pop off the rear wall of the space. He laid the wood aside, leaned in, and looked inside the space behind. He smiled with relief at the contents and reached inside to grab a handful of rubber-band-bound rolls of large-denomination bills. A half-dozen would do well till tomorrow. He replaced the wooden panel, closed the cabinet, and returned the screwdriver to the toolbox. Looking around the space, he smiled as he saw his old Bronco parked close to the end door, then the good side of his face sagged as he realized it was sitting on a trio of flattened Dick Cepek off-road tires. He told himself he'd get back to it.

As he looked around the space, he took the rubber bands off the cash—$30k would serve him well until the next day. He took one last look around, stepped toward the door, and returned to the Durango and his young assistant. There was work to do.

Carty stepped to the truck and motioned for the kid to roll the window down. The mariachi music was loud until the kid hit the *off* switch. Carty leaned in and said, "I'm gonna walk over to the house. Park in the back by the sliding doors there and wait for me." Carty walked haltingly past the derelict cars, two of which had been taken by various agencies as evidence in criminal cases against... well...him. The concrete block mixing buildings looked the same, but had been examined and sealed by whatever branch of officialdom had been in attendance. The fourth of the blockhouses, its windows and door shattered, the walls charred, and the roof detached from the upward blast, was a dark vision to him. He knew what had happened there, but this was the first time he had actually laid eyes on the site where he'd sustained his massive injuries. He stared at the shack for a while, rubbed the scarred side of his face, then snapped out of it and walked on through the dust and shattered glass. At the rear of the house, he just looked in through the kitchen window for a moment, then turned and walked back to the idling truck. To Carlo, he said, "Okay, pal, let's get the fuck out of here and run some errands. We got work to do."

As the kid maneuvered the Durango toward the driveway, he asked Carty, "Where do you need to go? Better than that, what do you need? I'll take you to get anything you want. My references are more current, and we can make the trip to get your stuff more efficient. Will that work for you?"

"Sure. Let's hit a hardware store or a K-Mart or somewhere. I need trash bags and some kinda baseball cap or a cowboy hat, and some other stuff. Gimme a pen an' some paper, and I'll make a list. You go in, I'll stay in the truck. Oh, and hang on a second..." Carty reached into his bag and brought out some of the money he'd rescued from the barn. "Here's the downstroke on your time. You're a good kid. I appreciate your help. Let's start with a nickel, okay?" He laid five hundred-dollar bills on the console between the seats.

"Oh, man! Thank you, Grant!" He picked up the bills, more money than he'd ever had in his hands at one time. "Let's get rolling and get you your stuff. I know a place you can stay, too."

Later as the truck made the transition to Charleston Boulevard from the freeway, Carlo looked over at Carty and asked, "Have you ever stayed at Arizona Charlie's over on Boulder Highway? It has a separation between the buildings and no hallways to share with other people. I know you want to be secluded and all. We can order food in if you want, instead of going to the restaurant to eat. What else do you want?"

"Yeah, that sounds great. They got a good casino. I used to go there sometimes. Check-in under your name, get a stove, a fridge, and two beds...y'know, a suite. You're a great kid, but I ain't sleepin' with you." He looked at the driver and smiled. "What kinda food you like, besides In & Out?"

"Good authentic Mexican, man, that's the best. I got a favorite place out on Nellis, really authentic stuff. You'll like it. We should hit that place tomorrow maybe. Oh, and I'd recommend we don't use large bills for the hotel and some of the other purchases. It'll just attract suspicion. Let's get a debit card at one of the check-cashing stores and use that. Way less hassle that way, trust me."

Carty looked at the kid and smiled. "Damn, Carlo. You know your way around, don't you?"

Carlo smiled. "You'll see, Grant."

———

After those errands had been completed and Carlo had checked in at Arizona Charley's, he drove to the east Las Vegas Walmart a few miles from the hotel. Carty gave Carlo a list of merchandise, some cash, and the debit card funded to four thousand dollars. Carlo went inside as Carty sat in the idling Durango with the A/C on medium to battle the ninety-degree afternoon. Carty watched the foot traffic in and out of the massive store and noted the number of Las Vegas Metro police vehicles cruising through the parking lot. The cops in Vegas were tough cats, and traffic stops on Boulder Highway were made on the tiniest justification. Well over a decade before, he had searched out the ranch property north of town in order to stay off the radar completely. As it turned out, that isolation had worked almost too well. Had Vinnie Bongelli not been in attendance the day of the explosion, Carty would have surely died. He wondered again what had happened to Bongelli. He wanted to settle up.

Carlo returned to the truck almost an hour later with sufficient food and supplies to provide solace and security for the week that he expected Carty to remain at the hotel. He hoped that they would part company within a few days, but he wanted to provide a cushion of readiness so that Carty wouldn't have to come into contact with the public.

Carty opened his door and went to the rear of the truck to open the tailgate. He helped load the cartful of plastic bagged food and *stuff* into the large plastic tubs he had bought, then shoved the tubs into the truck's rear compartment. He was well aware that he was making his burn-injured face visible to the public for the first time. That made him nervous, and he rushed back to the passenger seat, slamming the door after he entered.

————

Lloyd Ring sat in his office at Nellis Specialty Motors and considered his good fortune. His father-in-law had just dropped in to look at the dealership and had complimented Lloyd on the operation. There had been a rise in sales last month, attributed to a shift in the sales force, and the *new guys* had hit the ground running. The three salesmen had shown themselves well recently. Two were Latino, appropriate to the most recent market, and the other one was a *sophisticated* Black Air Force veteran, so the situation was covered regardless of the ethnic mix or language of his clientele.

Ring ran his finger down the list of accounts, checking off the car locations and customers as he went, noting those who seemed close to missing a payment. He opened his center drawer and unfolded the note he'd left in the coin tray. Where was this one now? Ring tapped in the code for the tracker he'd had installed on the black Durango that he'd lent Carty, waited a few seconds, and watched as the map image showed a wilderness area north of Las Vegas. Former travels had been mostly within town, with a trip to the desert for variety, and it looked as if the vehicle *rested* at Arizona Charley's on Boulder Highway. The truck was out for two more days, then it'd be time to settle up.

————

Carty was relaxing on the king-size bed after eating breakfast with Carlo. The TV was on in the bedroom, and he flipped through the dozens of channels trying to find something worth watching. What the hell had happened to friggin' television in his absence?

The cell phone rang that morning at nine sharp. Carty answered, "Yeah?" He looked across the room at Carlo, who was doing the post-breakfast cleanup.

"This is Robbie."

"Gotdamn. Robbie! Been a while, huh? How you doin', girl?"

"I'm fine. I'm looking forward to getting together with you. I'll be in Vegas in a few days. Are you able to travel? How's your health?"

"I'm still coming back from the dead, baby. Guess you knew all about that shitstorm, didn't you?"

"I'm so sorry about that, Grant. I really am. We were kept in the dark, completely. Bongelli told us nothing at all. If I'd known, you know I'd have come for you."

She sounded sincere, maybe a little plaintive. "Right. Sure thing. I drop from sight for six fucking years...you don't notice. Gotcha."

Pleadingly, she answered, "It is not like that at all, Grant. I'll explain it all to you after we get together. Look, we have new action in the works, lots of it, right here in L.A. You're in for a share if you want in, no questions asked. You have cred with everyone in the mix."

"Tell me about it."

"That will have to wait until we meet in person. Can you be ready to travel in three days?"

"Sure. No strings here that benefit me at all. I got my stash, I'm getting well, I'm ready to go. I'm at this place on Boulder Highway 'til the end of the week. Got my helper takin' care of me. Him and his mama have been real good to me."

"Well, cut him loose before we meet, and get rid of anything that ties you to that location. You were never there, okay?"

"I'm way ahead of you, Robbie. He's gone tomorrow. I'll rest up 'til you get here."

"Okay, Grant. I'll call you when I get to town. I'm driving my own car. We'll be in and out real easy like. You have much baggage?"

"Nah. Just a small bag of clothes and a coupla big tubs full of filthy lucre, babe. Nothing else to worry about."

"Okay. That sounds really good. Wait for my call. It'll be good to see you again."

## 8

Carty called across the room after he cut the phone. "Hey, Carlo! Where're we goin' this afternoon? You got anything planned?"

"Anywhere you want, Grant! What do you have in mind?"

"Coupla things. I wanna go get some clothes. Find me an indie men's clothing store, get me a suit, or at least some pants that cost over $20 a pair, maybe a shirt or two. Nothing against your mama. I like the stuff she got me, but I guess I'm tired o' lookin' like an eighth grader. Lookin' for a little upgrade, y'know?"

Carlo smiled. "I get it. My mom tends to infantilize all of us. There's a place up on Maryland Parkway we'll go to. It's a stand-alone store, locally owned, no mall traffic. Guys are cool there."

"Sounds good."

"Where else?"

"I'll get you to run down ta Wally World and get a coupla gas cans, two-gallon jobs, and fill 'em up. Then we gonna go back out to the ranch. I wanna close that account for good. Come back after you get 'em and pick me up."

"Gotcha, Grant. Gimme an hour."

———

The trip to the desert was unusual. Carlo parked the Durango between the house and the barn. He knew what was going to happen as soon as Carty told him to pop the tailgate but stay in the truck. Carty went to the rear, snagged the gas cans and a couple of leftover trash bags, and walked to the house. He stopped, looked around from a spot just outside the kitchen door, then kicked the door open and walked inside. Fifteen minutes later, he walked back to the truck, slammed the door, and said, "Change of plans. Let's get outta here, buddy." He had not gone to the barn.

———

Two days later, as Carlo washed the dishes after a hearty steak and scrambled-egg breakfast, Carty stood in the doorway to his bedroom and called, "Carlo? Time to cut the cord, buddy. Sit down over here, and let's talk, okay?" The younger man walked from the kitchenette to the dining room table and took a seat. He looked across the table as Carty reversed his chair to the opposite side and sat. There was a cheap vinyl satchel laying on the table next to the shiny charcoal-color pistol that Carlo had seen before. The pistol made him nervous.

"So, Carlo, been a hell of a week, huh?

Smiling, Carlo nodded in agreement. "Yeah, Grant. You really know how to put on a show."

"Well, you been a big help to me this week, but we gotta talk." He looked at the kid and frowned. "You know that I'm a bad guy, right? I am one evil son-of-a-bitch. I have done a lot of bad shit. Don't deny it, Carlo."

Carlo looked baffled, then smiled thinly. "All I will say is that you have been good to my mama and me. I have no complaints. You have been trustworthy, and I consider us friends. Am I mistaken in doing that, Grant?"

"Naw, man. We're buds. You're a good kid. But your mama told you to be careful around me, didn't she?"

"Well, yes. And I know some of the things that went on at that ranch years ago, but they do not concern me at all."

"Good answer, Carlo. Again. Back at the ranch, I had to kill some folks who crossed me. A lot of bad shit went down out there. I will warn you that if you go to the police about me, I will find you, wherever you are, and I will kill you. You feel me, Carlo? Then I'll find your mama, and y'all can have a group funeral. You read me?"

Carlo was frowning now. A little louder now, he spat back, "Grant, have I not been loyal to you this week? Have I not done everything you asked? Have I not watched your back? I don't deserve threats, do I?"

Carty reached across toward the kid, his fingers straight up in a *halt* motion. "Chill back, kid. I'm just telling you." He smiled. "Don't make me do that, you dig?" Carty grinned, still not feeling at ease. "No offense, little brother, I just gotta be clear." He picked the grey vinyl satchel from the floor and pushed it toward the other side of the table. "Anyway, Carlo, you been a big help to me this week. You set me free. I appreciate it. There's sixty-thousand bucks in there for you and your mama. Go buy you a new truck or get a degree or somethin', okay? There's still a few bucks on that debit card, too. That's your tip." He smiled.

Carlo opened the bag and looked inside at the banded cash. He smiled widely now as he looked back at Carty. "Grant, I don't know what to say. Thank you so much!"

Carty pointed at the kid with his scarred index finger. "Carlo, you DO know what to never say. Don't make me come after you. You know I will if I have to." He smiled now. "And with that, little brother, you are free to go. We're done, except for one last errand. I need you to take the black truck to this address. It's a drive-thru taco joint across from that little shopping center on Nellis. Put the key above the visor, leave the driver's door unlocked, and walk away. Call your mama, tell her to come pick you up there. You got that?" He tossed an envelope across the table. "Put that in the glove box. Give your mama a kiss for me, too." The good side of his face smiled thinly.

Still breathless from the largesse of the gift, Carlo smiled and said, "Yes, Grant. You can count on me. Anything else you need, ever, you give me a call."

Tired from the negotiations, Carty had risen and turned. He threw the kid a two-finger salute and walked back to his bed. He heard the door close as the kid left for the final time.

————

Roberta Thomas-Schwinn turned into the median lane in front of the Arizona Charlie's hotel resort complex on Boulder Highway and made a lap of the parking lot before she determined the proper location for her rendezvous with Grant Carty. She saw Carty, much thinner and more damaged than she'd imagined, as he approached her car. His grey slacks were tailored for his thin frame. He wore new shoes and a pale blue striped dress shirt. He carried a light grey sport coat over his left arm. He was escorted by a porter who towed a luggage cart carrying a couple of small bags and a pair of large plastic tubs encircled with bands of duct tape. With the tubs stashed in the trunk of the Maxima and the bags in the back seat, Carty tipped the porter a crisp twenty and took to the passenger seat.

Looking at Carty for the first time in years, Roberta was at a loss for words. The edgy young man with whom she'd been smitten in high school, the one to whom she'd given her virginity, the one whose son she'd bore, was gone. Her vantage as he looked out the windshield was his *bad side*, the gnarled scar tissue left after a high-temperature fire resulting from a meth lab explosion. He was rail-thin. They exchanged pleasantries and small talk as they sat in her car in the hotel parking lot for ten minutes, then Carty suggested firmly, "Robbie, let's get the fuck outa here."

# 9

The law firm I'd conferenced with on the first *Carty search* visit called me in for a consult and to attend a couple of meetings. It wasn't my favorite drill, but the pay was good, and I liked the case they were researching. A client's former employee had used a company's credit cards a few weeks after his departure, and we had to determine the sequence of events before and during his $56,000 spending spree. I determined that the simplest route was good old-fashioned embezzlement, with plenty of establishing documents to prove the crime. The client came away happy, and I came away with a great reference. Win-win. I stayed overnight and planned to drive back to SoCal the next morning, but again, Grant Carty got in the way.

Out of simple concern, I made a call to Carty's convalescent facility that Tuesday, asking to speak with the Director. He was said to be in a meeting with his management staff, so I asked the office manager about the status of Carty. The nice lady put me on hold for a few minutes then she came back to the line with the response, "Mister Carty left the facility last Thursday, Mister Street."

Oh, great. "Would you please ask Mr. Leggitt if I could have a few moments of his time this afternoon? It's really very important that I talk with him."

"Well, yes, sir. He has an opening at one-thirty, and I believe he will be leaving by three."

"I'll be there for the one-thirty slot, and I can't sufficiently stress how important it is that I speak with him."

"Noted, Mister Street."

———

At the executive administrative wing of Casa Arroyo, I rushed into Leggitt's office at sufficient a pace that he looked threatened. I leaned over my side of his desk, hoping that he would feel threatened, too. "What did I tell you, Leggitt? Did I not tell you that there was a good chance that Carty would skip? Do you remember that exchange?"

"Well, Mr. Street, I suppose you were right this time. How was I to know?"

"Perhaps listening would help. Okay, when did he skip out of here?"

"Last Thursday."

"Do you know how he left? Do you have security camera footage of the exits and your parking lots?"

"Why, yes, we do. It has monitors in the next room."

"I need to see the recordings from last Thursday, now! You just put a stone-cold killer out on the streets of Las Vegas." Within a half-hour, I had access to the footage that showed Carty hoofing it up and down the hallways of the facility. He displayed a limp toward his right side, but otherwise, he got along fairly well. The final parking lot footage showed a dark SUV parked in one of the outermost stalls of the parking lot, a silver compact sedan next to it. "Leggitt, whose car is that?" I pointed at the image.

"If I am not mistaken, that is one of our nurses for the south wing, Lupe Oswego. She worked nights on Carty's wing, I believe."

"Is she here today?"

"No, sir." He looked at a staff schedule on the wall behind his desk. "She has off until... No, she is on vacation for a week."

"I need her phone number and address. Now!"

I commandeered the bank of buttons, ran the recording forward, and watched the SUV back from the parking stall. From my head full of useless automotive knowledge and the grille shape, I concluded that the vehicle was a Dodge, probably a Durango. The fancy alloy rims suggested perhaps a late-decade R/T model. Those are pretty rare items. As the vehicle backed from the slot, I could see that it wore a Nevada temporary plate, but the resolution of the footage was low, so reading numbers was impossible. Now that I had the thread that would give the only clue, I had to find the source.

I knew from our earlier research that Carty had held automobile dealer's licenses for California and Nevada through the corporation that Vinnie Bongelli had established for him, and the dealership had run for several years as a front for the drug activity based at the ranch. Assembling those elements, I surmised that he would have dealt with other dealers situated at the low end of the car dealer food chain. The 'Buy Here-Pay Here' establishments, the ones that kept poor people poor for decades at a time, were plentiful in some parts of Las Vegas, mostly the Boulder Highway corridor, along Nellis Boulevard approaching the Air Force base, and on the northern reaches of Las Vegas Boulevard, the stretch that runs through North Las Vegas where *the strip* turns less sparkly and more desolate and desperate. In the interest of efficiency, I went back to the hotel, fired up my laptop, did some research, and made some calls. The results were iffy for the first two hours.

"You need a Durango? We can get you a Durango. Might take a few days, but if you give us a deposit...'

"Durango? Those things are kinda thirsty, ain't they? How 'bout a nice Hyundai Santa Fe? Or maybe an Explorer? We got three of those. Come on in, we'll set you right up. How's your credit? We carry our own paper."

The nineteenth call I made was to Nellis Specialty Motors,

appropriately on Nellis Blvd., a few miles north from my hotel. The smoky female voice at the other end purred, "Let me let you talk to the owner, sir. He knows the inventory inside and out."

I was put on hold for two minutes of eighties rock music before the gravelly voice responded, "I'm Lloyd Ring, I'm the owner here. How may I assist you?"

I chose *west Texas* as my duplicitous accent for the call. "How ya doin' Lloyd? My name's Street. Friend of mine said he saw a good lookin' black Durango at your place. I been lookin' for something like that myself. You still got that rig in stock?"

The voice on the other end of the line cleared its throat. "Well, Mr. Street, this may be your lucky day. That unit had been out for service and we just got it back yesterday. It's a real sweetheart! Black, R/T model, loaded, and yeah, it's got a Hemi! Bitchin' little truck! We don't see a lot of those."

"That's great! Thank you, Lloyd. I'll be right there! Don't you let it go nowhere!"

———

Fifteen minutes later, I rolled onto the property of the dealer. The dusty Dodge Durango was parked toward the rear of the lot, nose to the chain link fence, and as I reached the back of the lot, it was being tackled by the wash crew. It appeared to be the truck from the parking lot DVD. I looked it over, saw little of value, but decided to do a little detecting. The young Latino salesman who approached me seemed disappointed that I wasn't shopping for myself.

"Is the owner in? I talked to him on the phone a few minutes ago."

"He's in his office. Let me see if he's available."

Two minutes later, I shook hands across the desk with Lloyd Ring in his cramped office.

"What can I do for you, Mister Street? My boys are cleaning that

Durango you called about. It'll be ready for a test drive in ten or fifteen minutes."

I pushed the door shut. Ring noticed. I leaned across the desk toward him. He leaned away from me, and he looked a little scared.

"Tell me when you last saw Grant Carty."

Ring's chubby, florid face went pale. Quietly he muttered, "Oh, shit. I knew this would happen." He sagged a bit in his chair.

"Chill out, Lloyd, and answer the question. I want him, not you." I tossed him my business card.

He looked at my business card and seemed relieved. "Oh. You're not a real cop." He looked at me. "Okay. Look, here's the deal. I never saw him at all. He called me here, said he needed a set of wheels for a week. He and I used to do business, and he remembered my name after a lot of years, I guess. I dunno. No harm done, right? He came to me, not the other way around."

"Relax, Ring. I just want to know where he is now. You loaned him the Dodge, right?"

"Yeah. I did. He asked for it over the phone. Called me, said he needed some temporary wheels. I owed him some money from a long time ago, this was the payoff. I had my lot man take it to the hospital and drop it off. Carty called me two days ago, thanked me, and told me to pick it up yesterday, that he was done with it."

"Okay. Big-time Buy-Here Pay-Here mogul like you, Lloyd, you probably put a tracker on it, too, right? Ring up the code, Lloyd. Let me see it, and I might not have to call the cops on your ass for aiding and abetting a fugitive."

Lloyd cleared his throat again, turned to his right, tapped a few keys on his laptop, and turned the computer for me to see. I recognized the routes to the hospital and the ranch. A new aspect was the travel on Boulder Highway. He and I were getting chummier by then, so I asked him, "Where are these two stops, Lloyd?"

He looked at the screen. "That bottom one there is the big ol' Walmart at Boulder and Nellis, and that one's where they stayed those nights. That's Arizona Charlie's over on Boulder. Big fancy adobe-lookin' place. The other, looks like they had some stops more towards the strip. That one way out north, I have no idea."

"I know where it's at. Can you print this out for me?"

He looked at me and tilted his head. "What's in it for me, Street?"

Oh. He was one of those. I reached across the desk and put my right hand on his shoulder, my grip increasing slightly as I spoke in quiet, determined terms. "Well, Lloyd, how about I not mention your name as a co-conspirator in Carty's escape when I catch up to him and have him arrested? With a little luck, I can maybe get you a piece of the dozen bodies of the people he's murdered, too." I leaned closer, patted his shoulder, and squinted as I spoke quietly to him, "You've assembled a really good life here, buddy, and you have a great-looking family from the pictures I see. You work hard to keep bread on the table and keep all the balls in the air. I appreciate that. I'm guessing that's a big-time turnaround from when you were tight with Carty. Is that new lifestyle of yours worth a few minutes of conversation and a coupla sheets of fucking printer paper, Lloyd? We can sure as hell play it the other way if you want. No sweat."

Lloyd looked at me, eyes wide, swallowed, took a deep breath, and decided to go with the printer paper. "Sorry, Street." He turned back to the keyboard, tapped the appropriate keys, then seconds later, he took the warm paper from the printer tray and handed them to me. "That all you need?"

"That'll do for now." I tapped my card on his desk. "You will call me if you have any further contact with him, won't you?"

He nodded his head in the affirmative. After I left the offices, I walked back to the Durango and snapped a few pics of the tire tread to link to the images I'd taken near the barn at the ranch. They matched. I left and checked Arizona Charlie's with no luck at all. The valet remembered the Durango but hadn't seen Carty. He needn't have shown his face at the registration desk if he had an accomplice, and since the truck had no license number, it wouldn't be listed on any check-in documents. I still wanted to talk to their security staff, but it was close to the end of the shift and that could wait.

I looked up the name of the caretaker from Carty's former resting place and drove by the Oswego residence in North Las Vegas, a mile north of Sahara Avenue. The house was a tidy one-story of concrete block construction, the nicest of the homes on its street. The Nissan I had seen on the video from the hospital sat dusty in the driveway toward the rear of the house beside the carport. In the dust on the floor of the carport, there were tracks the width of the Sentra but also a wider set of tracks indicating a larger vehicle onsite as well.

There was a young Latina watering the dust and tending the shrubbery among the decorative rocks that formed the lawn of the house next door, so I waved at her and asked, "Pardon, ma'am, do you know the Oswego family who lives here?"

She rose from her shrub trimming, looked at me, smiled, and approached me. She was a striking young woman with dark eyes and a great smile. She wore short shorts and a bikini top. I do notice these things. She stopped on her side of the low picket fence and responded, "Yes, I do. They're great friends of mine. I date their son." She smiled again.

"Ah. He's a lucky guy." She smiled at that. "Would you know where they went, when they'll be back? I need to talk to Lupe regarding her work."

"Well, they went to Bakersfield for a few days. They have relatives there."

"Okay. That'll work for now. Do you have a number for Lupe or her son?"

"No, I'm sorry. I never needed one. They've been fifty feet away for our whole life."

I smiled. It was easy to smile at this lady. "I understand. Would you please give Lupe one of my cards when you see her next?" I reached into my shirt pocket, brought out a card, and offered it.

"Sure thing. I'm Lucia." She offered her hand, then looked at the card that I gave her. "You're up from L.A.?"

"Yes, I am. My business brings me here fairly often of late." I wiped a bead of sweat from my forehead. "I can't get used to the heat here. Thank God for good air conditioning."

"I've wanted to get to L.A. myself since I was six. I took lots of drama and dance classes in school. I'd like to try my hand. Do you know anyone in the business?"

"I know a few people, just casual friends. That can be a tough life." I smiled. "You certainly look like a star, but so does everyone else there. SoCal has the best-looking waiters and waitresses on the face of the earth, and they're all convinced that they're gonna be Al Pacino or Kim Basinger day after tomorrow. That almost never happens." Her facial expression showed her disappointment. "Sorry."

She tilted her head and asked, "No magic pill you can take to make it happen?"

"Not a one. I bet you could get a decent start here, if you signed on with one of the local talent agencies. You have to do it the way it's done, though. Get your headshots, make a demo tape, and start knocking on the doors of talent agents. Be professional about it even when others aren't. I think the public would love you in commercials." I smiled.

Her expression brightened. "Thanks! I'll give that a try."

"Break a leg!" I said, hoping she wouldn't. "Nice meeting you." I walked to the Mustang and started the next step of my day.

———

My next stop was the former Carty Ranch, twenty-six miles north of the Las Vegas Speedway complex off the 15, just past the tiny community of Caraway. The place had been raided by law enforcement operatives from five county, state, and federal agencies as our team was finalizing legalities in the courtroom in Riverside some weeks ago. In one fell swoop, our plan had changed the setting for crooked lawyer Vinnie Bongelli's victims. Carty had been rescued from his desert storage facility and taken to a place where real care could be rendered. Arnie Sutton—admittedly guilty for offloading Rick Damarow from a private plane at 6000 feet, but in prison long-term mostly because of Bongelli's laughable handling of his criminal case—had been treated to new counsel as his financial promises had finally been kept. Bongelli's estranged wife, no prize herself, had been granted her longed-for divorce in return for ample affidavit testimony on Bongelli's legal ramblings.

The storied desolate ranch had been central location for Shirley's operations while she cared for Carty, and had been the supposed/probable hiding place for the millions of dollars that Carty had withheld from his huge drug manufacturing and trafficking operations. There I found the evidence for many elements attached to the original impetus for the investigation, the double murder of Ronnie Connors and his wife almost fourteen years prior. My visit today was a simple research effort. I wanted to see what was left of the place and how the remaining elements lined up with what I'd been told by the other officials involved in the round-up.

I was always surprised by the lack of traffic after I left the Interstate. There had only been one SUV passing in the other direction after I left the off-ramp. I reached the driveway to the ranch by two that afternoon and drove through the dusty portal to the barn. The dust was as usual in the desert. A thick and car-abusing layer had settled on the Mustang by the time I'd arrived at the barn. There were signs of the law enforcement groups that had inspected the property, bright yellow crime scene tape, and bright red CRIME SCENE: DO NOT ENTER ribbons that crossed the door openings.

As I walked toward the barn, I took note of the deep tire tracks that seemed to stop near the walk-in door to the low side of the building. There had been one of those quick heavy rain showers a day before, so this indicated recent traffic intent on whatever was inside the place. Also, there looked to be two sets of shoe-prints emanating from the truck with a jumble of tracks from the barn to the vehicle, probably an SUV like my Tahoe. The seal at the door had been broken, so I went in myself, armed with my big-time cop flashlight and my unsnapped sidearm holster.

It was dark inside, so I flicked on the flashlight as I stopped and listened to the reassuring utter silence of the surroundings. As expected, the blue Yukon connected to the young adult son of a big San Bernardino car dealer, one of Carty's murder victims, had been removed. Carty's tricked-out Ford Bronco was still there, along with the dusty old Pettibone skip loader. Gun cabinets had been broken open and their contents removed, and the two old bicycles that had hung from the rafters had been taken as well after I told the authorities of my discovery. None of that was a surprise.

Looking around randomly, I spied some cabinetry on the far side of the largest room on the south side of the barn. They were twelve feet in length, well-constructed of stained and polished wood, and looked like they *belonged,* but two of the doors were ajar. I opened the doors further to see a misaligned rear wall...a false back to the cabinet. I pushed a loose panel aside and shone the light inside the deep cabinet. Dust patterns on the floor of the foot-deep compartment indicated something in cylinders of around three-inch diameters. There were a few broken rubber bands littering the shelves. Off in a far corner of the cabinet lay a curled single bill and one broken, dried-out rubber band. I reached inside the cabinet and snagged the bill, a fresh-if-dusty hundred.

An empty Hefty trash bag box, drawstring tall kitchen size, lay on the raised barn floor a few feet outside the cabinet. Looking at it, a scenario came to mind. Someone, I'll assume Carty, had come to the barn in the very recent past and had emptied the cabinets of a sizable stash of cash. This place had been Carty's empire for years, and he knew all his own hiding places. I spent a few minutes looking around the building and found a few similar spots, then looked inside the dusty Bronco. The rear seat was sitting askew, and there were a few spare bills in the rear cargo compartment. Had he been in a hurry, or had he had enough for his haul?

I had to give him credit. Carty was a clever boy—the imposing vehicle had apparently escaped the scrutiny of the searching hoards. I had never looked inside it either. Carty had hidden his ample stacks of cash, and when he retrieved it, maybe a few days prior to my arrival, he'd had help. I filed that info for consideration on the trip back home.

I snapped a few images of my finds and left the barn to walk to the tract house. It, too, showed signs of official search, and as usual, the examination had been none too careful. A desktop computer was absent from the spare bedroom, storage cabinet doors were left askew, and furniture had been shuffled in every room. The informal medical suite, Carty's abode for five years or so, had been searched aggressively and left a shambles.

I had participated in similar site searches during my early years as a police officer. Thinking back on those times and knowing the texture of many senior officers, I could almost hear the newbies being rushed with a supervisor's suggestion; "Ain't nothin' else in here, guys, let's wrap this up!" I felt that way, too, so without wrecking the place further, I let myself out the front door and walked around the house, back toward the car.

Curious about one more element, I detoured along the twin track path north 400 feet from the ranch proper to Carty's own private Potters' field. A week after the raid, while I was writing reports for the agencies involved, I was informed that an even dozen bodies had been disinterred from the plot. I had suggested probable identification for six sets of remains, and eventually, my suggestions had proven accurate. All there was left now was a rough plot cordoned off with ribbon-flagged sticks and, yeah, more crime scene tape. I walked back to the car and left the ranch with mixed feelings about the visit. After all the convolutions, I knew that I still needed to bring Carty to justice.

## 10

I was driving back from my three days in Vegas when it happened. I had dropped into the tiny stopover burg of Baker, reputedly the hottest place in the Continental US, home of a hundred-foot tall digital thermometer that often reads well over 100 degrees. I had waited until nearly dusk to leave town, and the quick stop made sense if only because of the Greek drive-thru where I glommed onto my official favorite I-15 road food—delicately french-fried Zucchini slices, a side of ranch dressing, and a Coke.

I drove across the street to the mammoth Arco station that sat at the corner at the end of the second Baker off-ramp and, such as it is, the town's main drag. Seems I always forgot to gas up in Nevada, with its lower gasoline taxes, but that evening I'd made the right choice. Pulling to the line of pumps, I aligned with the premium spout, ran my VISA in the pump's card receptacle, and stuck the nozzle into the appropriate spot on the quarter panel. I leaned on the car and sipped my Coke while fourteen gallons of deceased dinosaur drippings switched location.

Leaning as I was, my eyes wandering to the other side of the pumps and beyond. I wouldn't have normally stopped on the bland shape of a late-model silver Nissan Maxima but for its occupant—fortyish, thin and pale but heavily scarred on the side of his face. His hair was greying at the temples, but in the lighting of the gas station parking lot, he looked pretty decent. Hello, Grant Carty. Thank God for small favors.

My intention for the rest of the evening was decided right then and there. I would follow Carty and his companion, whoever it was, to whatever destination they chose. You lucked into a big one this time, Street.

Mobile surveillance is something of an art form, and I had learned a lot from my TV heroes. It was easier, for instance, in a modest gold '77 Firebird than it would ever be in a red-and-white striped gaudy-ass, noisy, slow Ford Torino, and far easier in a subtly tricked-out Dodge Dart 'vert than in a topless Olds Toronado, nineteen feet long with a head sticking up in the middle. In my case, I had cover; darkness, and the Mustang's variety of frontal lighting options, courtesy of my pal Zig's modifications. If I never rear-ended them, they wouldn't know I existed. Gassed up, I rolled toward the outer edge of the parking lot while the driver of the Nissan went inside to settle up and use the facilities like maybe 3000 other people on the average day at this location. By this time of the evening, the atmosphere inside was occasionally pretty foul, with a stench of either urine or bleach and disinfectant.

When she came from the convenience store, the driver carried a big plastic AM/PM bag, maybe some chips and snacks, perhaps a beer or two for Carty. She was a *solid-looking* woman somewhere in her thirties and dressed more *business casual* than *pretty*. I wondered where I'd seen her before. Eventually, the driver started the car and left the parking lot from the adjacent onramp to the southbound I-15. I gave them thirty seconds and made my own exit —zucchini and ranch dressing in my lap and Coke at the ready in the console cup holder. With her cruise control set at seventy and staying in the outer lane, the driver kept a quiet, steady pace. It was a boring drive for me—I'm usually at 85 or better on that stretch—

but hey, I was working. I passed the Nissan once on the stretch that approached the central Barstow exit, but taking the next off-ramp and waiting for them to pass below put me back into position.

## 11

After Roberta gassed up and went into the Arco to relieve herself in the disgusting women's restroom, she came back out and resumed the trip to LA. Soon after regaining the highway, she saw him stirring from his sleep in the passenger seat. After she saw him raise his head to look out the window, she asked quietly, "So, Grant, how are you feeling?"

His voice was still sleepy as he responded, "Like someone set me free after five fucking years in a closet, Robbie. I'm okay. Thanks for picking me up. Talk to me. Keep me awake. Where you say Bongelli is now?"

"He's in Federal custody, in a safe house, Thousand Oaks or Encino or somewhere, waiting for a Grand Jury to be empaneled. When the State and Federal cops raided his office in Riverside, we got out by the skin of our teeth through his side door with most of the files on discs and memory sticks. They haven't gotten to the Vegas office yet. You say you have money in the tubs, right?"

Carty grinned. "Baby, I am the six-million-dollar man, twice, with some change left over. Let's put that to work, quadruple it in a year or so, okay?"

"That works. Between the fire-sale buys of commercial property and cooking inside disguised properties instead of out in the sticks somewhere, we save a lot of production costs. Biggest issue so far is the transport guys occasionally getting stopped en route. We have lost the merch twice, but we bailed the drivers out pretty quickly. They know to not say a word."

"You say you got a place for me to live, so I can keep an eye on shit?"

Roberta glanced across at him. "Yes, we do. We just closed on it last week. Ten-unit apartment building above Sunset near Silver Lake. You get a nice two-bedroom, fully furnished, newly painted. There's even a killer view of the skyline of downtown L.A. on a clear night. I also found you a plastic surgeon, a good one. Gotta get you cleaned up and looking good again." She looked across at him. "Do the burns hurt, Grant?"

Lame question. "No, baby. Not anymore. They're just *there*, y'know? I got a face you could grate cheese on, and I probably scare the shit outta small children if I look at 'em sudden. After all this time, I'm used to it. Be good to get it fixed though." He paused. "Rob, when did you know what had happened to me?"

"Honey, I was clerking in Bongelli's office, finishing law school at UC Riverside at night. It was a real bitch to schedule, and Bongelli wasn't saying much. Hell, first couple of months after you got hurt, he wasn't there at all. They got his wife...or ex-wife now, I guess...to help after a while, she's a nurse and all, and after that, a little more came out about what had happened."

Carty was dismissive, if not forgiving. "Yeah. Whatever. I'm proud to see you took notes and tuned up the old system a bit. The property rehab setup sounds real good, long as no one gets too loud or anything. I'm proud of you for picking up where Bongelli left off. The crooked old bastard..."

Roberta was defensive of Bongelli. "Don't be so hard on Bongelli, Grant. He taught both of us almost everything we know about making money. I just tuned it up a bit to make it less visible, safer, and more profitable."

Somewhat absently, he said, "Yeah, you did good." Carty

watched out the window and exhaled heavily as the car traveled past new construction on the frontage roads beside the highway—restaurants and shopping centers like he'd never imagined would ever appear alongside this once-desolate stretch of Interstate highway south of Apple Valley. He watched out the window and imagined all the new potential customers.

Later, as the car blended into the traffic on the I-210 east of Los Angeles, she said, "One thing you have to do, Grant, is get to know your son. He's a good kid. You'll like him."

"What's he into?"

"He spends a lot of time with his friends, and we've hired some of them for the drug operation and the property renovation. He still lives with me. I suspect that will change soon, though."

Carty looked across the car and asked, "Was he any good in school?"

"He wasn't interested in what they were trying to teach him, but he did attend class, and he did graduate. I'm pretty sure he's hanging with some gang types, and hey, he's a kid. He'll take all he can get and sleep till noon if you let him. I've put him on one of the construction crews for a few days. I thought I'd set him up at your place, finishing the upper floors. You'll see what I mean when we get there."

"Gotta make him earn his keep. Can't have no slackers, they cost too damn much in the end. He into makin' meth?"

"He'd be open to anything that makes money." She looked at Carty. "I think he knows enough to avoid using himself. I hope so, anyway."

"Prob'ly knows just enough to get himself into a buncha shit. Lots of 'em like that. How's he treat you?"

Surprised at the question, Roberta frowned. "Usually, he's distant from me. I can understand that, really. He was ten years without a *dad* in the home after we left home with my folks in San Diego, then Lee and I split up just as they were starting to get along. Trey was sixteen, and Lee was teaching him how to drive in his old Corvette. Trey got pissed off at both of us, and the Corvette *mysteri-*

*ously* caught on fire after Lee moved out. Burned to the ground, and there was property video that showed my car at the scene. That little stunt cost me about forty grand, and to this day, Trey denies he did it. I'm pretty sure he had one of his friends torch it. I think the whole matter scared him a bit. I hope so."

"Well, maybe I can keep him busy, poundin' nails and paintin' walls, keep him out of the drug shit and off the streets."

Quietly, Roberta said, "I hope so."

"You think he's in a gang?"

"Maybe on the periphery of one. I let him use my new Chrysler 300 last year. He adopted it and made it into a clown car, so I stopped driving it. A description of a similar car came up on a BOLO from LAPD a while ago, but there was no license number given in the send. As a precaution, I took the plates off of it, and it stays parked at the condo. I keep an eye on things pretty well."

"You got *ears on* at the cops?"

"Oh yeah. We have a great ally there."

Carty looked at her. "Sounds like you have all the bases covered. I'm proud of you. I missed havin' you around, y'know?"

She looked across the car. "I wouldn't worry about that. You kept yourself busy, so did I. Life happens, y'know?"

Carty looked out the car window, took a deep breath, and said, "That's the plan."

**12**

Boring though it was, I stayed within view as the steady-as-she-goes pilot of the Nissan traveled toward L.A. At the bottom of the Cajon Pass near San Bernardino, she hung a right onto the 210 freeway toward Boomtown. Over an hour later, she turned off Sunset uphill into a neighborhood a mile and a half north of Dodger Stadium and drove to an odd-looking four-story apartment building perched onto a steep embankment above Sunset Boulevard near Silver Lake. The car stopped and idled for a moment, then the lights doused, and the doors opened. Both occupants went inside after unloading a clothing bag and a couple of large plastic tubs from the car's trunk.

As they worked, I watched from my vantage point up the hill. Using the field glasses from the *work bag* that I keep in my car behind the passenger seat, I again verified that Carty, in the somewhat scorched flesh, was back among us. I stayed until the Nissan driver departed, then until the lights in the apartment doused a little after eleven. Time for a game plan.

After the apartment house went dark, I drove home, calling Sarah as I drove. She was ready to leave when I arrived. I garaged the Mustang and drove the Tahoe back to the street facing the apartment house, parked a half-block away. We waited, watched, and talked for an hour, finally deciding that observing Carty in his new, undetermined role could result in a bigger bust in a short time. The more, the merrier.

Skeptical of being noticed by patrolling LAPD or neighborhood watch types, we drove around the neighborhood, studying the lay of the land. There were several homes for sale or rent in the neighborhood, and one, in particular, looked as if it would work swimmingly. We knocked off a little after two that morning and went back home to make some plans.

Had I been running solo on this deal, I might have arranged for every law enforcement agency within a hundred miles to fall on Carty simultaneously. That would have been gratifying to the max, and it would have enabled me to rub numerous noses in the dirt, having proven myself correct on many counts. With the background information we had on the additional players though, there was a great probability that there were grand plans afoot with his cohorts. I couldn't imagine Carty not putting his money back to work.

I had collected a very handsome reward for *selling* his part in the Connors double murders and finally locating him a while back, and I had done my job as assigned. I decided that night that I'd take the task a little further, invest some of my own money into this effort, and make sure that he didn't slip away again.

After the first sighting and the decision session in the Tahoe, Sarah and I shifted into high gear. I took a pre-paid six-month lease —low five figures—on a nice rental house, about two hundred feet as the crow flew from the suspect apartment building. After the business with the property owner was concluded, I rented some good furniture from a commercial outlet on Wilshire. Sarah agreed to be the *on-site operative,* and we hammered the house together in record time. Fortunately, she never had to be seen from the street, so her anonymity was secure. I spent a little cash on gadgets at Fry's Electronics in Burbank—a pair of big screen TVs, the mounting structures, a small satellite dish setup, and a stack of movie and TV series DVD sets, my hobby and a great way to kill time on what amounted to an extended stationary stake-out.

When I unloaded the Tahoe at the house, Sarah seemed impressed. When Zig showed up that evening to work his magic, he brought a collection of GoPro mini-cameras, a few boxes of wire, and some power tools to facilitate the expected long-distance snooping of the really shifty neighbor in the building by the curve down the street. Sarah had kept an eye on the apartment building for the afternoon, and now the new toys would keep her entertained, involved, and informed.

The living room's west-facing wall held two fifty-inch flat screens—one connected to the satellite system and disc player that Zig had brought, the other set to show images from the rental's exterior cameras, with all attached to a DVD recorder deck. One camera offered the flexibility of a joy-stick operation, split-screen viewing, and a zoom and capture function for still images of license plates and facial details. The fidelity of the recording was almost professional-level. The final addition was the thermal imager that I had used in the desert in the previous investigation. Sarah brought her expertise and numerous LAPD connections to national crime registries.

Per my order, the furniture rental truck arrived at 8 pm, and the new digs took shape within an hour. I'd let Sarah make the call selecting the furniture items. She'd been fairly conservative in the interest of keeping to a modest budget, but when I put in the order at the store, I'd added a few items, including a very nice recliner sofa and some serious lighting. She was genuinely appreciative. "Gotta take care of my peeps!" I'd said when she thanked me.

I mapped out the protocol. "Okay, let's get the drill down. Log the entries and exits from the building, every day. Cameras have time codes and loop recording, so you can let them do the work, just check it in the morning when you get up and do the transfer to the event disc for each day. Call me and Adam on the cells if anything extreme happens, and one of us will be here within an hour."

"Street, I'll be fine. Anything happens, I call you and Captain Fair, and we skull it out. You go do your thing. I'll be fine."

———

I'd had an appointment in the valley the next morning and stopped for a late breakfast with Ziggy. We usually tried to do this once a week. Our current favorite place for the meeting was an obscure waffle joint around the corner from his gun shop in the flats of Burbank. As we were finishing up, Zig asked, "Anything new on your guy from the ranch in the desert?"

"Still in the wind, officially, but he's in SoCal, with cash, making changes. We have his new abode under observation and a line on his plastic surgeon, but we'll sit on him for a while, see who else we can hit when we fall on him."

———

After my appointments, I ran some errands and stopped at the very cool Burbank location of Autobooks/Aerobooks to pick up an order. I drove back south on the 101 from the Valley, offed at Hollywood Boulevard, stopping at the Tommy's drive-thru on Hollywood for a bag of chili burgers that Sarah and I both loved. I followed the wide, busy street six miles east and south to the rental house. The traffic was light except for a Southland film crew—best cop show ever—working east of the 101, and the leisurely drive gave me time to think. When I got to the house, I had to park across the street and up the hill because a visitor's car, a dark blue Crown Vic Police Interceptor, filled the driveway. He and I had spoken at length, and I had explained the Carty connection. He had promised his cooperation with the takedown of Carty if it was needed.

I entered the house through the side door and walked through the kitchen, calling to announce my presence, to which Sarah responded, "We're in here." I had talked to Captain Fair often enough to know his style, and I knew he was on day shift, so he was now off-duty. I stopped at the refrigerator to snag a trio of Sam Adams, then I walked into the living room and joined Sarah and her boss.

I handed over the bottles, tore the Tommy's bag open on the coffee table, grabbed one of the burgers, and plopped onto the couch at the opposite end from Sarah. After her therapist session at my house had concluded an hour before, she'd taken a cab to her old hangout, the cop shop, for a visit and to get a ride to her new home.

"Adam! How are things at Bureaucracy Central?" I asked as I sat.

"You got that right, Street. Same as ever. I have some news for both of you."

Sarah and I dug into the Tommy's bag, and I slid an extra chili burger across the table to Adam. He looked at the mound of food, put up two fingers, and said, "Two minutes, guys!" He opened his briefcase and spread the contents across the coffee table.

"You have your sights on Grant Carty, right? And you suspect that his apartment house rehab down the street is a temporary cover for a meth-cooking operation. You're right. One of our ND cars tailed the transport car all the way to Warner Center, way out in the west valley, before we took him down. He bailed out in a coupla hours, but we took him and his load out of commission, which is the goal. LAPD Gangs and Narcotics are working together on this, and that is going well. You keep us fed with info, we'll keep the bulk off the streets. We'll keep the takedowns out of this 'hood until you wrap up your deal with Carty."

Sarah asked, "Did you look into who handled the bail?"

Adam answered, "Lawyer in Studio City is all I know."

Sarah looked at me, and I lifted my eyebrows. I explained, "We think there's a connection to Carty himself. He was a master cook in Nevada for years, and he was enabled and made successful by the system developed by his crooked attorney, who's now in FBI custody. It looks as if someone is taking the same system he developed and adapting it to a metropolitan environment."

I had been focused on Carty himself and had not given the

possible connection any thought. Finally, Sarah said, "Good point, Street." I looked at Adam.

"We'll take a look at that. Might be an interesting angle."

I said, "Give me the name of the law firm that posted the bail, and I'll check it out. I can get in and out of places easier than a badge can."

Adam took a post-it note, wrote a couple of lines, and handed me the pad. I took the top sheet and slid the pad back toward him.

I looked at Sarah. She seemed tired, so I made a move to close the session. "We appreciate your assistance with this, Adam. Thanks for your help with Sarah, too. That means a lot."

"No problem, guys. We appreciate the eyes on Carty. Department will fund Sarah's time, and I'll put in for funding to cover some of your costs here as well. No guarantees on timing, and we are still awaiting a decision on her status, but," he said as he rose from his chair, "we'll keep working all of it. Have a good evening." He looked at his burger. "Mind if I take this with me? My wife'd kill me if she knew I had this, but it'd be worth it. I'll zap it when I get back to the office. I love me some Tommy's!" We nodded in the affirmative, he touched Sarah's shoulder and smiled, then he walked to the front door and left the house.

I walked back in toward the coffee table where Sarah was attacking her burger. She and I had similar tastes in *informal* food, and the Tommy's fare was a favorite for both of us. I gave mine a minute in the microwave, put it on a plate with a side order of paper towels, and joined her on the couch. "Anything on TV this afternoon?"

"Just the traffic to and from the apartment house. Same six cooks for the second floor, same six construction workers for the third floor. Plumbing supply truck arrived at two, and that's all. Kinda boring."

## 13

The pretty brunette girl in the yellow '02 Camaro convertible drove past the address twice before she chose a parking slot two houses up the hill from the apartment building. She figured this john might become a *regular* and thought he might be a referral from one of her six *weeklies*. The income would put her closer to her goal, the figure that would enable her to go back to White Oak, Tennessee, buy the biggest house in town, and look down on the elementary teaching job and the dumb jock fiancé she'd left behind almost a year ago.

She locked the car, stopped to adjust her black leather skirt as she stepped to the sidewalk, and walked in her four-inch heels a half-block to the steps that led down to the first floor landing, about five feet below the street. She looked good, she knew she looked good, and she didn't mind that *her men* told her so and paid her quite well to look at and exercise their considerable fantasies with her. She knocked on the door, which was opened in a half-minute by a guy in a bathrobe. The room was dark, but it smelled clean. The shafts of light from opened blinds through a window behind the sofa on the other side of the room showed little dust in the air. The man stepped aside and motioned for her to enter. In her best *smoky* tone, she announced, "I'm Candice, we have an appointment." She stated it as a fact, not a question.

The man stepped aside to allow her to pass. The apartment was nicer than she expected, but she was surprised by the man's appearance. He was very thin, and the entire left side of his face had been burned away. The scar tissue was startling at first. "Yes, ma'am. Have a seat there on the sofa." He spoke with a very soft voice. She put her outsized and very expensive purse on the floor in front of the sofa before she sat with her legs crossed like the women on that cable news channel did. Leg shows always worked with johns, and she knew hers were worth the view.

His voice was rough but quiet. "So. I'm Grant. Thanks for stopping by. Damn, girl, you're hot." He leaned back on the shelf unit, looking as awkward as he felt. "Lemme be honest with you. It's been a while for me. I been laid up for a long time, wanna get back in the game, maybe build up a callous or two. Whataya best at?"

The girl smiled at him, her most perfect smile. She reached to put her manicured hand atop his, and in her most seductive southern voice, she murmured, "Grant, honey, let's do this. My first-time rate is $700 an hour, almost anything goes. No hurting allowed in either direction. More time, more money, cash up-front. We'll start with the basics and go from there. I'll talk you through it. You'll do fine. We'll have fun." She smiled her perfect smile.

At the invitation, Carty nodded to himself, then he rose and walked to the roll-top desk on the opposite side of the room. He opened a drawer and took out a roll of bills. He counted out a few, looked at her, smiled, and added a few more bills to the wad before he walked to her, hand out. She took the money, all hundreds, counted it, and smiled back at him. She put the money in her purse, closed the purse, and put it aside. She smiled up at him, took his hand, and rose from the sofa. "Have a bedroom, Grant?"

## 14

Two weeks before, I had spent a strenuous afternoon helping Dierdre move her considerable belongings from a storage facility in the San Fernando Valley to a stylish mid-century condo in the Beachwood Drive area of Hollywood. Located in 'The enclave's enclave,' as the realtor's ad had described it, the condo needed a little polishing before she would agree to move in. She had stayed at my place while the remodeling was accomplished, and we had gotten along swimmingly. I considered that a positive indication of future developments and not a bad thing even though we each enjoyed our *alone time*. Neither of us bothered the others' work. I liked that, too.

Now she was fully ensconced in her new place, and she had made a point of issuing an elaborate invitation for me to visit her and plan to spend the weekend. She made promises that she'd be *accommodating*. We'd have fun.

So she was, and we did.

I knew there was more to be found in Las Vegas, and I had other business there, so I needed another trip there the next week. I left Dierdre's on Monday mid-morning to go home to rest up for the Vegas trip the next morning. I left home by nine-thirty so I could weather the reverse rush hour on the 10, then cut north to the 15 for the quick trip across the desert. The Mustang took to the freeway like I had hoped it would. This time the steep climb northward up the Baker Grade out of the stopover burg was fun. The I-15 freeway reconstruction project that had slowed traffic through the mountain range for two years plus was nearing completion, so that stretch into Stateline came and went much faster than it had for recent trips. No law enforcement was in view on the last steep slope out of California toward the Nevada line, so I let the Mustang breathe, with a yellow late model Porsche Cayenne behind me, and we both topped 130 mph down the long hill and coasted across the state line. That was a blast. Always is.

I had a reservation at the Eastside Cannery, a trendy cubist structure out toward Henderson that I had discovered earlier that summer. I gave the Mustang to the *stick proficient* valet, checked in, stopped for a light lunch at the impressive buffet, then went to the room to shower, decompress, and make some local calls.

In my travels to Vegas during the Connors murder investigation, I had encountered a variety of interesting people connected with the convoluted history that surrounded those crimes. I called the ones from whom I wanted to try to glom some more information and made a dinner appointment with one of the keys to the success we had already found.

Roy Johnson was a retired high school football coach from San Diego. His adopted daughter had been the high school paramour of the convicted killer Arnie Sutton and the mother of Sutton's child. Roy had been a great help in unraveling the history of the players in that adolescent soap opera. We met for dinner at the Red Rock Resort out west of town. Roy was in his mid-60s, still healthy, attentive, and vital. He looked the part for his profession, a thick chest and shoulders above a relatively thin waist and legs. He wore a red polo shirt over black sweatpants and a new pair of silver Adidas running shoes. He had a healthy head of salt and pepper hair, cut close on the sides. His smile was wide as he approached from the parking lot toward the tall glass façade of the restaurant court of the massive resort.

"Mister Street, I'm so glad you called! We got the notice of Lylie's funding a few weeks back. I know that was your doing, so my wife and I wanted to thank you in person. It means a lot to us." We shook hands and walked into the din of the enormous casino facility. "Do you gamble, Mister Street?"

"Rarely. I did some a few years ago, won a lot of money. That enabled me to move to L.A. and open my business. I think I used up a lot of luck that time. I don't want to risk it again."

"Where's home?"

"Now, definitely California. Originally Atlantic City, New Jersey. I grew up watching all the old cop shows on TV. L.A. looked great in those, and I believed what I saw."

"Yeah. When we were in San Diego, they'd come there to film Simon & Simon a couple of times a year. Saw them filming at Horton Plaza downtown one time. The rest of that show was all L.A."

"You're right. A.J.'s canal house is in Venice. That'd be a tough commute every day. It's the magic of television!" Our menus had arrived. We perused them and gave our orders.

"Way back in the '70s, David Janssen did a really good show there in San Diego for a while. You're probably too young to know that one."

"Are you kidding? Harry O is a classic! One of the best ever, and maybe his best work ever as well. I have the series and the TV movies on DVD at home. He, Jim Rockford, and Joe Mannix made me want to come to L.A. in the first place."

Roy made a face when I mentioned L.A. I'd seen the expression before. "I don't know how you put up with that town. Vegas is bad enough."

I mentioned my Vegas pet peeve. "L.A. is a challenge. Vegas has its own plusses and minuses. The freeways and intersections here are incredible. You can watch a sunset waiting for the traffic light to change."

Roy laughed. "That is true. Cab fare taxes are responsible for that. The city lets the tourists pay for services for the rest of the resident population. It's a small inconvenience for a larger benefit. School taxes are low as well. That makes it easier than in California." Our salads arrived on big square plates, and the waiter brought our Coronas.

"So, how is Lylie doing?" I asked.

He beamed with pride. "Still knockin' it out of the park. She is one of the best kids I've ever seen, and I've seen a lot of 'em. Thank you for helpin' her mama, too. We really appreciate that. I'm glad she got away from that bunch she was with."

Between bites, I said, "I was glad to do it. She helped me immensely during that investigation, and I felt that was the least I could do for her. That brings us to today. I'm looking for some more information about the kids you knew back then—Carty, Arnie, and your daughter—but from a non-peer vantage point. Do you remember the girls that Carty hung with when he was in high school? I understand he was quite an operator."

"Yeah, he was. Like I first told you, Carty was two or three years older than the grade he was in. My wife says he'd been held back twice in grade school and once in junior high. The boy drove a truck to ninth grade, Mister Street, so he was way ahead in age and maturity. That made those little girls easy pickins, if ya know what I mean. Couple of 'em got in trouble, which I am sad to say is way more common now than it was then."

"Did the girls keep the babies or abort?"

"Well, you'd have to ask my daughter about that. She was closer to them than we were, and I'm sure she heard things that the teaching staff never would."

"Does anything else come to mind?"

"Well, just that Carty was one mean sumbitch back then. I know he had a couple of his friends beat up a kid who dissed him. And he did not graduate. He just kinda faded away, stopped coming to class. I would imagine his age and maturity—physical, not mental, mind you–got to him, and he felt out of place."

Our salads were devoured, then the main course, a fully-equipped brisket plate for me and sautéed jumbo shrimp for the coach, and we talked for a long while about life in general. He was a good commentator about the lives we all faced, and his remedies would have made him a natural for law enforcement. It was an elemental attitude that came with age, experience, and observation. He made sense. I hoped I did equally when I reached his age. After the food was dispensed with, he and I had a couple of draft beers and listened to some music from elsewhere in the courtyard. I hadn't learned a lot, but I don't always have to in order to feel sated.

I stayed and listened to the music after the coach left to drive home, then I made my way back to the cannery. I showered, cleaned up, and slept off the food and beer. The next morning came early, with a unique sun-streaked view of the distant Vegas Strip-area skyline from my eighth-floor west-facing room.

The coach had provided me with the new number for his daughter. She had departed her depressing circumstances working in a high-end cat-house in Pahrump, had moved back to Las Vegas, and had opened a hair and nail salon in one of the *quickie casinos* that had popped up around suburban Las Vegas. This particular plywood, stucco, foil, and neon palace sat toward the north end of the valley near the *loop* freeway and had a distinctly temporary feel to it. To an untrained eye, it was all glitter, classy in a *Vegas-y* though compact manner.

Our arm-twisting *settlement* with crooked lawyer Vinnie Bongelli's victim Arnie Sutton had liquidated a portion of Arnie's accumulated cash holdings at his suggestion after we clued him in on how Reanna and his daughter had been cheated. We had awarded Reanna Johnson just under $500,000 total, including a dozen years back child support and an enhanced amount for the support payments that had been defaulted on several years before as Sutton descended into addiction. I'd seen the delivery receipt for the courier letter, and I could've sworn I heard the whoops of elation from 310 miles away. Cagey gal that Reanna was, she cashed out a nice re-modeled tract foreclosure house in Henderson to live in and rented the hair and nail salon at the casino as a sure-fire income producer. The casino mostly catered to frosted-hair geriatrics from nearby retirement communities, and in her words, "Lord knows those ladies love to have their hair and nails done. God bless 'em."

I had given her a call that morning, and we agreed to meet for brunch at the casino. It was quarter after ten when I valeted the Mustang under the front canopy of the structure and made my way into the lobby. The room was alive with the sound effects one expects in Vegas—lots of bells and winner alarms going off amid the general hubbub of small-stakes gamblers. The visuals made it a prime recruiting ground for the AARP, and the average vintage of the attendees looked to be well past 65.

A vertical directory signboard pointed me toward a short hallway off to the left of the Registration area. The aroma of the hair chemicals and nail polish was pungent as I approached the third small storefront opening. The carved wooden sign above the portal read 'City Girl Hair and Nails.' From the hallway, I could see two tiny oriental ladies hard at work on a couple of blue-haired clients' hands. Reanna stood at the back of a barber's chair, preoccupied with the silvered hair of a male customer who may have been a casino employee.

I sat in one of the customers' chairs near the open entrance of the shop for about five minutes until Reanna finished her work. She took the wrap from the client's shoulders, professionally intent on talking to him to ensure his satisfaction with his haircut. It looked like the usual geriatric cut to me, close on the sides and thin on top, the style on which my dad had insisted for my siblings and myself during our childhoods. At the first opportunity, I had left that style far behind, only to straddle a mid-point during my cop career.

As she closed the register, she looked across the room at me, still intent on business. I rose from the chair and asked, "Can I get a trim?"

She looked at me and made the connection, then ran a couple of steps to hug me. "Street! How are you? It is so good to see you!

Come back here! Have a seat! We have some catching up to do! Let me fix that mop of yours. Your hair care here is free for life!"

I sat in the *cut chair*, and she started her work, spraying my hair to smooth it from the desert frizz that every Vegas visitor becomes familiar with. She talked a mile a minute, relating her departure from *that place* as soon as the Fed Ex envelope containing the six-figure check had arrived. I listened as she talked of using business connections from the brothel management in Pahrump to be able to get her Vegas business location and licensing in short order. That impressed me. "Oh, and I got a house last week! You have to come see it!" Her excitement was contagious, and in the stalls mirrors, I could see the tiny oriental women across the narrow shop look up and smile several times during her excited description of her recent acquisition. Finally, she asked, "So, what brings you to Sin City?"

"I came here to buy you brunch, catch up a bit, and ask some questions about the Carty of old and the women in his life when you knew him. I need some background, and you are my source of choice." I pointed at her in the mirror as she turned me for the inspection portion of the cut, and she smiled.

She looked at me in the mirror as she stood behind me with her hands on my shoulders. "That was a lifetime ago, Street, and the memories are nothing to brag about, but I'll tell you anything I know. Is the diner across the lobby okay? The food's good, and I can close up for an hour or so. How's the cut?"

"Looks great. You're good at your trade."

"Yes, I am. All of them." She took the wrap from my shoulders and laid it on the back of the chair as I rose. I took a pair of twenties from my shirt pocket and proffered them. "Street? Goddammit, your money is no good here. I owe you more than I could repay in a lifetime, so put that away! Buy lunch or something! Meet me right over there in fifteen minutes, and we'll talk." She raised up on her tiptoes and kissed me on the cheek, then whispered, "Quarter slots are good this morning. The machines here work best with coins."

I slipped a twenty into the tip jar, left the hair salon, and walked to the cashier's cage where, yes, I turned my other twenty into a couple rolls of quarters. I rolled through those in ten minutes but came out three bucks ahead through replays. Not bad. I cashed out at the cage again and walked with Reanna to the fifties-theme diner.

"How'd you do?" she asked.

"Made three bucks! Now I can move to Maui," I answered. We took a booth at the diner and looked at menus for a few minutes. "What's good here?"

"Clubs and subs, Street. All sandwiches, all fresh. Good stuff. They have sweet potato fries that I like a little too much, but everything's decent."

The waiter arrived, and we ordered. I noticed Reanna looking at me and asked her, "So what's going on? You made your escape from Pahrump in good order. I'm really proud of you for doing that. Looks as if you've found your niche."

She reached across and put her hand over mine. "Thank you for that! I had wanted to leave there for a year. I had some money saved up on my own, but you lit a fire under me. I owe you a lot for that."

"I need to pick your brain for a bit, and that'll settle the account just fine. I am wondering about Carty's later teenage years. You said he had a lot of girlfriends, and I have heard since that there was at least one pregnancy. Do you know what happened there? Is that girl, woman now, still in the area? Did she keep the child, abort, or give it up for adoption?"

Our salads arrived, and Reanna continued concentrating on the topic at hand as I started mine. "There was one girl, Roberta Thomas...Robbie. She was kinda plain, but she had big boobs by the time we were in eighth grade. She got to where she was desperate to be popular, and she tried too hard. We all felt sorry for her, even if we didn't really like her. Carty caught on and took advantage of her in every way. She gave him money, he screwed the crap out of her every chance he got, even in his car in the parking lot over lunch at school, and after a few months, here she came...

guess what? She's late, he's the only potential papa, and she is wanting more attention from everyone around her."

"He dumped her?" I asked, expecting the most obvious answer. I took another bite of salad. The cherry tomatoes were fresh and perfect.

"Shockingly, no. Her parents were very strict, and her dad really went after Carty. I know she kept the little boy. Carty helped with her and the baby for a while, at least. That was a surprise." She looked at me. "It was San Diego, dammit! There was just endless sex in that high school, lotsa really hot girls and tons of hunky guys, and they were big on doing what kids will do, y'know? The school nurse was always busy." She raised her eyebrows at that.

Changing the subject a bit, I asked her, "You and Arnie were together for all three years of high school, right?"

She clouded a bit at that question. "Yeah. He was two years ahead of me, and I guess I was anxious to give it up to a senior. We dated till after I graduated." She made a face. "Maybe not the greatest choice ever, huh?" She frowned at the memory. Our sandwiches arrived. We were quiet for a few minutes as we tackled the food, looking across at one another from time to time. Eventually, she took a break and asked, "You said a while back that you'd seen Arnie. How was he?"

"In a word? Bad. I doubt you'd recognize him. He's gone feral behind bars, face tatts and all. He weighs about a hundred and ten pounds, talks like a punk from deep in the 'hood. He will probably never make the return trip to adult life. He has a new lawyer though, so there is some tiny hope. Vinnie Bongelli was not his friend."

She made a disgusted face. "Shit, Bongelli was nobody's friend. How many victims were there, total, at the ranch?"

"At least a dozen. There are still new areas of his operation to uncover, and since Carty is back in the wind, we have work to do to get him rounded up again."

Reanna shot me a startled look. "Street, you didn't tell me that!"

"Just relax. We know where he is, he is being observed, and he's *contained* for now. He doesn't know we know about him. As he recovers, the state and federal agencies are trying to get all their ducks in a row to file multiple capital charges against him. I'm gonna help them clean up some other stuff he's connected with, and we'll give him more than enough rope to hang himself before we fall on him." I frowned. "It's complicated and probably a bit sketchy."

She had finished about half of her sandwich, as I'd come to expect in my many lunches with attractive women. She looked at me, smiled, and said, "Okay, Street, new subject."

"Yes, ma'am?"

"Are you dating anyone right now?"

I smiled. "Yes, I am. Beautiful young woman who works at one of the TV networks in L.A. We're doing well right now. I met her when I was on the Carty investigation. She was a victim in that, like you were. Carty had killed her father. It's early, but I see some real possibilities with her. I'm ready for permanent again." I read her expression, paused for a moment, and took a sip of iced tea. "And to address the subject that is on both of our minds right now, while under other circumstances I am certain that we could accomplish great things with one another, we both have issues in the way of that."

Reanna looked at me and frowned.

I continued. "I have my work and my friend in L.A., and you have your business, your daughter, and your new house. If you take some time to break from your old life, you can make your new life a hell of a lot more complete. You won't have to work at it and pretend like you used to." I took her hand. "You are a beautiful woman. Hang in, there'll be a good guy along in no time, and he'll ring you up like never before. I've seen it happen." I smiled at her.

"So, a room upstairs for the afternoon is out of the question."

I looked at her and smiled. "Truly tempting and quite flattering, but not today. How about dessert instead?"

She looked at me, her head tilted a bit. "Shit. How did you get so smart, Street?"

"I don't know that I am all that smart. In a lot of issues, I know I'm not smart at all. I'm lucky to know some people, though, who are really bright. I just pay attention to them and watch what's going on around me, and I know a little about people. Five years as a cop in Atlantic City helped, and I watched too much TV when I was a kid. My heroes taught me some good stuff."

Quietly, she said, "Yeah. They probably did."

We talked for a while. She described her new house and asked my recommendations for buying a compact SUV to replace her aging red Dodge Ram pickup. She seemed energized about her new business and her home, as well as having a shot at renewing her relationship with her daughter. Finally, the hour she had allotted was up. I paid the ticket and walked her back to her shop. She hugged me, and I left. She had given me some valuable information, and I knew what I had to do with it.

——————

The Clark County Sheriff's Department operates a morgue in the basement levels of the massive downtown law enforcement and administrative facility. The managerial structure topped out at Clark Griffin, who'd been Supervising Coroner for the last seven years. He granted me a brief interview that afternoon.

We met in his office. Griffin was a short man somewhere in his fifties, with horn rim glasses and greying temples. He wore a white lab coat with a few indeterminate stains at the waist level. After we met, he sat behind his desk and re-arranged a few piles of paperwork, looking for the reference to my case. "The identities of three of the bodies from the ranch were verified by the information that you provided us, Mister Street. Thank you for your assistance there. Several others were identified by papers and documents found on their person. Apparently, the murderer just plowed the bodies under after he shot them. The shooting victims were all dispatched in the same manner—shot in the back with a finishing shot at the base of the neck. This was a mean and determined executioner, but at least the deaths were quick."

I agreed. "From what I know of the killer, he just didn't want to be bothered with slow deaths. There was no altruism involved, just one mean, self-centered sumbitch."

He scratched his chin and answered, "Probably true. Anyway, we still have four unidentified subjects. Any ideas there?"

I looked at the list he handed me. "Most likely, from my vantage, they bought it in a meth lab explosion on the property in 2004. Look for Mexican nationals, perhaps with drug-related arrests in the Vegas area back from six years ago, '03, '04. Carty probably hired from the ranks of people he knew as customers. Metro cops may have info there. There should also be a Latino who was one of the shooters of the Connors."

"Well, yes, he is still on our list. Thank you for that. We'll look in that direction." He looked at me as he shifted in his chair. "That it? I have bodies to cut up."

"That's all I got. Thanks for your time." I rose, took his card, left one of my own, and left the offices. Back in the sweltering heat, I regained the car and sat with the A/C on high for a few minutes.

Officialdom dealt with, I noticed the Mustang was still caked with desert dust and grime, so I drove out toward the west end of Sahara Boulevard. to a privately-owned car wash and detail shop to have it cleaned properly for the trip back to L.A. I sat in the cooled lounge and made a few calls for the hour-plus the process took. Mustang restored to visual perfection, I stopped at a drive-thru on Sahara toward the freeway, had a great chicken sandwich and fresh coleslaw for dinner, then braved the freeway for the long trip. I was anxious to get home.

---

The next morning, I slept late, recuperating from my return trip from Vegas. There had been a steady bout of Santa Ana winds across the desert and a couple of wrecks near the base of the Cajon

Pass on the I-15 grade coming into San Bernardino, resulting in a six-hour trip, stop-and-go for well over sixty miles. It had been an exhausting day. I liked the new Mustang fine. It was fun to drive and rather fast if given the space to run. When I arrived home at 2:15 am, I showered, set the alarm for noon, and crashed. The phone woke me at eleven. Sarah.

"Street, you awake yet?"

"Yeah. I had to get up to answer the phone. Good morning. What's up?"

"Your little hottie in the yellow Camaro is back at Carty's. Third time this week. They must be getting along fine." I could hear the smile in Sarah's voice.

"She'll love him long time as long as the loot holds out. I suspect that'll be a while. Why don't you get her info, and maybe I can get an appointment myself? I'd like to talk to her."

"That body? Talking ain't her strong suit."

I smiled into the phone. "Well, gee, perhaps that bears investigation as well. I'll be over there by four to spell you. Is the construction crew still upstairs at the apartment building?"

"Yes. All the movement's on the top floor, so they're cooking on level three, all behind the blue tarp that's flapping in the gentle breeze."

"True enough. Maybe they've been watching Breaking Bad."

"Could be. See you later."

## 15

Vance Boyd had been Vinnie Bongelli's P.I., his street presence, as I latched onto Bongelli's network of duplicity in the previous months. He had followed me as I traveled around L.A. and the Inland Empire. He had tagged my GTO with an electronic locator before he tried to follow me all the way to Vegas. I'd easily defeated his attempts to tail me, had found his surveillance hardware on my car, had dispensed with his efforts in Las Vegas, and had probably harassed him a bit too much before I arranged a face-to-face meeting. Then I led him into a 120-day jail term when, at my behest, he t-boned a Las Vegas Metro PD Crown Vic. They get really upset when you do that.

One sunny afternoon as Vance Boyd was sitting in the exercise yard at the Las Vegas jail, his name was called on the PA system summoning him to the reception room. Taking a guard's directions, he arrived in the large room spotted with visiting families, friends, and legal reps sitting at circular steel tables. He looked around the room till his eyes fell on an extremely large but relatively friendly face, his former cellmate, Ross Caviglio.

"Hey, Ross! How you doin', brother?" Vance Boyd took a seat across the table from the huge man, 300 pounds if he was an ounce.

Ross had no chin. His face started its descent at his lower lip and kept a smooth line until it met his chest a couple of inches in front of his collarbone. His skin was newly tanned and clean-shaven. That day he wore a charcoal button collar shirt under a light grey sport coat atop some sharply-creased dark grey wool slacks. His head was shaved and polished to a fine luster. He had been Vance Boyd's first cellmate when he was brought to the facility. He and Ross had shared a cell for a week before his release.

"Aw, doin' okay for a fat man. Y'know, had to go get some real food after I got out, had to build up some energy an' get some sun. You said you could hook me up with..." he looked around furtively, "that work in L.A. I'm rested an' ready, bro."

Boyd smiled. "Oh, I can imagine, brother. What I can do is hook you up with my contact at the law office here in town. They'll provide you with the right names in Cali. I a'ready tol' the lawyer lady to watch for you. I said you was almost as good at this shit as I am." He smiled anxiously. "I was jokin' y'know..."

"I know you jokin', Boyd. I gotta get some cash flow goin'. Need to stack some green rectangles for the future, y'know? You say they pay well, right?

"They do. They tried like hell t' get me out of this mess, judge just didn't buy it."

"Hey, brah, this town got some badass judges." He chuckled. "Shit, they even nailed O.J! I'll call your people up. I'll do you a solid when you get outta here, okay? Count on it." He offered Vance Boyd his fist across the table.

## 16

The Sunset Starlight Motel was a small, fairly well-kept burnt-orange stucco two-story place just off Sunset in the Silver Lake area a mile from Dodger Stadium. While it had seen many decades and better days, it was currently clean and well-reviewed if you knew which sites to peruse. It had to be a popular spot if the Dodgers made the World Series. I had taken a room toward the south end of the ground floor in the late afternoon that Wednesday, purely for research purposes. I sat in a cheap half-round wood-and-vinyl chair at a wobbly formica-topped table in the surprisingly well-lit room and waited for the yellow Camaro to appear. That happened two minutes before the 4 o'clock appointment. I could see through the thin curtain as the young woman stood next to her car, gathered her large purse, adjusted her short skirt, and walked toward the door. She knocked, I answered.

She stepped into the doorjamb as I opened the door. She looked me up and down as I did her. "Wow. Look at you!" I said. She was a worthy target for stares. Close-up, she was a well-sculpted five-foot-six, great legs, and from what I could see, an *ample* but well-toned body. Her filmy white blouse was covered by a thin jacket that matched her skirt and high heels. For a woman in her profession, she was top-notch.

"You're Rick?"

"That'd be me." I smiled again. She stepped into the room and let the door close.

"Rick, are you a cop?" She stood a foot from me, her perfume bold and fresh in the slightly stale room.

"No, ma'am. They wouldn't have me." True enough, after a fashion. "Are you a cop? You certainly don't look like one."

"Thank you, Rick. No, I'm not a cop." She took a breath, walked to the side of the bed, and sat. She looked around the room as she said, "Let's get to it. My base rate is $600 an hour in full-hour blocks. Most things go, no hurting in either direction."

"Sounds cool to me." I pulled a half-dozen bills from my pants pocket and laid them on the bedspread, trying to concentrate on the matter at hand. She was a very attractive young woman.

She regarded the cash, stood, stepped close, and started unbuttoning my shirt. Damn. She purred, "Thank you. What do we have in mind, Rick?"

"As much as I hate to say it, I need to talk to you." She stiffened. I could relate. "I am not a cop. I'm a private ticket. I need some information from you. Your time is paid for, you can turn and walk out if you wish. I hope you don't." She stepped back and took a seat on the side of the bed, again sweeping her blouse and skirt smooth.

She looked at me, took a breath, then answered, "Okay, I'll play. What do you need to know?"

"You have a regular client, ground floor of the tall apartment house above Sunset past the curves a mile from here. Skinny guy, lotsa burn tissue. You know who I'm referring to?"

"Sure. Grant. What's he done?"

"That's not your concern, though you do need to be really careful around him. I assume you already know that."

"Sure. I'm careful regardless."

"Of course you are. Here's what I need you to do. I'll pay you every time we meet."

She looked at the money and didn't argue.

"Tell me about him."

She paused for a few seconds, then spoke right up. "Well, he pays well, and he's badly scarred from burns. He'd been laid up for a long time and wanted to get back in the game. He's not pretty, but he gets the job done. So do I. He's actually not all that bad. There are far worse. What has he done?"

"Once again, that's not your concern. I'm keeping an eye on him. If he says anything about his work or his friends, you tell me, okay?" She nodded in agreement. "Don't mention me to him, ever. He gets really mad and really nasty. You don't ever want to see that. Are you a good actress?"

She looked at me with a *get-real* face. "Yeah, I can handle that. He said he's having the first of his surgeries on Friday. Did you know that? He said he'd be down for five or six days, but he asked that I visit anyway." She grinned. "He likes to look, and he likes me on top."

Well, yeah. "Darlin', I can relate. If I can ask, how long have you been at this? Where are you from?"

"I came out almost a year ago. I'd just been dumped by my cheapskate asshole college quarterback fiancé and fired from my crummy-ass teaching job in White Oak, Tennessee. If I can make it here, I'll make it anywhere..."

"Wrong coast. You and Sinatra." I smiled. "Well, you are a major babe, and I'm sure you know that. With that mindset, you'll fit right in out here. Do you have a handler?"

"A pimp? No. No one but me and my stun gun." She patted her purse.

"Well, be careful out there, and look at some alternative work before long. Yours is not an easy or healthy pursuit. It will age you quickly, and it will rob you of your beauty and your youth. That'd be a shame. End of sermon. Here's my number, 24/7, if you ever need it." I handed a blank card with my number and a handwritten *Rick* on the face across to her.

She spoke softly. "So we're not gonna do it? We'd have fun, and the hour's funded." She smiled and fingered her blouse.

Whoa. I grinned. "Different time, different place, baby doll. I'm sorry for both of us." Back to business. Dammit. "Now tell me what you're gonna do next time you see Grant."

She laid out the procedure in order and remained smokin' hot in the process. Three minutes later, she stood, as did I. She stood on her tiptoes and kissed me on the cheek, then she left the room. I was tempted to take a cold shower myself, but I soon recovered and joined Zig in the idling Tahoe parked just outside the room.

Zig was himself a well-known critic of the female form. He looked across at me as I resumed the driver's seat. "Well, young man, what did we learn? That is one beautiful woman."

"Yes, she is. And probably underpriced as well." I shook my head and looked at him. "Zig, my friend, sometimes I find my own strength of will to be quite impressive."

"She better get out of that life. She won't stay that hot for long."

As I put the truck in gear to leave the motel parking lot, I said. "Do tell, Zig. Do tell."

———

I was at the rental pad at 8:30 that next morning, a Friday, when a dark grey Mercedes S-class sedan wearing livery plates and limo-tinted glass aft of the *B* pillar pulled to the curb in front of the apartment house. The driver left the big car idling at the curb, walked down the six steps to the front door of the ground-level apartment, knocked, and was answered by a casually dressed Carty, who carried a small grey zippered bag. The pair walked to the car, Carty entered the rear, and the driver pulled from the curb seconds later. I had parked the Mustang a half-block up the hill between the apartment house and our rental. I watched from the mirrors.

After they passed my point, I let the car idle for a few seconds until the Mercedes turned the corner at the top of the hill. I followed. The driver eventually worked his way to Sunset and then made his way past the downtown traffic to exit the freeway at the westbound Wilshire Boulevard ramp. I followed at a discreet distance. Bill Handel was bellowing away about some trivial dreck on KFI radio, and he helped keep me awake and my blood pressure up, so he served his purpose. "He's a lawyuh..."

Once on Wilshire, west from downtown, the Mercedes driver eventually turned onto a driveway that led to the rear of an immense block-long medical professional center. Numerous buildings of this type had been constructed between the mid-fifties and the late-sixties, developing into cutting-edge medical facilities serving adjacent hospitals. They had served well until medical professionals began moving to smaller, more intimate business park-style facilities. Now the huge eight-story building, with its gently curving facade that followed the mild curvature of the wide road in front, was something of a white elephant. I later found that it suffered a 45% vacancy rate and was back on the commercial real estate market.

One effect of the aging of the facility was that many of the newly-arrived foreign-trained doctors in the L.A. area chose the facility for their first offices. The occupant directory mounted along the bank of elevators inside the marble-floored lobby showed the names and the specialties of three dozen physicians. The information led me to the sole cosmetic surgeon's offices on the third floor. The doctor specialized in radical and corrective maxillofacial surgeries. I was told that he was in surgery for the day.

I went into his outer office and spoke to the receptionist, telling of a referral from a former patient and pointing to the nearly-healed shrapnel wound on my left temple, a remnant of a recent running gun battle with Carty's very own crooked lawyer in Riverside. The receptionist offered me a pamphlet that explained the consultation opportunities but also indicated that my scratch was less of an injury than the severe situations with which the doctor usually dealt. She offered another physician as a referral.

A little online research into complex plastic surgery hinted at a complicated procedure that involved skin grafts covering reconstructed and repositioned facial musculature and importation of some fat cells from the patient's own thighs and buttocks. Interesting premise. Recovery time for similar procedures ranged from two days to two weeks, but in all but the most serious instances, the recovery could be done at the patient's own home after a two-day on-site observation period. That suited our purposes just fine.

---

The next morning, I drove back to the rental house and consulted with Sarah about my plan for action at the apartment house in Carty's absence. It was Saturday, and the construction crews, as well as the cook crews, were absent. One of Sarah's drug cop friends had told her that after our last notification, the product from the apartment house cook had been intercepted during a traffic stop on Roscoe Boulevard, way out west in the San Fernando Valley. Sarah had become the LAPD's eyes on every shipment from the apartment building, and no one on the opposing team was any the wiser that it was anything but bum luck. Works for me. I wanted to have a look at the Carty-occupied floor and the upper levels as well. That was best done under the cover of darkness.

Sarah had done some online homework and had found the surgical suite in which Carty's doctor was working his magic. Used for numerous elective surgical purposes, it was managed by a different business entity on a different floor in that same Wilshire medical building. The surgical suite and the recovery room were booked for a forty-eight-hour period starting at noon that same Saturday.

That afternoon it started raining in L.A., effectively canceling, yet again, my weekend car detailing session with Dierdre. She agreed to arrive later. We'd make a *Sunday* of it. The storm would last for two days. Sustained rainfall in the L.A. basin was a rarity, and when the rare precipitation hits the city, it has several results. One of the less pleasant effects is that Angelinos forget how to drive. The LAPD was busy with myriad traffic accident write-ups, and ambulances bellowed their way in every direction on every major thoroughfare in the city, filled with fresh injuries and pursued by eager young attorneys. Insurance companies hated storms almost as much as personal injury attorneys and auto body shops loved them. When possible, I stayed off the road during storms. This time the rain would provide cover for my latest B and E adventure.

I'd done a bit of research on the apartment property I was preparing to enter. Built in 1953, it had gone through a dozen owners in a half-century plus. There seemed to have been some resistance to the building's outward appearance. That was understandable. Looking up from Sunset Boulevard, the concrete-block and stucco building was singularly unattractive, looking as if it were a big beige rectangular shoe box plopped on its end onto the side of the embankment sixty feet above the four busy lanes of Sunset. From a lower angle, it looked as if it would fall off its perch and tumble down the hill in a good earthquake.

In recent years, several ethnic restaurants had developed commercial spaces below the building on Sunset. Somewhere along the way, a concrete facing had been poured onto the near-vertical cliffside surface as an erosion control measure. That huge surface was eventually muraled in bright colors. Not unattractive, just *loud*, and evidence that many parts of L.A. were effectively Tijuana North.

After the building had been bought out of its most recent fore-closure, a construction permit had been obtained, ostensibly for remodeling. Unoccupied at night but for Carty, the building had been tented for painting, component upgrade, and pest control, but also to cover the cooking operation. I couldn't argue that the system wasn't clever. The current building permit, taken fifteen days after the property changed hands a month ago, showed a twelve-week remodel of the interior followed by fresh paint treatment outside.

Four stories of apartments translated to four, one-bedroom apartments on the first, third, and fourth floors. The second floor, which opened closest to street level, consisted of a two-bedroom unit, something over1000 square feet, with a laundry room, an

HVAC/utility room, and individual storage closets at the rear of that level. There were covered walkways and staircases to the upper and lower levels on both sides of the building. Perhaps the sole attractive feature of the place was that it had great views of Sunset Boulevard from its windows and the dramatic skyline of downtown L.A. to the south from some spots on the upper levels. It would have been worth the rent for the view alone if the place didn't look so tipsy from the exterior.

Sarah had kept an eye on the building all day and into the evening, and we decided that the time was right. I'd do my actual incursion Saturday at midnight, using the alley at the rear of our rental as the approach route. I did risk a trip home so I could change into appropriate skulking clothes. I chose a pair of dark grey khakis, a black long-sleeve t-shirt over dark blue deck shoes with no discernible tread pattern, and a dark blue *Spenser-edition* knit cap. I needed that anonymity. Hey, if the meth cookers or the serial murderer called the cops, I could get into real trouble!

I came back to the rental at ten o'clock that rainy evening. The weather forecast predicted a clearing by the next morning, but showers had persisted for ten straight hours. The balmy atmosphere felt dank as I walked west along the narrow back alley toward the hillside. The apartment house loomed to the right, a giant bright-blue tarp-covered rectangle stuck onto the side of the hill. The side street, fifty feet away to my right and slightly uphill, was dark and silent. I followed the walkway along the side of the building, picked a dark spot, and stood there silently for a few minutes. Then I went down to the basement level and looked into a window, verifying that there was no occupancy. I wanted to see if there was any interior noise or attention from the street in front of the building. I found the electric meters on the back wall next to the laundry room. Only Carty's space had any *live* power use, and only a little at that. Good to know.

One car that traveled past the house turned at the uphill curve, but nothing else happened as I waited. Even on Sunset Boulevard, a few dozen feet down the hill, traffic was sparse. I felt secure in replaying the stroll again later, with a little breaking-and-entering added. Walking back to the rental, still in the rain, I considered the tools for the job. I had everything I'd need, most of it in the trunk of the Mustang. I had raided my *gadget drawer* in the garage at home for a cleverly-designed lock-thwarting tool I'd bought from a guy in an alley years ago in Jersey, a couple of diffused flashlights, a bag of latex gloves, and a variety of Ziploc bags for the retrieval of evidence. Those were all automatic cargo when I skulked.

On went the shoulder rig, into the holster went the cop Glock. A couple of clips went into my back pocket. Backup was a loaded .22 that lived in an ankle holster. A really efficient stun gun held onto the back of my belt over my right hip, and a pair of cuffs sat in the other rear pocket. I didn't expect my B and E career to be violent, but I hate to be unprepared.

Final prep included a small video camera, an early *body cam* from Zig's latest inventory, one that would transmit back to the rental for Sarah's viewing enjoyment. The foray would also be recorded for future reference. Verbal communication would be via open cellphone with the Bluetooth unit clipped to my left ear. A final check of all systems seemed a bit overdone, but Sarah insisted. After that quick once over, I was given a pass and her thin cautious smile of approval.

Midnight came quickly. The rain had subsided for a half-hour or so, and the crowned pavement of the alley had already dried somewhat as I made my way to the apartment house. I stopped at the last telephone pole at the end of the alley to let a minivan pass on the street, then went to the lower side of the structure and entered the side landing. Given the tenting vinyl hanging from the sides of the structure, I was invisible.

Just inside the covered walkway, one floor up, was the door to Carty's apartment. I knelt to the left side of the door and inserted the business end of my lock-opening tool. I gave the trigger three squeezes and felt the internal *click* that indicated a positive result within the lock. Turning the lock, the door opened easily. I pulled the tool from the lock, let myself in, and closed the door, relocking the knob after it shut.

I had suggested when I heard of Carty's departure from the facility in Las Vegas that he would have some contact in L.A. provide for his housing. The Studio City contact that held the deed for the property was also the source for the furnishings and personal accouterments. The choices made displayed a definite feminine flair for color coordination and variety, an element that also suggested a familiarity to Carty, so that was probably the woman driving the Nissan. The furnishings were solid, if somewhat less than the quality of the stuff I'd sourced for our rental. I walked across the carpeted living room into the short hallway. The process reminded me a lot of my last similarly secretive foray in the desert house. This residence was smaller, less well-kept, and a bit dustier. It was a bachelor pad, what'd I expect?

I looked in the bathroom, recently cleaned, nothing special there, then I went across the hall to the first bedroom, the larger of the two. The bed was unmade but well-covered with a heavy comforter over the sheets and bedspread. Lotsa pillows too. A bedside table drawer held a lot of fresh condoms. Gratifying to see the multiple murderer was an advocate of safer sex. Casual clothes, maybe a week's worth, all specific to warm weather, hung in the closet. A nylon clothes hamper in the closet was half-full. After I slid the door open to look, I slid it back to the start point I'd established with the toe of my shoe. The room smelled of pot smoke more than the rest of the apartment, not an unexpected revelation. His stash rested in a plastic bin atop the dresser.

A quick peek at the empty second bedroom—nothing of value there—led to a look at the kitchen. Again, nothing special until I opened the double-door refrigerator. The crisper held a collection of plastic bags from numerous groceries and big box stores, all filled with rubber-banded rolls of bills. There were two layers of bags, varied denominations, and I saw nothing under twenties. My loose estimate came to three hundred grand. I shot pictures of the discovery, then shut the refrigerator door and looked at the rest of the decently-equipped kitchen. Inside the pantry door, there was a cloth grocery bag, again, filled with banded bills inside gallon-sized zip-loc bags. No more surprises were found lurking in the rest of the kitchen, and there was no more cold cash easily visible.

The living room was a quick study until I got to the large wooden roll-top desk. The tall document drawer to the right of the chair was packed with sorted manila folders, many packed with paperwork. Most pertained to his medical care, and all the bills were being paid in cash. Other folders were labeled with tabs lettered with addresses. I had my suspicions about the purpose, so I shot images of the labels for later reference. Looking inside the first, I found a collection of receipts and invoices for the renovation of an apartment complex on Balboa Boulevard in Northridge. Each of the documents were marked COPY.

Other folders contained invoices for chemicals that I recognized as being used in meth production, such as what was suspected to be happening upstairs in this same building. I'd get to that in a few minutes. Looking past the desk, I saw a new 32" flatscreen tv with the product labels still on the bottom of the screen. That was nothing unusual except at my house. I hate product labels, and at my place, they're stripped off as the item leaves its box. There was little else of interest. I'd never imagined Carty to be a big reader, but there was nothing in print in the living room other than business-related paperwork in the desk drawers. I'd expected to find some cheap porn or maybe a copy or two of Meth Cookers' Monthly, at least.

The drawer of the end table on the door side of the red vinyl sectional sofa held another box of condoms and a half-dozen bright yellow ballpoint pens from a local Credit Union. I pocketed another one of the pens from Nellis Specialty Motors in Las Vegas. I closed everything I'd opened and replaced the one chair I'd sat in to its original position, then I took a peek outside the window, seeing nothing but darkness on my side of the blue tarp.

Carefully and as silently as possible, I closed the door on the Carty abode and made my way up the tarp-sheltered stairway to the third floor. Two *front doors* were placed on each side of the building. Not a bad layout. I looked into the window of the first apartment I came to, seeing only clear plastic tarps and numerous construction tools—sawhorses, circular saws, and a tall grey hammer-finished metal tool chest. A stack of new drywall panels lay in the corner of the room. I passed on entering that unit, as well as the other two on that floor.

The rear apartment on the third floor was the real prize. A compact but fully-equipped meth lab occupied the *L*-shaped living and dining room areas, with the packing areas conveniently arranged in the kitchen. I let myself in, shot some images for the Narc cops, and went to the single bedroom. It was arranged with a cot and a small thrift-store desk and chair. A large green plastic tub held some production figures, seemingly a production schedule or goals thereof. Another plastic tub held remnants of a production batch, waiting for the next shift to pack the adjacent pile of tiny Ziploc bags. I pocketed a couple of the filled bags for future testing and examination.

The small bathroom, tiled in stylish—for 1958, maybe—shiny light-green ceramic rectangles, was dusty but for an unflushed, urine-spotted toilet and a pair of empty toilet paper rolls atop the tank. In the kitchen, the countertops had been removed, and appliance locations were empty, matching the bare subfloor.

Plastic sheeting draped from the walls was tacked to the ceiling and spread across the floor throughout the apartment. This practice had become the norm for cooks a couple of years prior, used in hopes of preventing the surrounding materials from absorbing the foul and increasingly identifiable odors of meth production. Flexible tubing exhausted the fumes from the cook-process out the front window. The building had no street neighbors on either side, and the eateries on Sunset brought their own aroma, so the usual cat-piss odor from these small-batch cooks was not a huge concern. I shot some images of the rooms and left that unit.

The renovation of the remaining apartments had not yet begun, so they were quick studies. Mission accomplished to the best of my knowledge, I made one final lap of the apartment building, then left by the side stairs to the south. I stood on the exposed walkway at a break in the blue tarping, maybe eighty feet above Sunset, and looked south toward the skyline of downtown L.A. That image was always fascinating to me, and that evening the ethereal glow was rimmed with the haze from the passing showers. I snapped a couple of images, then left the property to walk back to the rental house. Sarah had retired for the night, so I made certain that everything was closed up before I left and drove home.

## 17

Monday morning, at about eight am, Carty's sleep meds wore off. He opened his eyes, squinted, and looked around the room. He surmised that it was a recovery suite. He lay on a plush queen-size mattress, elevated about four feet off the floor on some kind of mechanized base. The room smelled clean behind the aroma of skin salve, fresh gauze, and adhesive. The lighting was muted, and the blinds were drawn. There were background sounds from the hallway past the closed double doors at the far end of the room. The air conditioning from the vents above the doors set up a bit of a draft.

Now fully awake, he could feel the adhesive of the gauze bandages tugging slightly on his face and neck and the stiffness of the altered skin beneath the cloth. His left jaw and that side of his face were still numb. He also discovered the video camera a few feet past the foot of the bed. He focused on it and made a hand motion inviting the observer to come into the room.

Fifteen seconds elapsed before the door opened, and a young oriental nurse entered. "And how are we feeling, Mister Grant?" She walked to the bed and started checking the monitors that were attached to his chest. He vaguely recalled having those same attachments when he was in the house in the desert and at the hospital facility in Vegas.

Carty felt his pulse race. He whispered, "I'm feelin' okay. Is the doctor in? I wanna get out of here soon as I can."

"Well, I think we can handle that right away. Doctor should be back in about a half-hour, and he will probably give you your walking papers then. Your clothes are in the closet right over there. I'll get these sensors off for you and leave you alone 'til he arrives." She pointed at the bedside rolling tray. "There's your call button if you need anything. You'll want to keep those wraps for two days. Either Doctor or one of us will get in touch with you to set a time for the proper removal."

After Carty used the restroom, he looked at his mummified face in the mirror, noting the bruising around the edges of the gauze. He washed his hands and then shed his flimsy hospital gown. He changed into his street clothes; a pair of tan khakis, a black t-shirt, and the pair of running shoes and socks, all courtesy of the nurse at the facility in Vegas. He smiled thinly as he thought of her. He ran a comb through his hair, walked across the room, and adjusted the blinds so he could look out the window. He was several floors above the busy morning traffic below. He didn't know exactly where he was, and he didn't really care, but he knew he was starting to feel a bit crowded.

He heard a knock at the door, and the Doctor strode into the room. "So, Mister Grant, how are we this morning?" His voice was cheery with the authentic Indian lilt as he motioned for his patient to take a seat on the side of the bed. "Have a seat, and let me take a peek. I am sure you're anxious to get home."

Carty made his way to the side of the bed, where he swiveled so that he could recline. "I'm feelin' decent, Doc. How did it turn out?"

"Oh, well, these first two procedures are just the start. If your healing goes well, we can probably accelerate the pace a bit. You are an excellent patient." He reached for the exam light and shone it into Carty's left eye, then the right, as he asked, "Are you feeling any pain? Is there much itching yet?"

"No pain. I can tell I'm still on local meds. Just a little itching. I expected some. You have anything that will help that? I don't wanna screw anything up, y'know?"

The doctor didn't answer, instead, he delicately pulled the gauze mask from Carty's right cheek, making a *Hmmm* sound as he pressed the cloth back into place. He backed up a step and said, "I think you'll be pleased, eventually. You may feel some itching in your calves at some point. We had to take some fat tissue from there to fill the voids in your cheek and below your jawline. There wasn't much there to take, I have to tell you!" He leaned back on his stool and looked at Carty. "You need to put on some weight. You want the rest of the package to be as handsome as the face, right?"

Carty had had enough of this. "Sure, doc. When can I get out of here?"

"I will call for the driver. He arrives at the top of the hour. I see you're already dressed. Good! I'll get you some pain pills. I have some samples of the anti-itch meds in my office. You can have some of those. Would you like breakfast while you wait? There's a cantina down on the third floor. Simple fare, really, but it's usually quite filling. It is part of the service here, there is no extra charge." He smiled again.

"That's okay. I'll send out for a pizza when I get home."

The doctor smiled. "Good idea. That will help with the weight gain!" He turned. "Very well. I will prepare your invoice for services so far."

"No need for paperwork, Doc. You quoted twenty-five large for this round, right?"

"Yes, sir. All-inclusive. Your balance is ten thousand dollars. You'll need a couple more of these captive sessions, then the minor tuning will commence."

"Hang on a second." Carty walked to the closet and took his briefcase from the shelf below the hanger rack. "Ten K. Got that right here." He handed the crisp white legal-size envelope to the surgeon. "All there, brother. I hope this comes out right over time." The doctor took the envelope without examining it. Carty spoke slower and squinted a bit as he reiterated, "And you understand, this is strictly off the books, right?"

"Oh yes. You are not the first patient to request that. Your wish is my command, Mister Grant."

## 18

When the town car driver dropped Carty back at the apartment house just after ten am on Monday, I was in an office at the LAPD North Hollywood precinct showing Captain Fair, his Gang Task Force, and Narcotics Division minions the pictures and samples from the apartment house. He had called in his drug-test specialist, who pronounced the meth sample I proffered to be about 65% purity. "Street, these small cooks don't get much over that strength. They have no chemists to speak of. They just pass the recipes around and make their own alterations at will. Purity is iffy at best. This looks to be a mid-level cook spot, not that big a threat. We can nab them after the transport is initiated and keep the stuff off the streets."

I had a suspicion I wanted to voice. "Consider this, though. Carty's reborn corporate entity now owns five residential properties in the San Fernando Valley area. These are multi-unit buildings of various ages and sizes, all mostly vacant, and all but one in the San Fernando Valley. There have been renewable ninety-day renovation permits pulled on three of the four so far. What if they're duplicating the process from our building in each of those locations?

This could be a larger operation than what we've found so far, and that would be plenty of new product on your streets."

Adam scratched his chin. "Might be worth looking into, but right now, we're strapped for manpower. We have four of my eleven officers out on leave or hospitalized, including that lady you're working with. While I can't authorize any obvious illegal activities, I would surely appreciate any information gained from same. We can re-visit direct action in a couple weeks."

"Thanks loads, Adam. Will you bail me out if I'm arrested for breaking and/or entering?"

He smiled a wide smile. "I'll think about it. Might depend on what you break."

"And where I enter? I have an even better idea. How about you accompany me when I do the potential B and E? That way, your knowledge and evidence would be first-hand as well. I'll let you hold the flashlight or something."

"Ah." He turned toward me. "Street, the current-day LAPD is primarily in the *reaction* business. You just bring me something I can react to, okay?"

"I'll try. Has there been any sign of the elusive Chrysler 300? Is the contract on Sarah still active? Has anyone been keeping an eye on her house?"

"No, yes, and yes, respectively. Our intel says the doers know she's above the sod, but they don't know where she is. Patrol drives by her house every couple hours. The garage door has been tagged. That'd drive her nuts."

"I understand. Stay in touch with Sarah. She'll keep you up to date on my borderline criminal activities. Carty should be back from his surgery today. He'll probably be down for a few days after he returns. And now that we know more about some of his operations, we can at least keep you better posted on the transports from the apartment building." I provided Adam with addresses of the other properties affected. Each of us promised we'd keep the other posted.

Later that afternoon, I drove past each of the Carty-connected locations and shot images of each of the available elevations. I talked to the managers of neighboring apartment complexes on Balboa, posing as a potential renter. Turned out that four buildings, each two-story, thirty- to fifty-unit complexes, had been built by a pair of energetic developers in the early '70s during one of many periodic construction frenzies in the San Fernando Valley. One of the complexes had fallen, extensively damaged, condemned, and later razed in the 1994 Northridge earthquake. The other three had changed hands to disparate owners numerous times in four decades. The specific down-market complex I was looking at had been damaged by fire a year before, and the tenants, mostly illegal aliens at that time, had vacated. The owner, bereft of rent payments, had fallen behind on his mortgage and had been bought out of foreclosure, appropriately at a *fire sale* rate, by one phase of the Carty corporate entity.

The developer's plan, according to the manager of a neighboring complex, was to rebuild and renovate the damaged units, upgrade the rest of the units, and re-open the complex as small condominiums, as had happened with several other complexes along the Balboa corridor. Large signs at each end of the frontage of the building told of newly renovated condos to be available in the near future.

I drove a block and a half to the local Target store, where I bought a baseball cap and a blue satin Dodgers logo jacket to wear over my khakis, polo shirt, and shoulder rig, trying to look the part of a potential renter. I parked at the curb in front behind a red F-150 and looked through a couple of first-floor windows of the vacant complex. As I walked around the corner toward the front entrance, I heard a woman's voice behind me.

"Hello? May I help you?" I turned to see a plain Caucasian woman, perhaps late thirties, five feet two inches and 170 pounds. Her face was pale and as featureless as a potato. She wore work boots, loose blue jeans, and a plaid man's wool shirt tucked in under her large bosom. She had a lot of dyed blonde hair tied in a ponytail and wore no makeup save for a bit of pink lip gloss. A half-smoked cigarette hung from her lips, and an accompanying pack was rolled in her t-shirt sleeve. I thought of a Jim Croce song verse.

"We have cameras at the perimeter here for security, so I saw you walking around looking in the windows. Do you need something?" She wasn't hostile, nor was she smiling. She stood with her hands at her waist.

I smiled and put my hands up. "Ya caught me! Sorry if I got onto your turf. I'm curious when these condos might be available. My sister is moving to town, and she'll be looking for something decent to buy. I used to live down the street about ten years ago. Just curious, I guess."

She replied, "Oh, okay. No problem, check back in about three months. We're just getting started with the rehab next week, and we have a lot to do." She shifted her stance. "There'll be twenty-eight brand new units, from efficiency to three bedroom/two bath. New pool and HVAC throughout, too. It'll be real nice."

"That sounds good. Are you involved in the build?"

She answered, "I'm a partner with the company that owns the property. We have a lot of irons in the fire."

"That's the only way to make it in L.A. now, isn't it? Do you have a card? I'd like to stay in touch. If I can't find a place for her to buy, she'll want to move in with me. Yikes!"

"Well, we can't have that, now can we?" She chuckled as she took a business card from the side pocket of her shirt. "We'll have a model unit finished in maybe eight or nine weeks. Call me back about then, and we'll let your sister pick her colors."

"She'll love hearing that. You may have made your first sale." I smiled at her as I took her card. We talked for a minute or two, then she went back around the corner toward the rear of the property, and I walked back to my Tahoe, wondering if I had just touched base with one of the principals in a very clever criminal enterprise.

Out of curiosity, I drove through the alley that ran behind the series of apartment complexes. Varying quantities of tenant parking spaces were laid out behind the complexes, some with security gates. The *backyard* of the 18560 address displayed a number of older mid-level import coupes, sedans, SUVs appropriate to construction workers, three pickup trucks of various ages and conditions, along with a few construction supply vehicles. Tarp-covered lumber was stacked near the side entrance door, and pallets holding buckets of roofing tar were stacked nearby.

I let the truck idle in gear and creep along the driveway as I powered the driver's door window down and shot some images of the vehicles in the parking area. More vehicles came into view as I rolled, but no midnight blue, late-model Chrysler 300 with tall aftermarket rims and lots of extra chrome trim.

———

Walking back into the apartment complex, Roberta stopped in her tracks and looked back, wondering, Where have I seen that guy before?

———

Back at the rental house, I parked in the driveway and entered through the side door into the kitchen. Sarah was standing at the refrigerator without her crutches and wearing her new prosthetic leg. She looked good. Without looking at me, she asked, "So, Street, you want a beer?"

"Yeah, that sounds good. We have some major news, and I need to ask you about the night of the shooting. Let's sit in the front room and talk."

Sarah frowned as she walked from the fridge. "One question, Street."

"Talk to me."

"I've never asked you. Did you ever get your jacket back?"

I smiled. "I did. It bit the dust in the process of your situation that night. Red satin event jackets don't absorb blood all that well, but they do make great pressure pads." I lifted my eyebrows. "I didn't mind a bit. It died a heroic death."

"I'm sorry to hear that, Street. Well, thank you again. I'm happy to still be around."

"I'm glad, too. I expect big things from this collaboration." I looked at her as she sipped her beer and asked, "How are you and the leg getting along now?"

"Better. The PT is helping a lot. I took a walk up the hill earlier today. I like this neighborhood. When this thing wraps, I might try to get a house near here. So, what else did you find in your travels?"

"I'm now certain that the renovation projects are the cover for the drug manufacturing and distribution activities. The apparatus for the manufacturing process, judging from the building down the street, is small and portable. If there's a problem with one location or if the demand is high, they have flexibility. They can pull up stakes and book to the next one, larger, smaller, whatever."

Sarah answered, "Good to be able to scoot if the heat turns up."

"Yes. I get the impression that the Balboa address was ramping up for production. Two of the trucks I saw there have also been parked down the street by *our* apartment house on a regular basis. I did some checking out there. The guy I spoke with at the North-ridge Fire Department says there was a kitchen fire that gutted one unit and caused smoke damage to five others. After the fire, the tenants vacated en masse. The owner was cash-strapped and under-insured. He eventually just walked away. He filed for bank-ruptcy on his property management LLC later that year. The building stood empty and boarded up for three years. The wire strippers took all the copper and the plumbing, and the taggers and the skateboarders had a few parties a week there as well. Finally, the city took notice. They condemned the place, put it up for auction, and it was sold for maybe fifteen cents on the dollar of its top value. Carty's corporation made the buy. It looks as if there are a dozen or more workers on site.

"Three months is really not all that long for a committed renovation of a damaged property of that size. Cleaning up some smoke damage, doing some painting, putting in new kitchens and wiring, and fixing the drywall would take a couple of months if they work at it 24/7, so it makes sense that they have a side crew putting at least part of the site to work for that extra timespan. Multiply that by however many locations they have, and you have a major-league meth production operation as well as a boost to renovation industry employment.

"But I'm a Gang Task Force officer. What you're suggesting is that the gangs who had a contract on me, who did try to kill me, are tied up with this narcotics operation."

"Sure. Why not? I don't have to tell you...gang types are usually all in on the drug business. It's easy money, and it keeps 'em in chromed-out Chrysler 300s with big silly wheels. Potential prosperity helps recruiting. A nice innocent construction job keeps 'em off the streets during the day. I'm also thinking the gang types provide an easy clientele for the apartment complexes and maybe, in the case of the Balboa address, the condos. Lotsa baby-mamas and their baby-babies. It could end up as a control mechanism for the management of the gangs, and what the hell, it may create an impressive cash flow as well."

"And eventually, the properties are sold off for a profit, and the principals involved go away fat and happy."

I grinned. "And others somewhat sedated."

"That, too."

"But the big story on that deal will happen soon enough. What we need to do now is find that Chrysler so that its driver and/or his passengers from that night can be identified and rounded up. If we can tie them to the drug operation and bag Carty sooner or later, it'll be a triple play."

Sarah asked, "What's your next step?"

"I want to learn a little more about the real estate business. The resident agent for the corporation that owns the apartment complexes is a principal in that law office. I'm pretty sure I talked to her today. I want to see where she hangs out."

## 19

At three pm that day, I parked the Mustang on the north side of the street, a half-block east of a condo complex on the south side of Aqua Vista Street in Studio City, and watched the traffic in and out of the address for an hour. I had driven by earlier, finding Roberta —Robbie—Thomas-Schwinn's complex to be pleasant enough. Thirty-odd one and two-bedroom condos filled a three-acre space that tapered toward the deep concrete drainage ditch that acts as a valley tributary of the L.A. River. California's soon-to-be outgoing Governor *Aahnold* had years before driven that same ditch as a cyborg on a Harley in a really cool movie. On balance, I had read once that during the rare rainy seasons, the plumbing and sewer systems in many such units backed up and caused considerable damage for the tenants. I also knew that Robert Blake had once lived two streets over, and the Brady Bunch house was right around the corner. Pick your poison, Angelinos.

Aqua Vista Street was a crowded westbound spur from Vineland Blvd. The curbs on both sides were packed with lines of parked cars, broken only by narrow driveways and open spaces allowing for fire hydrants. A City of L.A. meter maid crept her way down the opposite side of the street, examining license plates and marking tires for overtime occupancy. She looked expectantly across the street at me, sitting in my idling car, trying to look innocent, as she approached on the other side. I knew my number was soon to be up.

Eventually, the wide wrought iron gate to the condo complex started to clank open as a resident exited. I put the car in gear and made my way to enter as the other driver left, hoping to take a look around. I parked in an unmarked slot in the shade of some mature trees and made my way to the Property Manager's apartment on the second floor of the first building on the left, facing the driveway. I try to approach authority when I wish my daytime skulking to be semi-excused. Ray Trotter came to the door after I rang the bell. He was a six-foot-tall Caucasian in his early-to-mid forties. He had good skin, a strong jaw, bright white-capped teeth, and an aggressive head of salt-and-pepper hair. He looked kinda *Hollywood*. He spoke with a deep, booming voice. "Come on in! Welcome! How can I help you?"

I stuck to the story I'd concocted before. "I'm looking for a place for my sister who's moving to town soon. While I was exploring the other day, I saw the solid fencing and security measures used here. I'm impressed. I don't really want her living with me, but I want her to be safe, y'know?" Trotter smiled wide as he handed me a brochure for the complex.

"Well, I hope she'd be as happy here as the rest of us are. This is a great community. It's a little less *compact* than some of the newer addresses in this area. I've been here for over twenty years, and I have six units I use as rentals, but most of the units are owner-occupied. You'll also find that these units are better built than most in the area. There are some real toss-ups on this street. You don't want that in the event of a good quake." I shook my head as I listened and looked around the well-appointed apartment. On one wall in the living room was a collage of individual photos of Trotter and dozens of actors, some of whom I recognized. Zig called those *I Love Me Walls*. In L.A., everyone's an actor.

I asked, "What's the range of ages and incomes of the occupants here?"

"Oh, we run the gamut, from kids just starting out to the moderately wealthy. There's a successful attorney and her son who are my neighbors on the street side, and there are a couple of actors, besides me, in the mix as well. We have a few retirees, and they enjoy the peace and quiet here." He smiled. "I moved back after I got divorced...both times." Back to business, he started his conclusion. "The available units are listed on the back page of the brochure. I hope we can do business. Feel free to walk around and check the place out. Call me if I can help in any way."

We rose and shook hands. "Thanks. Shall do."

I ascended the stairs outside Trotter's apartment and made my way to the main path/sidewalk of the complex, looking at the cars and the appointments of the buildings and getting the general feel of the place. The address I had for Roberta Thomas-whatever was one of the two-story units that lined the frontage street of Aqua Vista. There was a line of carports behind the street-side condos, and the red F-150 I had seen parked in front of the Balboa apartment complex filled one of the spaces. A late-model grey Nissan Maxima—the car I'd seen in Baker with Carty as a passenger—took up the second space. Two stalls further down was, for the second time, the chromed-out, tall-rimmed dark blue Chrysler 300. I shot pics of the vehicles with my phone.

I stood there for a few seconds and considered the discovery, then walked back to the Mustang and left, pausing at the entry gate directory to take an image. This was getting good.

The trick to this whole operation was that we knew things they didn't know we knew. They, though, had the same advantage over us in some important aspects of the investigation.

Can't let that happen often or for very long...

Driving back to the rental house, I deconstructed the facts I knew and mulled the pressing needs. If Carty was working with Roberta and her law firm, what was his role? Was she the Robbie that Reanna had referred to as having birthed Carty's offspring?

If so, who and where was the kid?

Was she somehow connected to Bongelli's operations, prisoner management, financial manipulation, as well as real estate? With Bongelli stuck in a federal closet, who had taken possession of the system?

And, worst case scenario, was the Chrysler used in Sarah's shooting driven by Carty's kid? That would put Roberta and Carty at the base of the drug manufacture and trafficking operation and, perhaps, the kid involved in Sarah's attempted assassination. Heavy stuff all around.

## 20

A knock sounded at Carty's kitchen door as he was sipping a Pepsi. He opened the door and smiled when he recognized Marko, the cook who supervised the operations on the third floor. The young Mexican gave Carty a sheet of typing paper with a series of numbers written in pen. Carty looked at the paper and asked, "This is mine?"

Quietly, the younger man said in his heavy accent, "Yes, sir. Eight pounds. Ready to go."

Carty grinned thinly. "Okay, man. Make it happen, Be careful out there, y'hear?"

The Latino took his backpack to his car, an older Toyota Sienna minivan. He laid the backpack behind the front seat, started the car, and pulled from the curb.

———

From her perch in the living room, a half block up the hill, Sarah worked the joystick and the slide lever so that the license plate was clearly visible on the four-foot screen. She tapped the button for the still image and picked up her phone. Pressing the speed dial spot on the screen, she waited for the answer.

"Yates? Sarah. We have a roller from the Westley Place address. Blue Toyota Sienna, maybe late 90s, dented passenger side rear quarter panel, occupied once. Twenties, male, Latino, red Salsa band t-shirt and black cargo pants. License number 3-John-Kelly-Able,365." She paused to listen. "He should be hitting Sunset right about now. Let him ride, see where he goes. Take him down west of the 405."

Another pause, then, "Gotcha. Keep me posted."

———

Roberta stood at her kitchen sink and finished wiping the counter after clearing the table from the evening meal. Her son walked into the room and stepped to the refrigerator. The twenty-year-old gamer-wannabe was his usual sullen self, but at least he was home. "Trey, are you in for the evening?"

"Yeah, until I l-leave. What's up?"

Roberta turned and leaned against the kitchen counter. She watched as he selected an apple from the crisper. He was taller than his dad had been before his injury, and the resemblance to Grant Carty as a young man was striking. Just under six feet tall, with dark brown hair almost to his shoulders, with her hazel eyes. She knew he had some of his dad's traits of laziness and rage, but he'd finished high school on time and was a bit more mentally agile than the Grant she remembered. The boy had met his father only once, when he was two years old, and she wanted to correct that situation.

She asked him hesitatingly, "Are you going out tonight? I thought if you weren't, I'd ask you to go with me. There's someone I want you to meet."

He answered, his mouth full of apple, "Yeah, I guess. I can go out later. When d'you want to leave?"

"I'll call and set up the visit. Let's plan on quarter to eight." She grinned. "Be there or be square."

Past his apple, frowning, Trey mumbled, "Whatever that means." He turned and walked back to his bedroom.

---

At eight o'clock sharp, Roberta turned her silver Maxima off of Sunset and drove up the hill to the odd-looking apartment house planted into the hillside. She parked at the curb in front of the structure, and the pair walked to the front door of the street-level unit. She knocked on the front door, and within twenty seconds, Carty answered. "Hi, Robbie. Trey... Come on in, make yourself at home."

Roberta smiled and said, "Thank you, Grant."

Carty watched as Trey walked toward the sofa. "And you are Trey. I'm Grant. I'm your father." Trey looked him in the eye and then continued toward the couch. The two held their gaze as the younger man sat.

The kid hadn't said a word. He took his seat and finally asked, "What the fuck happened to you?"

Carty touched the side of his face. "This? I got blowed up, son, almost six years ago. Burned over about half my body. I used to look worse. Doctor's been fixin' me up. Whataya think?"

"How the fuck would I know? What do I have to compare it to? You haven't exactly been around for the first twenty years of my life, have you? Am I supposed to feel all warm and fuzzy now that you finally came around to show off your fucked up face?" He motioned to his mother. "Am I supposed to feel all proud because she was an easy piece of ass in high school, and I was the product?" He looked at his mother. "You shoulda swallowed."

With that comment, Carty stepped across from his stool and back-handed his newfound son across the face. The move was so quick that the kid was toppled sideways onto the floor. Carty leaned toward the kid's face and spoke through clenched teeth two inches away. "You little pissant! You never talk to this woman that way, you hear me? Stupid little piece of shit! I've put better than you in the ground!"

Roberta stood and all but pushed Carty back onto his stool. "Don't you ever raise a hand to him, Grant!" She went to her son and helped him back to a sitting position on the couch. "Are you okay, son? He didn't mean it. Any of it."

"The hell I didn't!" Carty still glared at the younger man. His voice was raspier now. "You apologize to your momma! You oughta worship the ground she stands on!"

She spat back at Carty, "You never lay a finger on him! Ever! That is not your place!" She looked back at her son. "Dammit, we have business to deal with here. Let's get on with it!"

Trey held his cheek, a trickle of blood wandered past his fingers. He would have a slice on his right cheek and a shiner below his right eye tomorrow. Breathless, he looked up at his mother and mumbled, "Sorry, Mom."

Raspy voiced, Carty said, "I'm sorry, son. I guess I'm not used to bein' with people yet."

Trey frowned as he looked toward the older man, but he refused to make eye contact. He'd settled scores before, and this wasn't over yet.

Roberta put her negotiating skills to work. "Trey, the reason I brought you here is we want you to take over the rehab job here and oversee the cooking being done upstairs. Your dad lives here while he has his surgeries, so you can help him out if he needs anything, too. It'll keep you busy. I want you off the streets." She looked at Carty. "Trey has done really well out at the place on Balboa. He's learned a lot about both sides of the business. He's a great detail painter, too."

"That right, son?"

Trey looked at his mother. "Yeah, I can do that. When do you want me to start?"

Roberta said, "How about Monday morning?" Trey looked

disappointed. "Eight, sharp! The workers will be in by then. You know how it all works. You'll do well."

"If you say so." He looked at her. "Any money involved?"

"Sure. I'll do a grand a week for each side of the work until this building is finished. Should take six-to-ten weeks. That sound about right?"

"Yeah. That'll do for now." Trey still refused to make eye contact with Carty.

## 21

It came to me as I lay on the couch in the den that Tuesday morning at 3 am. It had taken a while, too long really, to make the connection. The Godfather movies had been running on cable that evening, and I had *beered up* for an evening of binge-viewing, perhaps my thirtieth of the first two classics. I lay there on the couch as Michael Corleone stared out the back glass of his Tahoe lakeside home. I found the remote and killed the screen. I hit the light switch behind the sofa. I rose, walked across the room to the event board, and wrote LAWYER! on the surface in large red letters.

Roberta Thomas-Schwinn was the phantom girlfriend who'd borne Carty's son while in high school. She was the figure I'd seen looking out of Bongelli's office in Riverside on the day I'd served divorce papers before he got shut down at the courthouse. She'd been Carty's driver in the Maxima in Baker, and we had talked briefly outside the condo on Balboa. She was still connected to Carty, and in fact, she'd run the show after Bongelli's collapse. I had my work cut out for me, and I wondered if her memory was as sharp as mine. I had placed her in these times and places. Had she done the same for me?

———

Dierdre and I were growing closer, and we tried to spend any available time together. That afternoon we were parked at one of the Valley overlooks off Mulholland Drive. The sun was setting, and there was a slight breeze wafting through the open windows of the Mustang as we sat and listened to an oldies FM station playing softly on the radio.

Her head on my shoulder, she said, "Street, you have an old soul."

"Really? Perhaps. How did you come to that conclusion?"

"You leave clues all over. You have a wall full of old TV shows at home, half of them are older than you are. You love your Dad's old GTO enough to preserve it. You listen to old rock music...even this new car is an old-style pony car. You pattern your career after the old heroes of your childhood."

"Correct for the most part. And in my eye, I consider those things superior. They fit. You do the same thing sometimes, but you look a lot better doing it than most women I've seen."

"We're not talking about me here."

"Okay. And is this quirk something that appeals to you? We've been together for what, three months now? I think we suit one another rather well."

"We do indeed. You remind me a lot of my dad. You and he would have been friends."

"I wish I'd known him. I liked what I read from his file during the Carty investigation. I just wish he had been around to take his search a bit deeper. A little more information would probably have saved his life."

"I was mad at you when you first explained that to me."

"I know that. I could tell. I'm sorry I wasn't more delicate about it. That was wrong of me." A bird landed on the hood of the car, walked around a bit, chirped a few times at its reflection, then looked at us through the windshield. We watched it. Had we been in the GTO, I would have tapped the horn to forestall droppings. I'm mellowing.

"You did what you do. Delicacy is overrated sometimes."

"I tend to rip Band-Aids off quickly, too."

"I'll remember that." She smiled, then she leaned up and kissed me. The bird watched, twitched its head approvingly, and flew off. We watched the fading sunlight change the colors of the Valley for a while, quiet, and then she asked, "Street. Do we love one another?"

"Closest I've felt to it in a long time. I would guess I'm expected to be all tough and non-committal, now that I've been officially declared an *old soul*, but I'm not. Not at all. I'm ready for what I hope we're developing here. I hope it is love...because I do. I love you. I think I have for a while now. The question is whether it is mutual between us."

"But you're worried about being in love with someone. I can tell."

"I am. Look, one of my friends was recently mowed down because of her work. She had enemies, still unknown. Your dad—a good man who was serious about his profession–suffered a worse fate. Will you, at some point, be ready to share your life with that risk, no matter how much you love the person involved? Did your mom and dad ever discuss the danger he faced?"

"Yeah, they talked about it sometimes, but he'd been a Marine, so a little divorce work for some lawyer was a few steps back from serving in a war zone in the Middle East. Your work usually isn't that dangerous, is it?"

"Not usually. I try to keep it that way. I'm selective about the jobs I take, and I tend to call the cops or friends with larger guns...when danger raises its ugly head..." I spoke the last using a creepy TV announcer voice. Dierdre smiled.

"So you're not Joe Mannix."

"I am not. The locks on my home always work, and I take better care of my cars, among other things." In our time together, I had provided her with a proper education in the art of vintage TV.

"Yeah. He must've had Earl Schieb on speed dial."

"No, not Earl. Guy named Larry Watson. They mentioned him occasionally in the show. Real guy. Very cool. He started doing custom paint when he was fifteen in his parents' driveway in Downey back in the fifties. Had his own shop by the time he was seventeen, and he was a local legend by age twenty. His work was all over the car magazines, and he was making major money for his age and the time. He had a huge following. Great lookin' guy, too. He became a bit player in TV on the side, and he did paint and bodywork for producers and actors at Paramount Studios. He usually played a biker or a gang member or a dead biker or gang member. He married a former Miss Universe. I had heard about him for years, and I talked to him a few years ago on the phone, shortly before he died of brain cancer. He was such a cool guy, a California classic. I'd like to have known him better."

"What were we talking about? How did we get onto that guy?"

I answered, "Sorry. Simple. I have a head full of useless knowledge, and I use it artfully."

"Yes, you do. Often. That is not always a bad thing."

"It will be kinda annoying when I'm eighty."

She offered, "I will have stopped listening to you long before then." I had noticed that talk of the future had crept into our conversations. I realized that I'd missed that for a while.

I looked at her and smiled. "Yeah, I imagine so. I'm looking forward to that. I promise I'll listen to you at least some of the time until you're eighty. My folks could've used lessons in that."

"Let's model that part of the relationship after my parents. Mom always acted like she was interested in what Dad said. He kept up his end of the bargain by not being condescending. She was a great sounding board for him, and he for her. My friends were always jealous of how close they were. They were deeply in love, but they also acted as if they liked one another."

We sat together as the sun set and the lights twinkled on in the San Fernando Valley.

"So. Shall we head out? I don't want to waste your evening off watching the valley lights, come on. We could go to my place, catch a Fugitive episode, get you all turned on from that Janssen guy, and then get sweaty and horizontal for a while."

"You have such a way with words." She kissed me on the cheek, then whispered, "Feed me first, then you may have your way with me. A girl needs her strength. I'll give Dr. Kimble the night off."

"Goodie! Is the Daily Grille okay with you?"

"Works for me."

———

Adam Fair had called me that morning. "Street, just a head's up. We got a traffic stop on Van Nuys Boulevard last night, same car and driver Sarah mentioned parked at the apartment building. Driver did a rolling stop, and a traffic unit tapped him, found eight pounds of fresh meth on the floor by the back seat. You or Sarah want to see the guy or talk to him?"

"How long are you keeping him?"

"This is his third time under scrutiny. No bail, so he'll likely do a year at the Men's Central petri dish this time around. His attorney is pitching a fit. Judge says repeat offender, and an illegal, so he'd be a runner. He stays in the tank at very least 'til his trial."

"Thank God for small blessings. Think he'll turn on Carty?"

"I'm not sure he has ever seen him. Are you sure Carty's involved with the transport crew?"

"One can hope." Betting with myself, I asked, "Is the attorney the same one as before? Female, Studio City?"

"Let me see." He paused. "Yes. Same one. Roberta Thomas-Schwinn."

"Okay, let me know what he says. Keep me posted."

"Will do."

———

Captain Adam Fair sat in the back seat of the Tahoe that afternoon as we drove through the San Fernando Valley, showing him the various locations of the Thomas-Schwinn/Carty drug manufacturing system. We'd been on the game for five weeks, and I wanted his input regarding the time frame for the eventual official fall on the system. Sarah sat in the front passenger seat using binoculars to examine the building across Chandler Avenue from our perch.

Sarah rubbed her leg above her prosthetic as she opined, "Looks to me like the same type of situation as the one I'm watching and the Balboa address. Part remodeling, part drug lab operation. They haul out of here in the evenings, three nights a week, according to your informant."

Adam responded, "Yeah, at least that's what we're hoping. Three drivers have been nabbed so far, all emanating from one of these locations, according to your license numbers. We appreciate the heads-up on that. Anything new on your end?"

My turn. "I figured we needed information on the traffic patterns and the people and vehicles involved, so getting the plate numbers was a natural. Only other new item is that the attorney's kid is working at the place that Sarah's watching. We're liking him for being one of her shooters as well."

"Any sign of the tricked-out dark blue Chrysler 300?"

"I'm pretty sure it's parked in the carport behind the attorney's condo in Studio City. I have it as her kid's car. He seems the type for *bling*. The state registration comes back to her law office. I would like to draw him out in that specific car, apply some stress, and see what cracks. I figure two to three people in there shooting at her that night. Maybe one will talk. The car has been sitting since right after Sarah was attacked, and it may not have been cleaned since the shooting."

Adam's eyebrows lifted. "You think there may be material evidence inside it."

I touched my index finger to the tip of my nose. "He is driving his mom's Nissan Maxima, perhaps she is figuring that the tricked-out 300 is too hot and too easily identified after the shooting."

Adam looked at me. "Yep."

I continued. "My question is, how much longer are we going to play with these people? They have a big operation, we know where they're going with it, and even if your guys stop the haulers, some others have to be slipping through the net. That portion of whatever they are making needs to be stopped, too, right?

"Of course. Look, Street, my crew will be whole again, staff-wise, in a week, give or take a day or so. Let's get some more intel, make a solid case, and do it up right. Let's do one of these scouting trips weekly and plan on falling on them in two weeks, date TBA. Will you have your ducks in a row by then?"

"They'll be standing on the side of the road waiting to cross, brother. Don't let 'em get squished in traffic."

"Gotcha."

My cell phone rang a moment later. Catherine Gadsden's number appeared on the readout. I opened the phone and said, "I was just thinking that I hadn't heard from you in a few days. What is up?"

"Just a head's up, Street. Two more inmates working under Bongelli's system are making parole tomorrow, and guess who is handling their cases?"

"Let me guess. It's either *A*, what's left of Bongelli's law practice in Vegas, or *B*, Roberta Thomas-Schwinn. Final answer, I'll go with *B*."

"You win the new Buick. *B* is correct. And there's more."

"Why, how could there not be?"

"Get this, Street. Their landing address for official record purposes will be, drumroll please, one of the properties you mentioned, the Balboa address. I'm sending you the particulars."

"Ms. Gadsden, can we elope? I promise I will honor and cherish you forever, especially if you cooperate fully."

"That sounds like a threat, Street. I'll have to ask my husband and get back to you. Seven weeks married, the thrill may be gone, and there may be a slot open."

I frowned as I *got* the sentence, then I laughed. "I can tell the thrill is not gone, madam, by the way you worded that last sentence. I'll wait here while you blush."

A few seconds pause, then, "Omigod, Street. That was awful, wasn't it?" She laughed.

"Quite charming, actually, as I have come to expect from you. Proposal withdrawn. I thank you for the heads up."

Embarrassment still in her voice, she said, "Anytime, Street. Keep me posted."

Sarah looked back at Adam, smiled, and said, "Street gives good phone." She turned to me and asked, "What was all that about?"

I smiled. "Good stuff, Sarah. Good stuff." I looked at Adam. "We may be able to add to your list of arrestees from this deal, Adam. You may have a couple of soon-to-be three-strikers moving into the scenario."

The three of us concluded our day trip by dropping Adam off at the North Hollywood cop shop. I dropped Sarah at the rental house and drove home to do some paperwork and start preparing a deposition for a court hearing a few weeks away. Part of my work at times involves giving *expert witness* testimony in cases for which I had consulted for forensic studies. In this case, the court trial was a full two years removed from the investigation, so I had to brush up on the specifics well before the court date. Comes with the package.

Catherine's material on the parolees had arrived as expected. My initial reading verified a couple of suspicions about the operations taking place there. The prospects for the future made me smile. They would serve as dependable predictors of the action at the Balboa address and would make for an easy *get* whenever the LAPD decided to do their thing.

## 22

Roberta had left the apartment house, driving her F-150 five minutes before the girl in the yellow Camaro took the newly vacated parking spot at the curb. She left the car and walked to the door of the Carty apartment. As usual, she was stunning, a dark red leather shorty jacket over a filmy black blouse over a short leather skirt that matched the jacket. Her dark hair was pulled back into a ponytail behind a wide red hairband. Her heels were four-inch Italian imports, and her purse cost more than the engagement ring she had received from her beau in White Oak, Tennessee. This was her second visit this week. The two pairs of eyes observing from the *smoking area* two floors above watched appreciatively as she approached.

Carty opened the door, greeted her warmly, and closed the front door as he hugged her, his hands making their way to her rear end after less than ten seconds. "Hi, baby doll! Man, you look good enough to eat!"

She smiled coyly at him. "Well, if that's what you're into." She smiled up at him, "Your surgeries are going great, Grant! I can't tell you how great that work looks."

"You think so? Well, thank you, baby doll. Doc seems to be a good one. I like his work. I have a few more sessions with him, and then the fine-tuning will start."

She put her hand to his cheek and stroked the refurbished surface ever so delicately with the first knuckle of her index finger. "It feels good," she whispered. "You're gonna be a really handsome dude here before long. Are we doing the usual business this afternoon?"

"Sure thing, baby doll." Carty reached toward the end table next to the sofa, opened the drawer, withdrew a folded-closed manila envelope, and handed it to her. "There's a little extra in it this time. I know this place is out of your way. You live way out in West Hollywood, doncha?"

His *personal* remark made her flinch a bit, and she changed the subject. She placed the envelope in her purse as she rose from the sofa. He stared, transfixed. She turned slowly toward him and put her dainty, manicured index finger on his lips. His gaze shifted to her suspended breasts, and he smiled. She whispered, "We don't discuss personal information, Grant." She smiled and changed the subject. "How 'bout you take me into the bedroom and show me how strong you're becoming?"

---

Carty answered the door fifteen minutes after the girl left. He looked tired but happy as Trey stood on the landing outside the kitchen door.

"Yo, Grant! Just a head's up, man. Plumber's comin' tomorrow for the kitchens on the upper floors. If I'm not here yet, they may knock on your door. You have all the keys, right?"

"Yeah, Trey, I do. No sweat. How'd the cook go?"

"We should have five pounds by tomorrow evening. Mom's hiring a second car and driver for escort, so the haul doesn't get snatched like before."

"Probably a good idea. Maybe she needs a *jam car* like the old bootleggers used to use."

"Yeah. Whatever." Trey looked at Carty. "You look a little tired. You getting enough rest?"

"Um, yeah." Carty smiled. "I guess I just had a workout."

"Is that what she was? Okay. Damn, man, she's hot! I saw her leave. We heard a lot next floor up."

Carty smiled. "Oh yeah, sorry 'bout that. She brings out the beast, y'know?"

"Okay... Anyway, I'll see you tomorrow. Have a good evening."

"Alright, son. And hold up a minute. Let's you an' me have dinner some night, okay? Someplace down in town. I wanna start showin' off the new face."

"Yeah, I guess so. Let me know when, and I'll try to make it."

"Sure thing. 'Night."

As the door closed, Trey walked from the building to the street and regained his mom's Maxima. He patted his shirt pocket, feeling the tiny Ziploc bag within. It was time to try the product.

———

I had been curious about the condition of the suspect Chrysler 300. Later that evening, I donned my skulking clothes and penlight and drove to the Aqua Vista Street condo. Again, I lucked out and met a car exiting the property. I parked in one of the Visitors' slots and tried to look casual. I soon made my way along the shrubbery toward the row of carports at the rear of the two-story street-side condos.

I lucked out this time because the red Ford F-150's height shielded the lower Chrysler from view. The big dark blue car was dirty from sitting. A wildfire in the mountains to the north had dumped ash through much of the valley, and dust rivulets had dried on the car body from the recent rain showers. The car had been stationary for a while.

I rubbed the passenger side window with the sleeve of my jacket and shone the penlight inside, then lifted the driver's door handle. The interior courtesy lamps lit, verifying that the car had a decent battery strength. From my vantage, I could see a cluttered interior and some metallic objects on the passenger front floor. This bore further inspection.

Just then, the kitchen door of the next condo opened as a really bright carport light turned on. A middle-aged black man exited the condo and walked toward his Lincoln Town car. I quickly ducked to the ground between the vehicles. The condo door opened again, and a female voice called, "Get me some Ben & Jerry's from the 7-Eleven, too, Jack."

*Jack* grunted a response, and the kitchen door closed. The Lincoln door opened and closed, the car started, and *Jack* left his parking space. All fine, except that my perch was lit far too brightly for my comfort. I froze in place. The Lincoln drove away, and after thirty very long seconds, the carport light doused automatically. I now reasoned that some—but not all—of the carports had motion sensor lighting. Make a note, Street.

Now carrying a tension headache, I skulked back to the Mustang, sat quietly for a couple of minutes, gauging reaction from within the complex. Sensing none, I started the car and quickly left for the trip home.

## 23

Early the next afternoon, I walked into the living room of the rental house to pitch an idea. Sarah sat in the big recliner watching an episode of Adam-12 on cable, but she muted the sound when she saw me looking toward her. "What's up, Street?"

"How are you and Reed and Malloy getting along?"

"We're all good. They haven't changed a bit in 40 years or so. Inspirational stuff, lots of LAPD troops got their initial push from those guys."

"Were you one of them?"

"Not really. When I was comin' up, channels 5, 9, 11, and 13 here played reruns constantly. I think Adam-12 was on a couple of hours a day for a while. I was more into The Rookies myself. That Georg Stanford Brown was hot!" She looked at me. "It's a black thing, y'understand."

I chuckled. "Of course! I bet you had to deprogram from Aaron Spelling cop tactics before you arrived at the academy. 'Check your hair, take a shot' doesn't cut it in the real world, does it?"

"You have a point, Street. T.J. Hooker was not a proper training officer 'cept for Adrian Zmed. They were a perfect pair. His hair was even more hokey than Shatner's toupee. What else is up?"

"Question...do you know any good car thieves?"

She looked at me and frowned. "I know some folks who are good at car theft. The rest is a value judgment, I guess. What do you need?"

"Well, it strikes me that your buds at the LAPD want to wait on getting the drug deal shut down, so that gives us time to deal with your shooting. I'm pretty sure I know where the car I saw that night is located, and I suspect that it has not been moved recently. Additionally, it may not have been cleaned since your shooting. If it just happened to get lifted, then recovered by your friends at the cop shop, might they decide to search the car for evidence?"

"But of course. Even a remote suspicion of a cop shooting, they'd take a very close look." She paused. "I didn't hear you plan a car theft, did I, Street?"

I gave her my best *shocked* look. "Who, me? Of course not. Never happened."

"How would you propose to pull this off?"

"Well, the kid is driving his mom's Maxima to the apartment house every day, and mommy dearest is at her law office or at one of her properties all day long. She drives her F-150. The Chrysler is, for all intents and purposes, left out in the open, just waiting to get nabbed. Easily recovered by the police, of course, just a few blocks away from home, and taken to impound...they run prints, and if they find shells, drugs, guns, or gunshot residue, they pull the kid in and sweat him. Maybe if they find prints, they can get his homies in the box, too..." I looked at her. "You, of course, know absolutely nothing about the unfortunate theft of the Chrysler except for heroically participating in the roundup."

"Interesting concept, Street. Let me know how it turns out." She rubbed her leg above the prosthetic, smiled at me, and shook her head. She consulted her phone for a number and wrote the number on a Post-it note. She said, "Let me get you a nice cold beer," then she pulled the note from the pad. She reached across the space between the chairs and placed it on the arm of my chair, then she rose and walked to the kitchen, smiling and touching my arm as she passed.

# 24

Trey Thomas met his friend Pablo at the crowded, noisy Tommy's burger joint near Silver Lake. As Pablo took the passenger seat in the silver Maxima, he asked Trey, "So, you bring the shit?"

Trey said nothing. He looked sideways at his friend, smiled thinly, and raised the tiny Ziploc bag from his shirt pocket. "Whataya think, I'd forget you? I said I'd bring it."

Pablo, looking around the parking lot, asked, "Where're we gonna do it?"

"Let's get some food. I'll pull off the lot and park on the street down by the lake. Shit, we prob'ly be the *least high* people there."

Pablo nodded in agreement. "'Kay. You brought the shit, I'll spring f'the chow. I'll get chili fries. Wonder if the grease'll soak up the high?"

"That ain't how it works, brah."

———

A half-hour later, Trey and his friend Pablo sat in the reclined front seats of the Maxima in a meth-induced fog, staring up at the sky through the open sunroof.

Trey opened his eyes and inhaled deeply. "Oooooohhhh, shit, man. That is incredible. Thass like nothin' EVER, man! How long's th' high last?"

Pablo looked at his friend. "What, T-man, you never been high before?"

Trey swiveled his head on the headrest to look at his friend. "I been high from smokin', just not w'dis shit. How long does it last?"

"An hour, maybe two if it's primo shit. This ain't that great. We be back on the turf in a while. Your first time? Thass hot, bro. So how much more'o this can you get?"

"I can get some more. I do'wanna overdo it. I do'wanna be a regular user either. My ol' man runs the production, and he can be tough."

Pablo asked, "Zat the ol' man that sliced yer cheek? Gave you a black eye? You do' even know his ass for a month! What the fuck you owe him?"

"You have a point." Trey took a bite of the cold burger and chewed slowly. His tongue was numb. He wasn't sure he liked that.

## 25

Robert Carl Teef was a young black man, maybe 5'3" and 120 pounds soaking wet. He was wearing a red satin cast jacket commemorating a TV series I'd never seen and had a fairly impressive '70s style Afro. He looked to be in his indeterminate twenties. A clean-cut black man, secure in his world as he approached my booth in the restaurant at *the Garland* on Vineland, a third of a mile north of Ventura Boulevard. "You Street?" he asked as he slid into the booth.

"I'm him."

"Lovely Sarah set this meet up. She a great lady."

I nodded in the affirmative. "We agree on that."

"Haven't seen her lately. Understand she got shot up."

"She did. Ever hear anything about that?"

"Hell no. You a friend of hers, too?"

"I am. I'm helping her get back to full-on Sarah. She got hurt bad."

"Sorry to hear that. She good people, even if she's a cop."

"It can happen. You hang with any gang types?"

"Used to. Got nabbed liftin' a bad-ass Trans Am back when I was fifteen, an initiation thing. She saw I was scared shitless and spoke up for me a coupla times. She made sure I got a fair shake. Sent me to Juvie for two years, and she stayed in touch with me while I's inside. After I got out, she got me a couple jobs, made a hell of a referral a couple years ago. Now I work over at Universal in the transpo crew, do some movie an' TV cars...hero car stuff, y'know?"

"Good for you. You're good at your work?"

"Man, don't even ask. I am the best."

"Know your way around a Slim Jim?" I knew his answer already.

"Poppin' locks? Shit, man, I's born with one o' those at the end o' my arm."

"Okay. Our potential subject is an oh-eight Chrysler 300, a car that may have been used in Sarah's shooting. It's stashed under a carport about a quarter-mile away, inside a security fence at a condo complex."

He frowned. "And Sarah's cool with me doin' this?"

"She gave me your name."

He smiled. "Awright! That'll work. You gonna help?"

"I'll be nearby. I'll help you get inside the fence. I have a magnetized license plate you can use. You pop the lock, throw on the plate, snag the car, and drive out."

His head tilted as he asked, "This place has cameras?"

"It does."

"Does the PoPo know this is happening?"

I grinned. "The ones that matter will. You're safe. Pop the car, drive it three blocks, park it, I pick you up, and drop you back where you started. Cops find the car, take it to impound, and hopefully find what they need to find. If not, 'Hello, Madam, we recovered your car.'"

Teef held up his right hand. "Whoa. I don' wanna know nothin' else. We on. What's your budget?"

I started high, per Sarah's suggestion. "A nickel okay?"

His eyes widened as he smiled. "Five hunnert? That'll work. When you wanna do this?"

"As soon as you finish lunch."

He perused the menu. "You buyin' that too, ain'tcha?"

I smiled. "You drive a hard bargain. Order whatever you want."

---

Five hours later, an LAPD dispatcher sent a patrol unit which found a dust-streaked dark blue '08 Chrysler 300 with extra chrome appliques and tall, shiny-but-filthy rims sitting in the parking lot of an old grocery store on Moorpark Avenue. Seems an anonymous caller complained that the car was parked in a handicapped parking space with no authorization placard hanging from the inside mirror. Oh, the horror! In some areas of L.A., that offense could have sent the car to the crusher and the owner to jail. I watched from my Tahoe, parked two slots to the north and across the driveway, with Sarah sitting shotgun, observing.

Sarah pointed out, "Street, that car is filthy. What self-respecting drug gang shooter worth his *twenty-twos* lets his ride get that fuckin' dirty?"

I looked at her. "Be glad. Be very glad. There may be evidence that connects the car with your shooting. I'm a witness to the car moments after you went down, two inside, half a mile from your house just before I found you. You said they shot from inside the car, so gunshot residue and maybe even shells or cartridges may be inside. And what about drug paraphernalia? Tying the kid to his mom and Carty would not be the worst thing ever, would it? Least we can do is hope."

"Yeah. C'mon, Street. I know what you're thinkin' most of the time. You're off the job for a while now, but you still got the chops." She smiled. "Well, most of them, anyway."

I chuckled. "Okay, if you say so..."

## 26

Roberta arrived at her condo on Aqua Vista Street that evening and noticed that the Chrysler was not in its parking stall. She pulled her F-150 into her carport and phoned her son from her cell. "Son, where are you?"

"I'm just leavin' the apartment building. What's up?"

"Did you take the Chrysler?"

Exasperated, Trey answered louder, "No, Mom. You said not to, remember? I'm in your boring-ass Nissan."

"Well, the Chrysler is missing. If you didn't take it, it's been stolen. I'll have to call the police. When will you be home?"

"Might be a while. I got plans."

"Alright. Make it an early night, though. This has me worried."

"Ma, just call the cops. They'll find it for you." The phone clicked as he disconnected.

Roberta started to press the digits for 9-1-1, then stopped, recalling the clever ad campaign, *9-1-1's Busy*. Instead, she called directory assistance and obtained the number for the North Hollywood branch HQ of the LAPD. The responding officer taking the information told her that there may be a patrol unit or detectives by in the next few days to take images of the crime scene. Roberta thanked the officer and gave her mobile number, promising to meet the officers on-site when they arrived.

———

At the same moment that Roberta was closing her phone, the tow company flatbed dropped the dirt-streaked Chrysler 300 just inside the second garage door of the LAPD Crime Lab in downtown L.A. Captain Adam Fair descended the stairs from the raised observation area and approached the Crime Lab supervisor. They greeted one another, did a blue-gloved fist bump, and then Fair looked inside the open driver's door. He backed away when the tech asked, "What do you want from this one, Adam? What are we looking for?"

"Dan, I just want a straight-up look for gunshot residue, drugs, something we can pull the driver in for. We think this may be the car used in Sarah's shooting."

"Oh, yeah. I remember hearing about that one. How's she doing?"

"She's progressing." He looked at the car. "This is a quiet deal, okay? Give me the first and only call, and let me know what you find."

"Gotcha, man. You see Sarah, tell her we're praying for her. You'll hear from me, full report on the car by this time tomorrow."

"'Preciate, ya, brother..."

———

With Sarah's help, I got some inside information on Trey Thomas. He had been nabbed for pot possession twice while he was in high school in Riverside and had been caught in a stolen car as a passenger the year before. Both instances of pot possession had been dismissed, and the other had become a ticket for joy-riding. If you're going to venture into a life of petty crime, it helps to have a newly minted, fairly sharp attorney for a mom. There was no evidence that he had any contact with his estranged father until he started spending time at the apartment house. We were both curious how that was going when Sarah's long lens showed that the young man had a serious egg under his left eye and a slice on his cheek after the first apparent meeting with dear old Dad. It would make an interesting story if and when we got to have a chat with him in person.

Trey had been born in San Diego to a sixteen-year-old high-school junior, Roberta Thomas, who, in turn, had been something of an unfortunate case. My witness and confidant for adolescent life in San Diego during the Grant Carty era had described Ms. Thomas as a victim and not all that popular or attractive except on a per-use basis by Carty himself. When she announced herself pregnant by him, Carty had manned up and paid child support. Again an element arranged by the ringleader and master of ceremonies for the whole operation—Vinnie Bongelli.

Bongelli had taken the new mom, by now estranged from her parents, under his wing. He had given her a stipend from Carty's earnings early on, then a job as a secretary in his front office, then as a law clerk in his practice. She had shown promise and a flexible intellect, so he provided her with a middling legal education at a local UC school, which eventually led to a career of her own. Trey, now twenty, was an emerging punk by that time, his thuggery heretofore undetected by his always-preoccupied mom.

Roberta had finally been suspicious of her son's activities a month and a half prior and sufficiently attentive of her son that she picked up on his potential involvement in the cop shooting east of Hollywood. That was a shock to her, and she had no proof, but she couldn't convince herself that he hadn't been the perp. When she heard of the APB on a tricked-out Chrysler 300, she'd locked down the car and temporarily cracked down on her son's movements.

## 27

In juggling her law practice duties with multiple real estate development projects and the fledgling drug operation, a few things had slipped past Roberta. Now, for instance, she was concerned about the theft of the unattended Chrysler. That, she thought, could be trouble.

Another *bother* was the guy she'd talked to outside the Balboa apartment project. She had an uneasy feeling about him...for whatever reason. She couldn't place him, but she knew their paths had crossed, at least briefly, at some previous point. She just couldn't recall where.

At 5:30 that day, Roberta walked to the first available service counter at the North Hollywood headquarters of the LAPD. She stood there for a minute before her presence was acknowledged. The officer on duty, Evan Gollehon, was a thirteen-year veteran motorcycle officer working desk duty while his sprained elbow was healing. "Yes, ma'am, what can we do for you this afternoon?"

"I need to report a stolen car. It was taken from my carport at my condo, inside a security fence, at an Aqua Vista Drive address. All the pertinent information is right there." She handed the officer a single sheet of printer paper with all the worthy facts neatly typed, an 8x10 color photo, and her business card clipped to the top right corner.

The officer lifted the paper and looked at it. He looked past it at the complainant, and his eyes narrowed. "Okay, Ms. Schwinn, thank you for this. Can't say I hold out a lot of hope. Car as fancy and new as this is probably in Mexico in about 600 pieces by now. I hate to be mean about it, I just don't want to have you hold out much hope. Your insurance company knows about the theft already, do they?"

"Yes, of course. It is fully insured, but my son loves the car, so we're hoping it can be recovered."

The officer looked at the monitor as he typed the VIN into the computer, seeing the note, "RECOVERED, SEALED, HOLD FOR EVIDENCE, per Cpt. Fair, EYES ONLY," in response. He looked back at Roberta, using his most earnest face. "I understand completely, Ms. Schwinn. You never can tell though, we may have good news for you at some point. We will call you first thing if we find something. Thank you for coming in."

Roberta walked back to her F-150 in the parking lot of the LAPD station, unlocked the truck, and sat sipping her leftover Starbucks coffee as the air conditioning cooled the truck cab. There were suspicions swirling around in her head that evening, and she tried to put them in some semblance of order as she sat there. After draining the tall cup, she placed it inside a plastic grocery bag laying on the rear floor behind the passenger seat, shook off her concerns, and drove home to her condo on Aqua Vista Street.

———

At quarter after seven that evening, Carty walked to Roberta's F-150 as it idled in front of the apartment house, opened the passenger door, and climbed inside. "How you doin', darlin'?"

"Fine, Grant. Thanks for joining me for this. I really appreciate it. You've been cooped up in that apartment for weeks now. Let's get you out in some fresh air!" She looked across the cab of the truck as she waited at a stoplight on Sunset. "I can't get over how good your face is starting to look!"

"Well yeah, that little doctor dude is workin' out really good. He gives me plenty of attention. For what he charges, I guess he damn well better, huh?"

"He's certainly not shy about his prices. Working *off the books*, he doesn't have to be. If he's this good, he's worth every penny."

He looked across the truck cab at her. Roberta had stopped at her condo and changed into a modest pale pink pants suit. She wore a thin pearl necklace, and her hair was combed back to fall at her shoulders, making her look younger than her years. Her makeup was fresh, her perfume faint. Carty said, smiling, "Robbie, you lookin' real good tonight."

She glanced across at him, "Thank you, Grant. I appreciate that."

---

Carty sat across from Roberta at their table in the upscale Ventura Boulevard Italian restaurant. "So, what are we celebrating this evening besides me lookin' like a matinee idol?" He smiled at his own joke.

"I just wanted to get you out of that apartment for a few hours. We have a little business to discuss, and I want your input on what's going down with Trey lately."

"All I see is, he slow-walks finish work on those apartments just like every other guy workin' on that building. He fits right in with the beaners he's supervising. Place will look real good in a coupla weeks. We can put it on the market, an' I can move out, get something a little bigger.

"Okay. I was wondering if you wanted to look at some other properties to buy, fix, and flip. We can afford it now, with one of the first Chandler Avenue complex sales closing next week. The timing is okay on that one. We'll clear about $600k. If we do enough on that end, maybe we can get out of the other business altogether. That'd be nice, wouldn't it?"

"What, you want out already? Seems to me like it's startin' to look good. Why stop now that we're starting to show some momentum?"

"Well, I just get nervous. A third of our hauls are being nabbed already. I don't think it's worth all the risk anymore. And..." she paused, "I don't want Trey involved in it anymore. I fear he'll start using."

Carty nodded. "So... You don't want him to follow in my footsteps." He looked at her. "I understand that. I got way too far off the path. Too much money, too much freedom, too much everything else, too. I fucked up, and it goddam near killed me."

"Well, Trey is not going down that path. How about you raise your game a bit, go straight, and make some real, honest money in real estate? You could be an example to Trey."

"What's next? You want me to take Trey camping, teach him how to start a campfire, and change a tire on his car?" Carty smiled. "If I tried to get started with that, he'd probably be 30 before it took hold. I am not your basic daddy figure, babe. Five years flat on my back in a bed in a house in the middle o' th' fuckin' desert filtered a decade of *grownup* out of me. How about your ex-husband? Was he any better than I'd be?"

"Maybe a little. He and Trey hate one another. He was a little too milquetoast to cut the mustard with Trey, or me for that matter."

"Good for him. Okay. So, what else are we talking about tonight?"

"I am in the process of getting you some new ID. When that happens, we'll set you up with a credit union account, and build a credit file from that. It'll be like you're a real grownup—ID, credit, all the goodies. You're gonna want to get out in the world soon as your face is better. Got any plans for down the road?"

Carty noticed the slight but let it slide. "Part of that depends on you. Get me that ID. Let me go out and see what I can stir up. I'll try to steer Trey away from crooked shit if you want me to, but you gotta understand, that's what's in my blood. Let's be real here. Me doin' *straight* is not gonna stay afloat for long. Probably better that I take a hike after the face starts to work again. I guess I'll try to stay under the radar and try to not get busted for nothing. There's probably a price on my head in Nevada. Can't get caught there anymore." He looked around the restaurant, then at her. "Much as I miss stuff like this, I don't have that much experience with it. The ghosts from my past are tying my ass down. That desert shit really fucked me up." The waiter had brought a bottle of wine. Carty sipped his water.

She commented, "You look tired. Do you sleep at all?"

"Some. Not a lot, and not every night. Four, five hours at a time maybe. I sleep best when the doctor's got me bound and gagged." Carty smiled thinly and said. "You're lookin' a little tired yourself. Ever'thing going okay?"

"Yeah, I suppose. I told you the Chrysler got stolen, didn't I?"

"You mentioned it on the phone. That's the car you gave Trey, right?"

"Yes. I'm hoping it comes back in one piece."

"It's just a car. It's insured, isn't it?"

"Of course. Trey drove it for a few months. LAPD has a BOLO out for a car like that for being used in a police officer shooting a few weeks ago. I made him park the car until I get word that it's not his they're looking for. I'm worried about the influence some of his friends may have on him. I don't want him to start using."

"You already said that. Will you please chill out? He's a smart enough kid. He's not on anything, far as I can tell. It's just a business to him. Just a job. And besides, he has a good lawyer." He smiled again.

"Yeah, he does, doesn't he?" At that moment, the waiter brought a wide silver tray holding the main course to the aisle beside the table.

After the dinner was completed, the pair sat in their booth and made small talk as they sipped wine. Roberta opined on the diminishing quality of the men in her life.

Carty frowned and smiled simultaneously. "You mean to tell me that with all the guys you deal with every day, all those lawyers and clerks and judges and legal aid dudes, not to mention your clients, there ain't been any of 'em make a move on you? They all blind or what? You're a good-lookin' woman."

Roberta brushed a lock of hair from her forehead and touched his hand at the middle of the table. "Thanks, Grant. A woman needs an ego boost once in a while. A good energetic roll in the hay works sometimes too." She looked at him and smiled thinly.

Carty sipped his third glass of wine, starting to feel its effects, his first alcohol since his immersion had ended. "You got that right. I got this girl comes by couple/three times a week. She stays an hour or two, I'm seein' stars for the next 24 straight. God, what a body that girl's got. She knows how to operate that sumbitch, too. I ain't never seen nothin' like it."

Roberta was sipping her wine as he talked, but now she stopped and looked at him squarely as he spoke. "So...you're dating someone."

Carty smiled behind his wine glass. "Naw. Ain't *datin'* her, Robbie. I'm a client. She's a pro."

"Oh. I see."

"Yeah. It's all business. Don't need no beginners don't know what the fuck they doin'. Don't have no pain-in-the-ass hurt *feelins* to deal with either. From now on out, I'm all about the *strange*. Ya get right down to it. I guess I just pay her to leave." Carty smiled, oblivious to the pair of enraged eyes staring at him from across the table.

Roberta, realities a bit clearer now, looked at her watch...her plans for the evening and overnight suddenly scrubbed. She checked her watch. "Look at the time. How about we wrap this up? Do you need anything else?"

Carty put his empty wine glass on the table. "Naw, Robbie. I'm good. This has been great. Let's make this a reg'lar thing."

As she rose from her seat, Roberta took the ticket from the table and curtly answered, "Sure."

## 28

Downtown, at the LAPD CID garage, Adam Fair walked to the side of the stall to consult with the shop supervisor, Gabe Quinlan. They stood next to the dark blue Chrysler 300, and Quinlan shuffled the contents of the shallow tray holding tagged Ziploc bags on the hood of the car. Fair asked, "What did you find?"

"These cats didn't clean their car at all. Gunpowder residue on and around the passenger side front door panel matches the one spent shotgun shell wedged under the front edge of the passenger seat, same position. Cash, twenty-two hundred in small bills, in the center console glove box. Found six pot blunts in a baggie under the driver's seat, and more than a little powder cocaine under the passenger side front floor mat, a half-ounce of same in a baggie in the fold-down armrest in the back seat. Car smells strongly of stale cannabis, to the extent that it makes your eyes water to walk past it if the windows are rolled up. You said a kid drives this thing?"

"Yeah. Driver's a twenty-year-old. Connected to Sarah's shooting, maybe."

Quinlan shook his head. "Well, he's gotta be glad he's not my kid. After I came off of the contact high, I'd probably arrange for a visit from someone like you."

"I hear you, brother. All the forms done on this?"

"Yeah. Faxed it to your office right before you arrived. Photo info is on its way as well. There is a lot for you to digest in those forms. Now you notice we did wash it. We had fingerprint powder all over it, old-school style. We were teaching some academy types as they came through here."

"That's fine, Gabe. Have the flatbed take the car to NoHo HQ by this evening."

"You got it, brother boss."

Fair smiled at the reference. "You're getting pretty good at this, y'know?"

"Sheeeit! Who you callin' *good*? I'm waaay better'n THAT!"

"Yeah." Adam Fair paused and smiled. "You are. Thanks for the help, man." After a fist bump, Adam Fair walked toward the stairs to exit the garage facility. After he stripped off his blue latex exam gloves, he raised his cell phone and tapped the face for Street's number.

I was returning from a trip to Mission Viejo to visit and interview a new potential attorney-client when Adam Fair called me with the findings from the exam of the Chrysler. He had a lot to say, and so far, it was exactly what we needed. I invited him to the rental house for a confab with Sarah and myself that evening. We set the appointment for seven pm.

I went home, took a shower, and changed clothes before I fixed a late lunch—pastrami and Swiss on deli rye, warmed on a flat press on the stove till melted, some shredded coleslaw, half a dill pickle, and a Sprite to drink. I sat at the desk and tapped out a fee proposal for the law firm I'd left two hours ago. I tried to artfully mask the *I-405 surcharge* within the *additional services* area of the quote, hoping they'd take the hint and opt for long-distance remote service.

# 29

The sting from the previous night's rejection set aside for the moment, Roberta set to work on her plan for security for her trafficking drivers. When Ross Caviglio entered her office that afternoon, he was indeed intimidating. A recent parolee from the Las Vegas Metro Correctional facility, Roberta had paid no attention when the *friendly* referral had been made by the Vegas satellite operation. Now here was this giant, in her office acting as if she owed him some gratitude or a job.

She looked at the large neckless man from her safe perch behind her desk in her office. "Okay, so it says here you were just paroled from the Metro Jail in Vegas. You were there on what charge?"

The wicker client chair creaked with the man's weight and bulk. "Iss complicated. I was workin' for a guy doin' mobile security for his runners outta North Vegas, an' I caused a cop car to hit a parked truck. It was just an accident, but I pulled forty-five days from it. I was a cellie with a fella there, says he was a PI, worked for this attorney all over Southern Cal. Couldn't find the attorney, Bongelli, his name was. I asked around some more, and the answers led me here. You used to work for this Bongelli out in Riverside." Ross folded his hands in his lap and waited for an answer.

"I did. When the office out there closed, I moved to Studio City and opened this one. So just to be clear, you ran interference for drug runners in Vegas."

"North Vegas. Yes, ma'am."

"That's interesting. What would the cost of your service be, and what does it include?"

"You have an expensive product in respectable quantity to be transported locally. You give me a time and place for pickup and delivery, I make it happen. I am paid weekly, a flat fee that is negotiable and expenses directly attributable to the work."

"Where do you source the vehicles?"

"Usually eBay, locally, but real spread out. You should never know what they are or where they come from. You know nothing of my end of the operation. I pick up, I deliver, we settle up the next morning."

"And you run it all. We don't have to lift a finger other than paying you."

"Precisely. In the event of a disturbing development, I will expect you to offer legal services just as you do with your other workers." Ross smiled, showing a row of capped teeth. "I have done this a lot, ma'am. I am very good at it. I've never lost a shipment, and I can move anything you want moved. I unnastan' you also do apartments and condos. I need a place to crash, too. Been in a motel for three days over on Victory in Burbank. It's a little tight."

"We do indeed. I can fix you up with a nice place. This sounds good. Call me later this afternoon, and I may have something for you. We'll talk numbers then."

The huge man rose, the wicker chair giving a sigh of relief. "You have my number. Call me when you have a decision. Thank you for your time."

Roberta lay in her bed that night, watching the digital clock on the wall next to the drawer change to 1:00, then 1:01. Her sleep patterns had hit a wall recently, and she had faces and places wandering through her mind. She closed her eyes, and for whatever reason, she saw the face of the guy she'd talked to at the Balboa reno project. She thought she'd recognized him from somewhere, but it was from a while ago. Riverside maybe? Bongelli's office? But when? Under what circumstances? Maybe she'd had a class with him. She gave up. She rolled onto her side and closed her eyes as her cheek lay against the cool pillowcase. She waited for the little blue sleeping pills, three of them this time, to take hold.

She awoke again as the digits showed 3:26, with an image in her mind. She was at Bongelli's office before the fall, and there was a man in the parking lot leaning against the fender of Bongelli's new silver Mercedes shortly after he had taken delivery. She couldn't see the face clearly from that distance, but she knew...she just knew. The big fall started shortly thereafter.

## 30

I looked across the car at Sarah as we were leaving home for a trip to the rental house. I asked her, "We've been jerkin' around with this crap for too long. You ready to make something happen?"

"Like what?"

"I want to get a look at the operations at one of these condo projects."

"How do you plan to do that?'

"Just a little subterfuge. Have you ever seen anyone coming out a door, not hold the door open when they see a guy's got an armload of cardboard boxes? It's a common courtesy. You will always want to try to be courteous, and seeing the boxes, 90% of the time, leads them to not look at your face. They just open the door and go on about their business."

Sarah countered, "What if they don't? You're on a construction project. Why wouldn't you be using a cart like everyone else?"

"I don't need heavy boxes. Just something big enough to be awkward to carry. Put on a ball cap and some cargo pants, look like I'm busy and in a hurry, I'm golden."

And I was...almost. I drove the Tahoe to the Balboa location in Northridge, arrived at 4:50 that Wednesday afternoon. I scarfed some clean electrical component boxes from the dumpster in the alley, enough to look a little tipsy as I carried them in my arms. A couple of blank five-sheet invoice forms peeked out from between the top two boxes. I also had a lapel camera and digital recorder tucked inside the collar of my dark grey jacket. Someone's name —*Fred*—was shown on the oval patch above my breast pocket. I'd been *Fred* a few times before. We had driven past the complex before the visit, and I didn't see the red F-150, so I felt certain that I would be a stranger to anyone inside.

I left Sarah in the idling Tahoe, parked just outside the perimeter wall of the complex, and approached the walk-in door on the south-facing wall of the building. A coverall-wearing Latino was standing in the dark hallway smoking a joint. He saw me standing at the door and pushed it open for me to pass.

"Thanks, pard. Boss in?"

"Si. In the apartment next to the pool."

"Thanks, bro." I made the twelve strides to the outer layer of apartments and hung a right toward a wooden table with a circular saw sitting in the middle.

Two men were standing next to it checking measurements on some trim moldings. One of them looked at my *load* and pointed toward the row of apartments behind the pool. "'Lettrics? I think that goes back to unit 24. They been waitin' for ya."

I mumbled my thanks as I stood toward him so that the camera could get a clear view of the man's face and the gang tattoos on the side of his neck. I waved and turned to walk toward his referral. As I walked across the concrete courtyard, I looked around the facility. There were two stories of apartments, most one-bedroom units on the small side, with the occasional extra front window indicating the *DeLuxe* two-bedroom spread.

I arrived at Unit 24 to find a closed door and plastic wrap covering the inside window surfaces. Compressor noise from inside hinted at a painting project. Fine with me. I deposited the empty boxes on the table next to the door and walked the inner perimeter of the facility, getting an eyeful of the layout, noting the three units at the rear of the courtyard, plastic-wrapped more fully than the rest. Given the system I'd seen at the Sunset apartment building, I could safely assume that was where the cooking or mixing and cutting was taking place. Duly noted. Also duly noted, the lady I'd encountered previously, entering the same side portal I'd used moments ago. Time to go. I tapped my Bluetooth headset, and Sarah picked up.

"Sarah!" I whispered urgently. "Front entrance, thirty seconds!" and I made my way to the wide entrance portal, walking past the two rows of gold-toned metal USPS lockboxes and through the front gate. I may have heard a voice raised behind me. Not the stealthy escape I'd wished for, but you gotta go with what ya got.

As I ascended the three steps to the front sidewalk, Sarah pulled the Tahoe to the curb, and I took the passenger seat, then she merged into the sparse afternoon traffic on southbound Balboa. Sarah looked at me and asked, "How'd it go?"

"About as expected. Moderate renovation nearing completion, and they're cooking in, looks like three units, southwest rear corner, ground floor." I looked at her. "I don't know that Fair would send troops to raid the place at this point."

"If it looked like a sure thing, he might. He may need more evidence."

"I have the camera footage. Let's see what that shows."

———————

The sturdy lady Street had seen enter the courtyard approached the two men cutting moldings at the circular saw on the work table. "Gluckman, the guy who was just here...went out the front gate... who was that?"

Ron Gluckman, parolee from Chowchilla State Prison after five years in for a home invasion robbery, looked at Roberta and stepped back. "I have no idea, ma'am. Just a guy in here making a delivery. Had some boxes of 'lettric stuff. Took them to number 24, I think."

Roberta stormed across the concrete, past the empty pool, to the unit on the opposite side of the facility. She knocked on the door, and a young Latino in painter's overalls answered the door. "Did you just see a man here delivering some boxes?"

Lorenzo looked at Roberta with questioning eyes. "I din' see anyone, Ma'am."

Roberta looked at the array of packaging on the table and looked past the front entrance of the facility. "Where is the invoice for the delivery about five minutes ago?"

Roberta turned to the next workman and started to speak. Lorenzo Garcia, the painting foreman for the interior, protested to her. "Ma'am, there hasn't been a delivery here since this morning. We have everything we need, and you know that I tell you what to order when we need supplies."

This satisfied Roberta momentarily. "Okay, guys. Get back to work. Keep your eyes open." The Latinos looked at one another, shrugged, and returned to work.

———

Later, we watched the clandestine video that I'd made at the Balboa address. It showed nothing that we hadn't known before, so I filed the stick, and we moved on.

## 31

The first *accompanied* drug haul from the apartment house took place that Thursday night, dutifully observed courtesy of Sarah and her zoom-lens camera. The hauler drove an aging white Toyota Corolla sedan, and the escort had a decade-old Ford Expedition 4x4. The escort from LAPD, a new charcoal Dodge Charger that looked like a cop's rendition of *sneaky*, picked up the pair of vehicles on Ventura as they traveled west from the 405 interchange. At one point, the pickup slowed with the Charger two cars behind at an intersection as the traffic light changed. The Toyota, ahead of the escorts, scooted across the intersection as the light changed and disappeared into the labyrinth of side streets that make up the trendy, expensive neighborhoods of Encino. Score one for the bad guys. I've pulled the same stunt myself when followed.

A second attempt ended somewhat differently. Late the next night, the same Expedition was recognized and pulled over for switched license plates, a burned-out license plate light, and a cracked tail light lens. As the officer approached the truck, the driver's window powered down, and the driver's silhouette became visible. The young LAPD officer, suspecting trouble, stopped her approach and called for backup after commanding the driver to turn off the truck and show his hands.

The Expedition driver, a large Caucasian male with a shaved head, responded by revving the truck, slamming it into reverse, and climbing the nose of the Ford Crown Vic patrol unit. The *loaded* receiver hitch on the truck did an instant destructo number on the radiator and front facia of the big Ford. He then put the 4WD truck into drive and took off, leaving the steaming police vehicle immobile and the female officer crouching behind the open driver's door, firing five rounds into the fleeing truck. The next morning, the owner of a Sun Valley wrecking yard called the L.A. County Sheriff's to report a shot-up, burned-out Expedition parked just outside his chained parking lot entrance. The Toyota? Poofed without a trace.

————

Adam arrived at the rental in his personal car, a nondescript dark-red Ford Explorer. He parked in the driveway behind my Mustang and walked up the front steps. Dressed in civvies, he looked like anyone other than a powerful Law Enforcement professional on a mission. Sarah greeted him at the door, and we took our places in the living room.

He looked at Sarah as he took his seat, leaning forward to lay out an array of photos on the coffee table. "Okay, Sarah, we think this is the evidence we need to go get this guy, but I want your input. Looks as if Street's buddy, Trey Thomas, was driving, and a younger guy, one of our gang-boy wannabes, was shooting from the passenger seat. This may have been part of an initiation."

"Prints we have are for an Abel Juarez. Age sixteen. Juvie record, looks as if he was a courier and an errand boy for the Wheeler Street Reds crowd for a year or so out in Panorama City. Nabbed twice by age fifteen, charges were reduced, and he was sent home. He has a mom and five siblings there. His dad, Roberto, has been incarcerated since the kid was four, so he's been adrift for a long time. Looks as if you had some contact a year or so ago with one of the seniors from Wheeler Street, guy went to prison for a solid twenty. Good job there, but I'm bettin' they had eyes in court that got stuck on you, hence the attack."

He cleared his throat and continued, specifying evidence pics as he spoke. "Now, the shell we found under the front corner of the passenger seat of the Chrysler shows a match to the powders on the door upholstery, same position. That's the shotgun—"

Sarah interjected, "That's what took my leg. Oh, I remember that just fine."

Adam responded, "Yes, it is. Now you also said there were other shots from—"

Sarah finished the sentence for him. "From a pistol. I think it sounded like a semi-automatic, but I may be wrong. I was a little busy at the time."

"Okay, you were right about that." Adam continued, "There were four shell casings on the floor, .40 caliber, and some more residue in the door panel but more toward the front of the door. He was firing from the driver's seat. Your wounds indicate two hits, side abdomen, through-and-through, and two found in the fence next to the sidewalk. You were lucky there. Could've been far worse."

"Yeah, Adam, I really lucked out, just lost the leg." I heard a tinge of sarcasm in Sarah's voice as I looked at her. "I know I saw two shooters. One shotgun, one pistol, both from inside the passenger side front door of the car."

"So I think we lucked out, but there was more. Inside the center console storage bin, we found these. Gang-deployed hit men are a lesser breed now, it seems." He smiled as he slid the new picture toward us. "These clowns wore earplugs—that foam style with the gel coating that you push into place, leaving..." he pointed at the next picture, "...a perfect print from the index fingers of one Trey Thomas and the thumbs of one Abel Juarez combined with powder imprints, same subjects, index and partial thumbs, both hands from the sides of the plugs as they were removed after the shootings. The powder traces all matched as well."

Sarah smiled for the first time in that meeting. "What a break that is! That shit never happens!"

"You are right!" I had never heard Adam so enthused. "We don't have the guns, but we have the car, the shells, the cartridge, the powder residue. And now the perfect prints on the earplugs just about slam the holding cell door on the tender pink fingers of Trey Thomas and Abel Juarez. And as the guy who gets to call the shots on all this shit, I am delegating you, Madam Sarah, to decide the method of shutdown for these guys. Take your time, let me know what you want to do and when. I expect this to be a good bust, and it is all on you. Make us proud." He rose from his chair. "And now, you'll have to excuse me. I have a school function with my little girl, and I am never late to those. Don't get up. Let's talk tomorrow."

————

We were on an errand run the next morning, with Sarah mapping possible takedown sites for the upcoming event, when Sarah looked at me from across the Mustang and asked a question.

"Street, how soon do you think I could go to my house? I'm fine campin' out at the rental, but I need some of my own stuff. You think we could make that happen?"

"Fair says there is suspected gang activity near there, and your garage door has been tagged. Maybe if I went by and checked it out first? You cool with that?"

She pursed her lips. "If we have to do it that way, fine."

"Okay. I'll run by there early tomorrow morning and see what's what, and if it's okay, I'll come get you."

She smiled. "Probably best to do it while the little darlings are sleeping. Any time before two in the afternoon should work."

I was glad to see her sense of humor had returned. I tried for a change of subject. "You and the leg are getting along well, I see. Hopefully, we can wrap this deal up soon, and you can get on with your life. What was the final review board decision?"

"Released from service, wounded in action, my choice of desk duty to my twenty or out now, buyout TBA, regular city pension after I hit twenty. I haven't decided yet."

"Well, keep me posted. I'll go to the house tomorrow morning... check things out. If it looks good, I'll come back and get you if that's what you want."

She handed me the brass key. "I'll be waiting."

———

I was out running errands the next morning when I took a drive through Los Feliz, eventually crossing Sunset to arrive in front of Sarah's house. The dry, late summer/early fall heat had scorched off whatever green her lawn and shrubbery had worn, and the siding wore ash, dust, and soot from the Valencia wildfires that had darkened the sky in the area a week prior. I walked up the short path to the three steps to the front door. I looked around the street again before I entered. Seeing no Gatling guns pointing in my direction, I unlocked and entered.

Knowing Sarah for a while as a dedicated law enforcement professional and one hell of a pool player and seeing how well she kept the rental, I knew that she would be annoyed no end at how dusty her home was. I walked through the house and saw nothing obvious except the damaged frame of the French doors that opened onto the back patio. There were two sets of faint footprints in the dust on the very handsome dark, hardwood floors in the living room and kitchen. The prints looked to be new athletic shoes of an average size, leading to the kitchen door that led to the garage. As I passed the kitchen sink, still containing our weeks-old coffee cups, I picked up a stale-sour scent that I dreaded.

I snatched a kitchen towel with my left hand. I wet it under the faucet and un-holstered my Glock with my right after I turned the knob and opened the door. Inside the darkened one-and-a-half-car garage sat the usual detritus of suburban living and a near-new dark charcoal KIA Soul. The windows of the KIA were sweaty, to such an extent that I knew what to expect. With the towel over my mouth and nose, I stepped closer to the little car to see a plastic trash bag-covered corpse. The exposed head was that of a young Latino man, medium-tone skin with a fluffy *natural* haircut. I could see no open wounds, leaving that to the body cops who would visit within the next hour.

After a walk around the car, I re-entered the kitchen and started making calls from my cell. Adam Fair first up via the burner phone. "Adam, I'm at Sarah's house, and there's a new inhabitant. Who do you know in the murder cops?"

"I know 'em all, Street. Want me to roll up, too?"

"Absolutely. Kid's probably a gang type, you may have him on file. You know the address?"

"Oh yeah. See you in fifteen."

"Ditto. Bring a flatbed tow. DB's in the garage. Tell your peeps to park in the alley."

"Gotcha."

My next call was, predictably, to Sarah. "Hey, kid. I'm at your abode, got some news."

"Uh oh. It's bad. I can hear it in your voice."

"You know me well. Short strokes, I will be by within the hour to bring you here. House has been entered, not visibly damaged. There's a dead kid in the front passenger seat of your car. Maybe seventeen, eighteen years old, Latino male. Been there a week at the most, kinda messy. The rest of your home is intact. Not good, but not as bad as it could be." I waited a solid ten seconds for a response.

"Geez. Okay, Street, thanks for going there for me." I could hear the strain in her voice. Quietly, she finished, "I'll be here."

Within the next ten minutes, I could hear the siren of Adam's big black Crown Vic as it warbled its way up Sunset Boulevard into east Hollywood. He turned the sound effects off as he turned off Sunset rolling toward the alley behind the houses. He coasted two houses past Sarah's, left his car with the package-shelf cop lights winking, and walked decisively toward the side of the garage, where we met with a handshake.

"Whataya got, Street?"

"Follow me." As we walked back through the house to the garage, I pointed out the footprints on the hardwood floors. We walked wide of the impressions toward the kitchen door into the garage. I picked up the kitchen towel as I passed the sink, readying myself for the stench. I could tell that Adam simply held his breath.

He took a good long look at the body, walked around the car, stepped back into the kitchen, and exhaled. "Yeah, that looks like one of ours. Second-gen gangsta, poor little bastard." Adam found the garage door opener, and the garage flooded with sunlight. As the door raised, the Coroner's van stopped in front of the garage. The timing was eerie.

"Adam, I gotta ask. How do you do that? Your elements arrive at exactly the right time as you raise the garage door. That's just weird. We always had to wait a half-hour for anyone from support services to show up. How do you make that happen?"

"Heh heh... Street, brother, ya gotta know...these are my peeps. I am in control! I'm good to them, they're good to me. Not a big deal." He smiled a proud smile for a second, then he returned to the grim duty at hand.

"Well, I'm impressed. I'm going to go get Sarah. We'll be back in a bit." Adam was already pointing the crew to the search priorities and assigning jobs. He waved me off, and I left. When I arrived at the rental house, Sarah was waiting, visibly upset.

"So how bad is it?" she queried as she shut the door to the Tahoe, took the passenger seat, and strapped in.

There was no need to sugarcoat the facts. "Want it straight?" She nodded. "The house was entered but not damaged except that they jimmied the French doors to the patio. Someone tagged your garage door, and there is a pre-packaged corpse in the front passenger seat of your KIA. He's really ripe and probably a little soupy, so the car's done. Call the insurance guy. It's a bio/hazmat site inside. Aside from that, the house is unmolested to my eyes. You will probably disagree."

"Okay. Thanks, Street." Sarah exhaled heavily and shook her

head but was quiet for the remainder of our trip, looking out the side window of the truck as we drove north on Sunset. We arrived at her house, and I parked again on the street in front. Out of caution, I stood outside the Tahoe and scoped the street north and south, checking for lookie-loos, still curious about a closely-positioned hostile observer. None was apparent. Sarah, wearing a blue Dodgers logo hoodie, walked smoothly onto the lawn, to the porch, and into the house. No one who had witnessed the scene in front that evening all those weeks ago would have thought it the same woman.

Inside the house, the air of activity was vibrant, a dozen officers and techs examining and photographing anything that Adam pointed out, focusing on the garage, the car, and the inert passenger inside. The decision had been made that the car would be studied here but shipped to the Crime Lab, where the CSI techs could remove the body intact with no *spillage* of the contents in Sarah's garage. The flatbed tow rig came and went. Thank the ever-thoughtful Adam for small favors.

Adam and Sarah greeted one another warmly, she looked at facial photos of the dead kid then the two sat at her kitchen table and quietly discussed the situation. I made myself scarce and sat in the beige leather recliner in the living room, perusing a copy of Road and Track magazine. Hey, I know my place. After ten minutes on site, the hum of activity had quelled. The techs spoke to Adam and were released from the site study. Sarah rose and walked to me.

"Street, I'm gonna get some clothes and a few things and get the hell out of here. This place creeps me out now."

"Well, let me take the truck out to the alley so you can load out back. Take your time, and let me help if you need it. We'll get it done."

"Thanks, C."

Adam Fair looked at me from the kitchen table, caught my attention, and motioned me to join him as he rose to walk toward the garage. "Street, you know how upset she is now. It's gonna be a rough next coupla days. We're on this thing real heavy, we'll get it cleared up. Please keep an eye on her, and let me know how she's doing." We walked through the garage toward the alley where his Crown Vic was parked as he continued. "Somehow, the gang types know she's alive and in hiding. The deceased kid was probably a recruit who screwed up some assignment. They mighta had Sarah's hit man do him as an initiation. We ought to figure that out via street intel in the next 24."

"Anything I can do, let me know."

"I know, and I appreciate your help. Just try to keep her on an even keel, okay? She's shook now, rightfully so, but they got me pissed off, too. We'll get this straightened out soon."

He offered a fist bump, then he folded himself into his big sedan and pulled out. I walked through the side yard of the house next door, retrieved the Tahoe, and moved it to the alley. Sarah and I half-filled the rear cargo bay behind the second seat with filled Hefty Bags, then she locked up the house, and we departed. Back at the rental, I backed the truck up to the side door that opened into the kitchen and helped her unload. Not surprisingly, her clothes went directly into the laundry hamper as she silently went about her tasks. I knew not to break the silence.

After an hour at the rental, Sarah walked into the living room. I could hear the washing machine from the laundry room, and she had showered and dressed in the interim. She walked into the room wearing a handsome dark blue denim outfit, looked at me, and asked, "So, Street, where you want to go to dinner tonight? I'm buyin'!"

## 32

Trey was taking a smoke break on the outer third-floor walkway of the apartment building when the girl left his dad's apartment at two that afternoon. His compadre and occasional meth-snorting partner, Chino, nudged him as they watched her walk to her yellow Camaro. "Would you look at the ass on that? Your old man tappin' that?"

"Way more than tappin', bro. Payin' the price, too."

"You an' him gettin' along now? Your shiner's almost gone."

"We're about the same, I guess. I stay out of his way. Better like that, y'know?"

"He still owes you though, for that slice on yer cheek."

Trey looked at him and nodded. "He does indeed. I have an idea. Let's go for a ride."

Chino nodded in agreement as the yellow Camaro pulled away from the curb.

––––––––

We settled on a new steak and seafood place in Encino, a couple of miles west of the 405. The food was good, but it takes a couple of sessions before a restaurant goes on my *hot list*. Sarah was recovering nicely from the trauma of her home being invaded by strangers, but she was less than adamant about the future.

"I'll have a moving company take all my stuff out and store it, get a little paint work done, and it goes on the market. I have no other choice." She sighed as she picked up her wine glass. "I don't want to, but once the incursion is made, the address is known by every gang shithead from here to Detroit. Those assholes gossip like old ladies in a rest home."

"When we wrap this stuff up maybe I can help you relocate. You have lots of decisions to make in the short term," I offered.

"Oh, don't I know it? We make plans, God laughs."

"I have it on good authority that He's not laughing at you, Sarah. No one is. You are one of the strongest people I've ever encountered. That will not change. Seems to me your future is your call. If you wanted to stay with the LAPD, what kind of job would they give you?"

"I've been offered an administrative position, duty approvals, and budgets, procurements, stuff like that. It sounds good, but I think I'm cubicle-phobic. I need to be out in the air, such as it is. Pay is a little better, so I'm thinking about it. This city is not getting less expensive to live in."

"True that. Where else would you like to go?" I sipped my draft beer as she pondered.

"I honestly don't know. I have a sister in Florida, my folks are retired in East Tennessee. I know things are easier back there." She squinted. "I go there to visit though, I get so goddam bored...and truth be told, I'm just not that close to them."

"Oh, I can relate to that. Seems to me you have time to consider your options. Anything I can do to help, let me know."

"Only thing right now, I need to find a car. I figured I'd ask your help with that."

I answered, "No problem. Any time."

Our dinners arrived on a big chrome tray at the table side, broiled sea bass for me and blackened Alaskan salmon for Sarah. I was envious of her choice, but it was all good. There would be a *next time*.

As we walked a block on Ventura to the Tahoe, Sara mentioned, "Oh, Street. Did I tell you about the last visit to Carty of that hottie in the yellow Camaro? Yesterday morning, four hours."

We reached the truck, I opened her door, then walked around and took the driver's seat. "You mentioned it in passing. Yesterday, right?" Reminded, I opened the center console and pulled one of my burner phones out. I opened it and looked at the readout, seeing the girl's number. "Oh, geez. I missed her call yesterday evening." I pressed for voice mail and listened for a few seconds, then hit the speed dial and waited for an answer.

The girl answered, speaking softly. "Rick?"

"Yes! I see you called yesterday. Sorry it took me so long to get back. What's up?"

"Um, I need to talk to you. I got hurt yesterday, and I need some help."

"Where are you? I'll be there this evening." She gave me an address in the flats of West L.A., a tenth-floor security condo in an upmarket area just off Wilshire. I had briefly searched the area when I first arrived in L.A. before I found my house, and I knew the rents in an area high-rise to be in the mid-four-figures monthly.

Of course, I had to consider that the woman was an element of the ongoing drama surrounding Carty, and as such, she was not exactly a proven ally. I had no idea what I would be walking into. Caution ruled the day, lest I get my ass shot off, or worse.

"Give me till eight, and I'm bringing a friend with me." I waited for a response. "She's a trusted ally in my work. Is that okay?"

In her soft voice, she answered, but I detected a strain. The *sexy* was no longer there. "Sure. I'll be waiting. Call when you get here, and I'll ring you in."

We disconnected, and I turned to Sarah and updated her on the ongoing situation with the girl. Sarah had thoughts similar to mine. "That's a rough trade. They don't all stay cute and sexy for long. If she was careless for a minute, there's no telling what went down. I know some policewomen in the sex crimes unit, and there are counselors if she needs them, but we need more info. I'll go with you."

"Great. That's where I was headed."

I chose the Mustang for the trip, knowing that parking in the area would be tight. Packing my shoulder rig under my most-recent dark-blue sport coat and the .22 at my ankle, I felt secure in talking to a 115-pound female, but I was glad that Sarah had my back. We parked a half-block away and strode to the front landing of the building between the twin two-story waterfalls, where we rang in. The elevator took us to the tenth floor, and a short stint brought us to unit 10-C. Sarah rang the bell, and the girl answered seconds later.

I really didn't know what to expect, but she looked quite good when the door opened. She had a black turtleneck sweater and a pair of filmy white linen pants. She was barefoot on the thick carpeting, and her hair was tied into a ponytail. She looked like she was about 19...and really cute. "Rick? Come in," she said, and she stepped aside to let us pass.

The apartment was large and plushly appointed. The living room featured leather and suede upholstered sofas facing a west-ward window-wall with a wondrous view toward the coast and an open deck with lounge chairs and pillows with an impressive fire-place to one side. She led us to the sunken living room, and we sat. I introduced myself and Sarah using her first name. She introduced herself as Heather Lynn Loomis.

I said, "Just call me *Street*. So, tell us what happened."

Her voice was strained. "I feel like such an idiot. I was followed home, pure and simple. They knocked on the door, and I opened it, thinking it was a neighbor. It wasn't."

As Sarah withdrew a digital recorder from her handbag, she asked, "Tell us what happened, in order if you would. I'm going to record you." She noted the date, time, and source subject, then laid the recorder on the coffee table in front of Heather.

"That's fine. Two young guys forced their way in, overpowered me, and...um...we had sex." She looked at me. "You know what I do, and I don't know that *rape* is the right word. I saw what they intended to do, and instead of fighting and getting hurt seriously, I...well...I did what I do." She looked at me, embarrassed and, I thought, maybe a little defiant.

Sarah spoke up. "If it was a home invasion though, if they entered the building without permission, if they forced their way in here and overpowered you, it is rape. Rape is about the violence, not the sex. Realistically though, you may have problems in court if this gets that far. Do you have any injuries?"

"Yes. I cover up well, I guess."

"Let's go into the bathroom, and let me see. Is that okay, Street? I'll get photos for the sex crimes interview later." Heather Lynn Loomis looked at me.

I responded, "Do your thing."

Heather said, "Mister Street, if you'd like a drink, feel free. The bar's at the counter."

The two women walked to the bathroom, off the large soft-beige bedroom. I looked around the room from my sofa perch, then I got up and walked to the compact bar, took a glass and a few ice cubes, and ran some tap water. I didn't spot a great quantity of hard liquor, just a dozen bottles of wine in a countertop cooler. Apparently, pretty young women from White Oak, Tennessee, didn't cotton much to hard liquor.

Sarah and Heather emerged from the bathroom after about ten minutes. Sarah and I conferred on the sofa while we looked at pictures on her camera. She had extensive bruising on her breasts and a few scratches on her abdomen though none that would leave a scar. Heather stood at the bar and poured a large glass of white wine. When she resumed her chair, I started with my questions.

"You were followed here. Do you know where the other car picked you up?"

"I think it was right as I left Grant's place. He's the one you know, isn't he?"

"Let's just say I know *of* Grant. We're not buddies."

She spoke softly, "Okay. Anyway, I had been to his apartment three times this week, and twice, a younger guy came to the door for him as we were wrapping up. I recognized the voice. He has a bit of a speech impediment. I taught school back home, I recognize those things."

"Good," I said. "Any other details about him? Tattoos? Piercings?"

"He had a couple of tatts on his upper arms, but he also had an old black eye. Kinda greenish grey, almost healed. And a cut below that, also almost healed."

"Ah. The other guy?" I asked.

"Latino, heavy accent. Not as tall as the other one, and he had an odor. Like cats or something. It was gross."

Sarah and I exchanged a glance. Both of us mouthing cook.

She offered, "And yes, they did use condoms. They're in a Ziploc in the trash can in the bathroom. All of them. I insisted."

Sarah was impressed. "Smart lady! Way to take charge! There'll be an officer here in the next 24 to take those from you. They'll open a file, but it can take years to go through the court system. I have every confidence these two will be dispatched long before that ever becomes an issue for you." Sarah tilted her head toward me as she finished.

Heather said quietly to both of us, "Thank you."

I chimed in. "Change of subject: Are you going to take some time off to heal?"

"Yes. My guys expect visual perfection, and they won't like bruises. I may go to a girlfriend's place in Malibu for ten days, rest up, get back in shape."

I offered, "That's probably a good idea. You have my cell number. If anything else comes to mind, let me know."

"I will." She sipped her wine, holding the glass with both hands, looking at me with a practiced gaze over the rim. God, this woman was hot...

Sarah asked, "One more thing, sorry that I have to ask, do you have any convictions for prostitution anywhere? We haven't talked about that. If this did go to court, that would be an element."

"No, of course not." She looked at me and grinned. "As far as anyone knows, I'm just a pretty southern girl who likes having sex."

Hey now. I looked at Sarah and then turned to Heather. "Okay. Let's stay in touch. Let me know when you hear from your friend Grant. We're pretty certain the two attackers followed you from his apartment building, so you want to cut him off altogether. We'll handle them."

Sarah added, "There will be a policewoman friend of mine call you or visit here in the next 24 hours to get that Ziploc bag and perhaps some more details—time, date, stuff like that in case you want to go further with a complaint. That's always an option for you."

"No, I'll just chalk it up to an occupational hazard." She frowned, then looked at me.

She knew what I was going to say next. I stood, and Sarah followed. I may have exhaled a little too heavily. Exasperated, I said, "Well then, you need a new occupation. Stay in touch."

Quietly, she said, "I will. Thank you for your time."

———

Back in the car, Sarah shook her head and looked at me. "That is one lucky girl. Those guys frightened her. Maybe not enough to make her quit *ho-dom*, but they scared her. She loves the money right now, and she also has the hots for a certain PI I know. She asked me about you."

"I suppose I should be flattered. What did you tell her?"

"Oh, I said you were happily married to a reformed nymphomaniac who keeps you worn flat out. She was crestfallen by the news. She wouldn't want to break up a happy family."

I laughed. "Clever! Thank you. I'll try to keep my cover story intact. Maybe Dierdre can fill that role. I'll ask."

"You like her, too, though. I can tell."

"Nah, it's different. I think she's gorgeous, and she's sexy as hell, and she's probably quite good at her work, but women like her get burned out too quickly. The ones I've known through my work, including one I encountered during the Connors thing, seem to eventually get desperate for attention outside the bedroom. It's like that's all they know. And she might have other issues as well." I looked across at Sarah. "Another time, another place. Dammit." I smiled at Sarah as I stopped for the traffic light at Sunset and La Cienega.

"Yep. Well," said Sarah, "since you are not hopelessly smitten, I'm gonna do a complete package on her, check her out back home in Tennessee, too. All that. Make sure we're not being played. I got a look at her Tennessee driver's license and California ID while we were talking, as part of the cop thing."

"Good call, officer!"

"You think Carty's kid and the other one from the apartment house are the doers in this, don'cha?"

But of course. "More than likely. Black eye, speech pattern, tatts, cat piss aroma, the time frame. It all fits. The kid and his dad are not pals, judging from the shiner, so it may have even been a revenge thing. Then again, she's cutting Carty off, and he's not going to like that a little bit. Maybe good ol' Dad can take care of this matter himself."

"That...would be ironic."

"Wouldn't it though?" I was spit-balling ideas now. "Okay, back to Trey: what about the other *dad*? Last name Schwinn. Apparently, he and Roberta were together for a few years, split up a year or so ago. I'm bettin' he has an opinion or two about Trey. Perhaps a perspective on the mom as well. I think he was another attorney in Riverside in Bongelli's law office."

"I'll look him up when I get home." She caught herself. "Or rather...back to the rental, though that's more *home* now than my place." She frowned as she said it.

"That'll pass. You'll get back to normal soon. Take your time, decide what you want to do, and you can get a new place. The buyers' market is getting a little stronger now. You could probably get a great deal. Your old place is nice and in a decent area, and you have equity in it. A little paint and polish, you will come out pretty good on it when it sells. You'll be in great shape, regardless. We can keep the rental for up to a year if needed."

"Yeah. I guess."

Back at the rental, Sarah sourced Lee Schwinn, we looked online for a replacement for her KIA, and we talked for a couple of hours. She had been through a lot, a few things courtesy of our current working arrangement, but she was a major ally and a good friend. I valued her counsel and her loyalty.

## 33

That next Tuesday, I checked out Lee Schwinn with my compadre in Riverside, Catherine Gadsden. She had offered mixed reviews. It seems Lee Schwinn and Roberta Thomas had met when they worked together at the Bongelli Law Firm in Riverside, he as a shiny new law school grad, and she in varying jobs before she passed the bar exam three years prior. Bongelli's unique legal practice had been quite lucrative for Bongelli himself, but he'd also paid his associates well for their involvement in his numerous duplicities.

Lee Schwinn was a small man, five-foot-five and maybe 140 pounds. After the Bongelli escape, he had been jobless for a while before snagging a spot in the firm he shared with two other attorneys, both at least a decade older than his 34 years. Business for the junior partner in a small civil law firm was spotty at best, so he seemed to jump at the chance to interview a new potential client. He stood from behind his desk, impressively dressed in a new dark blue suit, looking as successful as he hoped to be someday. I walked into his office with my briefcase clutched tightly to my side and requested that we get down to business quickly.

"This conference is confidential, right?" I asked, portraying a nervous *innocent*.

"Absolutely, unless you'd prefer we be joined by an associate of mine. I see no need for that until we make some progress with the basics. You have an hour of consultation, as requested. Please proceed."

I reverted to my normal charming self as I took the chair opposite him. "Trey Thomas." I flipped my business card to his side of the desk.

Schwinn frowned as he perused the card. "What about him?"

"You were his stepfather for a period of time before you and Roberta split up a while back. I would like to get a little information about him. He is starting to be involved in some bad stuff in L.A. He may be in way over his head, and I need a little perspective in order to make a fair decision about the path to take with him. You may be in a position to help him."

Lee turned serious. "If he needs help, Mister Street, you're talking to the exact wrong person. If he were drowning, I would probably be the first to toss him an anchor. I wouldn't be the only one, just the first. Trust me on that."

"Interesting way to put it."

He smiled and chuckled once as he tapped the corner of my card on his desk pad. "I have never been more serious in my life, Mister Street. That little bastard decided to destroy my marriage to his mother, and he did so with some flair. I'll be blunt. I have my own issues, and Robbie is certainly no real prize either, but the kid screwed what she and I had, and then he decided to try to destroy me personally as well. After I caught him in the act of publicly sabotaging me, the little fucker destroyed something that meant a lot to me." He motioned to a picture on the wall behind his desk, below his diploma, his certification, and license documents. "Do you know much about cars, Mister Street?"

I ventured, "Car guy since birth. I was brought home from the hospital in a '69 GTO, and I still have the car."

He grinned. "Nice. Then you can probably understand. You are one of a few. I saved every penny I could for over a decade, ate deviled ham and saltines for dinner more often than I want to admit, and at long last, I bought my dream car.' He counted features off on his fingers. "A 1971 Corvette LT1 roadster. Close ratio four speed. Posi, that great metallic orange color they had that year. Tan leather." He raised an index finger. "And it was the only one made that year in that color combination with the factory luggage rack, the FM radio, gold-line tires, finned wheel covers, and a black vinyl top on the hardtop together on the Monroney sticker. NCRS documented. Eleven thousand one-owner miles. I bought it out of a Holmby Hills estate sale, I friggin' stole it! I paid 44,000 hard-earned dollars a decade ago, it was worth two to three times that at the top of the market."

"Okay. Sounds magnificent."

The topic had awakened a passion in the man. "Oh, it was. And I used that car to teach that kid how to drive. Did a great job of it. Kids today don't understand stick shifts at all, they don't want to be bothered with the extra effort of a clutch pedal. Some of 'em get all confused, and some just aren't coordinated worth a shit. But when we were done, that kid could speed shift like Dick friggin' Landy."

"There's bad news coming. I can tell."

He looked straight at me, didn't bat an eye. "Yeah, there is. His mom and I were on our way to an amicable divorce. Five years in, we both understood that we were far better as acquaintances and professional associates than we ever would be as man and wife. She had ghosts and memories that haunted her, some via Grant Carty, and she couldn't get over them or let them go. That asshole still lived inside her head, and that killed our relationship. Trey sided with her. He felt slighted, and he blamed me. He acted out. One night after we split up, he came to my house, and he burned that car to the ground as it sat in my driveway outside my garage." He exhaled heavily. Set a lit propane torch under the rocker panel. Took about ten minutes to totally ignite the car."

"Wow. I am sorry for your loss."

"Thank you. It was insured, of course, but that is beside the point. To properly address your query, I have to ask what the accusation against him might be."

"There are several. Most serious is the attempted murder of an LAPD Gang Task Force officer. Secondary, the home invasion and rape of a young woman just days ago, and lastly, his heavy involvement in drug manufacturing via mommy dearest and dear old dad."

Lee continued. "That's right. The mysterious and elusive Grant Carty is back above the sod. That's bad. We were working for Bongelli's firm, doing all that paperwork for all of those scam corporations he formed on behalf of his many prisoner clients, and we finally figured out what was going down out in Nevada. You're the guy who got Bongelli taken down, aren't you?"

I smiled. "That's me."

"That was a clever deal. Some of us had to scramble like cockroaches there at the end," he grinned, "but that needed to happen anyway. Thank you for doing that. That was a long time coming. You probably saved a few lives by taking him down the way you did."

"Yeah. I live to serve." I smiled and lifted an eyebrow. Lee *got it* and smiled back. "So, Trey…"

"Just an evil little sonofabitch." He paused. "Yes! I just called my *ex* a bitch! That never happens in a lawyer's office, does it?" His mood was improving, his voice lighter. "And now that his dad is running around loose, there will be more trouble and more victims. Robbie will probably be among them. She is still smitten." He paused. "Please. Take both father and son down, by whatever means necessary."

"I'll give that a shot. Thank you for your time."

## 34

Trey walked from the *cooking* apartment to the external stairway of the building carrying the plastic garbage bag from the kitchen. His mom had made a pass through the building that morning, demanding that the remodeling detritus be cleaned. The testing quality of the product had fallen, again, this time below 60%, and the distributor handling the westernmost part of the San Fernando Valley had refused an order. Roberta was not accustomed to the client being critical of the stuff—'it's dirtbag meth, there ARE no standards,' she'd said—and in the end, she had spoken ill of the buyers and their reputation. The phone chat had grown heated and the rhetoric more bitter with each salvo, so now there was one less sale venue to worry about.

Trey had started using the *apartment house product* three or four nights a week himself. He and a friend would take their leave at five in the evening and would eventually gravitate toward their quiet space, this time a steep side street off Cahuenga above the 101 freeway between a fenced, whitewashed garage facility on one corner and a small L.A. City Firehouse on the other. The fifteen-degree incline and the mass of car lights passing on the freeway had enhanced his high when he was *only* smoking pot, it would work with this stuff, too. Right?

The friend had brought his own product to this latest foray, far stronger than the *dirtbag meth* originally provided. Trey finally rolled into the Aqua Vista condo address at 2:20 am, blasted to a mere remnant of his normal self.

————

Roberta walked down the hallway at her condo the next morning at 8 am and knocked on Trey's bedroom door. "Trey? Are you in there? Are you awake?" She turned the knob, and surprisingly, the door opened. Trey lay across the bedspread, face down, shirt off. She noticed the new tattoo that stretched across his shoulders, indecipherable to her eyes, as she shook him awake. His body odor was heavy and not at all pleasant. Louder, she called, "Trey! Wake up!"

With the new motion and noise, Trey raised up on his elbows and turned to face her. "Mmmmyeh. Eh, Mom. What time is it?" He yawned, exhaling a stench toward Roberta that prompted her to turn her head away. He squinted into the sunlight as she raised the blinds.

"Trey! Wake up! It's after eight!" She returned to the side of his bed and pulled him up by his upper arm. "Sit up, goddammit!"

Now he raised up on his elbows and turned over to face her. The right side of his hair, peppered with sweat as he retired hours before, stuck vertically above his ear. Roberta was standing with her hands at her waist in what Trey had for years called her *mom pose*. That was never a positive development. She started in as he yawned again and regained some semblance of awareness. "What time did you come in this morning, Trey?"

He squinted and rubbed his left eye. "Um, I donno. Maybe two?"

"Do you recall anything unusual happening as you drove in?"

As his head cleared, he could tell she was really pissed. He was still foggy when he answered, "Um. No. Like what?"

"Oh, like taking the driver's side off the Nissan against the pole in the carport as you drove in! I was leaving for work, and I just saw it! Goddam it, Trey! We are not doing this again! You are paying the deductible this time, and you're paying to fix the post in the carport, too!" She clenched her teeth. "Now get your ass up! Take a shower and clean up! Get to work! We'll hash this out tonight!" Twenty seconds later, he heard the kitchen door slam, and her truck start and leave.

————————

Carty exited the Mercedes Town Car after his latest four-day session at the cosmetic surgeon and walked to his front door. He keyed the lock and let himself in. Once inside, he walked down the hall to the bathroom, stripped, and took a shower, careful to avoid getting the facial gauze wrap wet. He had a hard time sleeping the night before, dealing with business strategy hassles and the new discomfort stemming from the more serious and precise surgeries now being performed. Roberta had called his cell an hour ago, freaking out, something about Trey wrecking her car or on drugs or some shit. Damn kid.

Carty also knew he had to get back on track with the call girl. It'd been a week since he'd seen her, and dammit, he missed her *machinations*. Girl had skills. He walked through the construction site upstairs from his apartment. The upstairs crew had been working for three hours by the time he had arrived. The framing on the top floor was finished, and those apartments were ready for sheetrock. The work was starting to look good. He hadn't seen Trey at all yet that morning. He walked back downstairs and took a nap on the couch in the living room for an hour until the kid made an appearance.

Carty answered the door when Trey knocked, stepping aside to let the kid enter. "Your mama called a while ago screaming into the phone, somethin' about you crashin' her car. What the fuck did you do, boy?"

"I took out a pole in the carport when I drove in last night." He dropped his chin toward his chest and looked up at Carty.

"You mean this morning, doncha? 'Bout two-twenty or so? That's what she said."

"Yeah, I g-guess."

"Let's walk out and see what you did."

"It's parked on the other side of the s-street."

The pair walked to the outer porch at the kitchen door and looked toward the street. Carty looked at the car and then at Trey. "Yeah. It's crashed, ain't it? Whataya gonna do about that?"

"I guess I'll pay the deductible and get it fixed."

"Yeah, I guess you will. There's a body shop down the hill on Sunset. We can get an estimate there this afternoon.' He looked at the kid for a few seconds, frowned, then spoke. "Y'know what, Trey? On second thought, fuck it. You're takin' a day off. You been workin' real hard for weeks now. Let's you 'n me take a ride."

Trey looked at Carty, a bit suspicious now. What was the catch? "Where we goin'?"

Grant closed and locked his apartment door, and the pair walked toward the street. "Well, I want you to help me do some shopping. I'm gonna need a set of wheels here in a few days, an' I doubt yer mama's taught you the finer points of car shopping. You can tag along with me, give me some input maybe." He looked at the kid. "You can drive. We'll look at some rides, stop and drop this one off at th' body shop on the way back." He paused. "Your crowd's not into cars, are they?" They reached the wounded Nissan, and Carty took the passenger seat.

As Trey took his seat and started the car, he answered, "Some of us are. Man, if we ever get the Chrysler back, I'll show you what we did with that one. It's mondo bitchin'."

"Well, yer mama tol' me about that one. Sounds like you overplayed yer hand there, maybe. Kinda chromey, wasn't it?"

"Oh, yeah. Had some chrome ten-spoke 22s on it. Chrome on the roof posts 'n shit. Mesh screen grille, and it's a Hemi. Stylin'."

Carty answered, "And, memorable to anyone around in case

you run a red light or go four miles an hour too fast on the Ventura freeway. Dial it back just a tad, man, you can get away with lots more shit an' you won't spend so much time at the side o' the road with Five-Oh behind you runnin' yer numbers. They used ta pull me over in my Bronco ever' hour on the hour! *The man* knew my ride like th' back o' his hand. They knew it was me, and they kept busy hassling me. Ya read me?"

The kid nodded. "Makes sense." He added, "Is that why you moved to the desert?"

"One of the reasons, sure. We was gettin' big, slingin', makin' an' transportin' our product. Civilization got in the way. Then I got hooked—money, drugs, bitches... I had it goin' on in ever' direction, my step-bro helpin' me." Carty looked ahead and pointed at the turn lane off of Hollywood Boulevard. "Get on the 101 up here. Let's hit Van Nuys Boulevard, and we'll look there. Where was I?" He paused. "Oh yeah. Then this little rich kid pissant came around, gettin' in our shit, wantin' ta sling alongside o' us. Not happnin'. Annoying as hell."

"What'd you do?"

"We dealt with him. Never saw his pasty ass ever again."

"Sounds as if you handled it. Got it outta the way."

Carty looked across the car at his son. "We did that." The two traveled a few miles in silence. "I gotta say, Trey, you are a decent driver." He tapped the kid on his shoulder and laughed, then added louder, "Well, when you're not wiping the side off your mama's car. Were you high or what?"

Trey smiled. "Maybe a little. It happened, awright. I do' need to rehash it 25 times. I did it. I screwed up. I'll fix it."

"Steppin' up! Good on ya, kid!" Carty watched as the scenery passed. The steep hillsides on each side of the tired old 101 freeway, one of the first ever built in the L.A. basin, gave way to the panorama of the San Fernando Valley. The car made the transition to the first of the curves that took the freeway toward the ocean. There was another wildfire near the coast, and smoke hung like a gauze drapery over the western landscape. As they made progress westward, Carty asked, "So if you had yer choice, Trey, what would you want to do in yer life? Whataya wanna be, now that yer growin' up?"

Trey thought, *I wanna get high again, asshole, just like I was last night*, but he demurred. "I'm not sure. The construction thing is as good as any right now, I guess."

"Do you think you'd ever want to live outside L.A.?"

"Where, like San Diego? Riverside? Somewhere like that?"

Carty laughed. "There's places other than Southern California, y'know? A whole big country. Hell, a whole big world!"

"Meh. I'm good here. Which exit do I take?"

"Hit yer outside lane, Van Nuys Boulevard north. Stay to your right at the ramp up here."

"Now that we're here, where are we going?"

"I want to look at a truck that's for sale up here a ways. Might not buy anything just yet. I wanna check it out first." Trey stopped at the light at the bottom of the ramp and signaled the turn. The small independent used car lot sat on a quiet corner a half-mile north of the freeway off-ramp. Carty told Trey to park at the curb on the narrow side street. The vehicle in question sat next to the sidewalk, a late-model Dodge Ram stretch-cab pickup, a 4x4, bright blue, lifted, sitting tall on Dick Cepek off-road tires and chrome rims. A chrome roll bar and a bank of driving lights rose from behind the cab. Chrome running boards hung below the cab, and a colorful graphic stripe swept down the bodyside. The two men sat in the car and gazed at the beast. Trey spoke up first.

"Shit, man, I thought you were all about low-key! How is that low-key?"

Carty chuckled. "Yeah, I guess yer right. They could sure as hell see me comin' in that, couldn't they?" He smiled and rubbed the gauze that still covered the left side of his face. "Someone gets all pissy about something, ya just run their ass over."

"Prob'ly pass everythin' but a gas station, too, huh?" Trey laughed.

Carty chuckled. "Good point." He tapped his son on the upper arm as they laughed. "Oh well, it looked good in the Auto Trader. I had this badass Bronco years ago. Maybe I'm done with that phase of my life. Let's boogie on outta here. Maybe get some lunch. You like In & Out? I think there's one on the other side of the freeway." Trey started the car and made a U-turn to regain Van Nuys Boulevard as Carty made a call from his cell. There was no answer.

The burgundy Mustang coupe that had been following them since they'd left the apartment house made the same move.

———

My cell rang as I followed the damaged Maxima into the parking lot at the In & Out on Van Nuys Boulevard. I silently congratulated the criminalistic Cartys on their taste in fast food as I picked up.

"Sarah! What's up?"

"Hey, Street. Just got a call from Adam. They got the final report on the Chrysler and an ID on the dead kid in my car. He just sent it to me. He's coming by here tonight to discuss it with us. You up for that?"

"Sure thing. I'll be done with *Bo and Luke* Carty by then. I suspect that Carty is about to buy a car, either for himself or for the kid. Carty on wheels may be tougher to keep an eye on."

Sarah chimed in as well. "I would imagine so. I just wanna wrap this shit up! We all need to get back to living a normal professional life instead of waiting for them to get off the dime."

I agreed, "True for me as well. I suspect that Trey is sampling his product a bit. His mom's Maxima lost its driver's side sheet metal last night. Maybe they're shopping for a replacement. Father and son bonding can be sooo important!" I heard her laugh. "See you in a bit."

———

Inside the Maxima, Grant and Trey were scarfing down the last of their lunch. Carty looked across at his son. "Okay, Trey, lemme know what you think. I wanna buy your mom a new car. This one's what, four years old? An' it's all beat up now and got what, how many miles?"

Trey looked at the odometer. "Says 72,092 here."

"Awright, it's old and beat up. Let's find something she'd like, and I'll cash it out. Get this one fixed and curbstone it. I think she deserves that. How 'bout you?"

Trey gave it a noncommittal, "Yeah, fine."

"What does she like? What's her favorite color?"

"She's into blues. She likes blue."

"Okay, what kinda car? Foreign or domestic?"

"She liked her Chrysler. Probably domestic."

"Hmmm. But she also likes this thing enough to put 72-k on it as a daily driver. I have an idea. Go right on Van Nuys an' let's check something else out."

## 35

I spent the afternoon tailing the Carty twins, five hours total, during which Carty senior stopped at the Van Nuys Infiniti dealer and procured a handsome new dark blue G35 sedan. Feeling a bit daring, I parked at the curb, donned my Dodger cap, walked into the showroom through the customer lounge, and checked out the action while thumbing through a brochure and trying the hot-looking G37 coupe on for size. Tempting, sure, and I'd even rent one the next time work took me to the east coast, but I had already spent my yearly *car allowance* budget that year, twice.

Trey was healing from his black eye rather well, and he seemed to take to the idea of making a purchase with his dad's money. Carty, the left side of his face still wearing the surgical dressings from his most recent operations, coached his son on the purchase of the impressive sedan, even haggling a bit, then arranged for its delivery to Roberta's law office later that afternoon. Following these two wasn't all that difficult. Trey tended to be a decent wheelman, and I could hang back a bit because the pounded Maxima was easily spotted from a distance. The new Mustang was fairly anonymous looking unless you really knew your cars, so the possibility of being spotted in Trey's mirror was not a major issue.

After their business was concluded, the Cartys regained their Maxima from the side lot. I followed them back to the Sunset Bl. body shop where the car was left for repairs. From my parking space, a half-block from the independent body shop just blocks from the apartment house, I watched as the car was consigned for repairs. I heard Carty talking to Trey as they waited outside the body shop, smiling and giving him a congratulatory pat on the shoulder. "You did good, son. You drove a hard bargain with that ol' boy! I'm impressed. Let's get back to your mama's office before the car gets there. I want to see her face when she sees it."

———

From Studio City, I took the 101 home to change clothes and return calls for a half-hour, then headed back for the rental house. Sarah was building a fairly impressive spaghetti dinner for the two of us, and I gifted her a decent bottle of wine in return. While we ate, we shared our day's experiences. She had deciphered the intent of the newly added escort driver for the *delivery team* and had noted the plate numbers and identities of the players, advising her LAPD contacts of the discovery. She had learned of the earlier confrontation with the patrol officer on Ventura Boulevard, had made the connections, and passed the word. She was proving to be an excellent detective.

Adam Fair arrived a little after six that evening as I was clearing the table and loading the dishwasher. He and Sarah talked in the living room and reviewed video images as I finished, then I joined them.

Adam was his usual friendly, informative self as I took a seat across from his position on the couch. "I see Sarah's got you in the kitchen, Street! Better watch that!"

"It was a fair exchange, Adam. This woman is a serious Italian chef." Sarah smiled proudly. "I understand you've brought us some news."

He handed me a manila folder with eleven pages of print and

nine printed images. "I did. That is our analysis of that Chrysler you turned us onto. We're certain it was the car used in the attack on Sarah. The gunpowder residue on the passenger side front door upholstery matched the type of powder used in the ejected shell we found under the corner of the front passenger seat, which also correlated with the type used in her attack." He passed me the pictures and the printed reports.

I offered, "I'd suspected the car was the one I saw that night. I'm glad that worked out. Is there a connection with the kid found in her garage?"

"There is." Adam passed me a thin file describing the young man. "Kid's a gang wannabe, and we suspect that Sarah's shooting was his initiation. When Sarah survived, his killing was some other kid's initiation. Lately, these assholes are getting meaner and calling orders that are far more violent. And Sarah, last night we grabbed up one of the guys who came into your house. Crime lab said that a sharp kid at the M.E. facility had found his fingerprint on the trash bag the dead kid was wrapped in. He'll be talking with us over the next few days."

But, I thought, "One thing I wonder...how would they have known she survived?"

"Good question. You know how tight our security was regarding her whereabouts. You called the rules on that. It's neither of us three, and word is airtight outside of us. Could be that they planted that kid at her house out of frustration because they don't know where she really is. In any case, we can feel secure that our secrecy is working. This place is a perfect location for her. Tight as a drum."

He paused, cleared his throat, took a sip of iced tea, and continued, "And since it's Trey's car, and he was presumably driving, we're going to pull him in. I have an idea of how to arrange that since we have the car in our possession. Wondering if you two might want to play along?"

At this point, Sarah chimed in, updating Adam on our more recent discoveries about young Mr. Thomas' behavior, those regarding the attack on Ms. Loomis.

"Wow. That's more bad news for the little fella, huh?" He leaned back and thought for a moment, then asked Sarah, "Do you think she would pick him from a lineup? And could we nab the other kid from the meth lab?"

Sarah answered quickly. "Maybe to the first question, definitely to the second."

I responded, "It's a big maybe. She's a high-end call girl, very independent, has a select clientele, and has never been nabbed for her activities. We think she's looking at other career opportunities, and we'd like to keep her out of it if possible."

Sarah looked at me, smiled, and said to Adam, "Street's got her in *Save* mode. He thinks she's cute. And he's right."

My turn, again. "But I think she'd do a line-up or a photo array, especially if both her attackers were present. It takes so long for rape cases to get to court, the perps will be long gone and in the system by then. She may be gone from L.A. by then as well."

Adam pursed his lips. "Well, let's look at that then. Street, his mom's an attorney. I met her at the station. She's full of herself, but she's also quite competent, from what I understand. She'll bail him out as soon as he's arraigned, won't she?"

I answered, "Absolutely. That's why stacking as much as possible against him will work. If we can draw Carty out as well, maybe get him good and mad about his kid attacking his girlfriend, you can get him in the same sweep. The charges against him are being finalized in Nevada next week. It's past time for him to go away, too."

"Yeah. It is." Adam looked at Sarah, then at me, and counted on his fingers. "So, we'd be cleaning up Sarah's shooting, the killing of the gang kid, the call girl's attack, potentially routing the drug network, and bringing in a multiple murderer all at the same time." He looked at me again. "You brought us this whole deal, Street, you're our on-site eyeball, so I'll need your statement before we roll. We'll let you have Carty, he's not on our radar as much as the drug types and the cop shooter."

I smiled. "I appreciate that."

Adam said as he looked at his printed agenda, "This is gonna take some arranging. Let me start talking to some of my people, see what we can put together. If this shit's spread out all over the valley, we'll need LAPD SWAT and the DEA as well. I almost dread that."

Sarah had an opinion. "Adam, let's take it in stages. Get Trey first, sweat him regarding my shooting and the dead kid at my house, get our rape victim to ID him so we can take him and the other kid down about the attack on her. If mom and dad are distracted, the drug operation will be easier to tackle, right?"

I added, "And Adam, please try to find the leak regarding Sarah's survival as well. That has me worried." I looked at her. "She still has a price on her head."

Adam exhaled, stood, and walked toward the front door. "Okay, you two. I'm outta time. We have work to do, plans to make, and secrets to keep. Stay in touch." Sarah and I rose, he shook my hand, touched Sarah on the shoulder, and left the house.

––––––––––––

The door to Roberta's office was a frosted-glass affair with a dark-toned wood frame that had stayed when the previous tenant, an *independent film producer*, had moved out. It was, in her mind, fairly handsome, and it was the only element of the office that she'd not stripped to the bare framework and replaced before she had taken occupancy. One of the biggest porn production houses in the world was headquartered a mile away, a business whose bank of counsel she had met twice in court in the last year. She was fairly certain that the former tenant in her office had been in the same business on a smaller scale. She reasoned that even with her own sordid operations, there had to be at least one line she would not cross.

Her receptionist had alerted her to her visitor before the frosted door darkened with the shape and color of her son Trey's form before she heard a knock. She called, "Come in, Trey." Trey strode through the door and took a seat in the client chair opposite her. She had already decided to ease off on the confrontations for now.

"Son," she allowed, "to what do I owe the pleasure? Did you and your dad spend the day together? How was it?"

"W-we had a good time. And I...um...I wanted to make up to you for wreckin' your car. I'm sorry that happened. Anyway, Dad and I got you a p-present. A gift. Come see it." He smiled more in that sentence than she'd seen him smile in months, he'd said the word *dad*, and his stuttering had lessened, so he wasn't nervous. Maybe he was just, finally, *happy*?

"Okay, Trey. What have you two been up to?" She smiled as she rose from her chair and walked toward the door. She had already seen the delivery receipt, and she had an idea of what was afoot. Together they walked outside to the ten-slot parking lot at the rear of the building. There stood Carty, his arms open for her. He took her hand and then hugged her.

He whispered in her ear as he held her, "Robbie, I know I was rude the other night. I wasn't thinkin' about what I was sayin', and I want to apologize." He separated from her and continued. "Since this damn kid trashed your ride, he and I thought we'd get you this. We know you go outta your way to take care of both of us, and this is a small token of our thanks." He walked her to the driver's door and handed her the key fob. She looked at the well-polished sedan and smiled.

"Grant! I don't know what to say. It's beautiful. Are you sure?" She looked at him. As he nodded, she added, "Thank you! Thank you both!" She opened the door and looked inside, getting a whiff of the butter-colored leather, then took her place behind the steering wheel. Grant had walked around to the passenger side and took that seat as she adjusted the driver's perch. "Grant, this is gorgeous. Thank you both!" Trey, standing at the passenger side, smiled through the open sunroof.

Trey offered, "They had about a d-dozen of 'em at the dealer, but this was the best-lookin' one of all of them."

Carty said, "Yeah, Trey liked the rims. He picked it out." Quieter, he added, "Oh, and your Maxima is at the body shop. Trey's payin' the deductible, like he promised. I'll curbstone it for ya when it comes back."

Roberta smiled and said again, "Thank you, guys! This is perfect. I mean it. Now, if you'll excuse me, I'm expecting a business call inside. Can we have dinner tonight to celebrate this? I'll buy, anywhere you two want to go."

Grant took the hint, and before he left the passenger seat, he reached up toward the switch panel above the mirror and pushed the button that closed the sunroof. "Sure thing, darlin'. Let's plan on that then. Call me, and I'll meet you."

"Take my pickup, Trey, drop Grant off at his place, and leave it at the condo. I'll be along after work. And be careful." Her tone of voice indicated that her anger over his behavior might not yet be placated.

## 36

After Adam left the rental house, Sarah and I talked about tactics for the approaching battles and gave one another a few ideas. It was a conversation that would continue for several days. I hit the highway south and rushed home to prepare for the evening's festivities among high-powered TV network executives, a guest of Dierdre at her network's rollout of fall TV series. Numerous actors and media big shots would be in attendance, and my attendance had been deemed mandatory by my own rising star. Dierdre had received considerable praise for her work with the net's ten-o'clock news with the local affiliate, though in fairness, there was no shield between the network brass and the management of the L.A. channel.

The dress code had been established earlier in the week, so after I showered and pummeled myself into *presentableness,* I waited patiently until seven pm, when the stunning purple Challenger SRT8 and its more stunning pilot, prepped to the max and wearing a short purple thing that I referred to as *that dress,* burbled into my driveway. I strode from the patio chair, took my place in the shotgun position, and we were off. I sat and watched her drive the new mount, rowing the six-speed stick like a veteran Can-Am race driver. I have to say I was impressed. We made great time to Hollywood Boulevard.

Dierdre drove to her reserved parking space in the bowels of the massive theatre auditorium and retail facility at the Hollywood and Highland intersection. In truth, much of Hollywood would need massive urban renewal just to raise it to the level of *dump,* but this site, not yet a decade old, was borderline amazing.

I cooled my heels in a hallway behind the stage for a few minutes and watched as Dierdre did her exec thing, directing the stage crew regarding spoken show introductions and gently admonishing others about cues, timing, and stage lighting. Finally, she shed her executive role and joined me for a stroll into the ballroom, saying, "This is where they've held the Emmys and the Academy Awards presentations. I love this room!" As soon as she was recognized by other staffers, the whole kiss-kiss thing went on for a half-hour as I was introduced to numerous of her co-workers.

Casts of several shows I was unfamiliar with said 'hi', and I had a nice conversation with the station's very attractive and mildly flirtatious evening *weather girl.* She was a striking young ash blonde and former USC cheerleader about whom I had been warned. "She's just looking for a future divorce settlement or three." I had a nice chat with her, though I did revert back to college freshman dialog for context. She was, as Zig would say, *fun to look at* and, I suspected, a great example of cosmetic artistry.

Several station execs were introduced, and one of her female cohorts surmised, "You're that cop that Dee is always talking about. I can see the draw, girl."

I smiled and corrected her. "I'm not a real cop, I'm a private ticket."

"Oh, that's right. She did say that. Nice to meet you." She walked away as if I'd asked for a loan. The network programming chiefs were introduced and were quite positive in their interactions with *Ms. King.* One of the older guys hugged her a bit too tightly for my taste, but relented when he saw me watching with a stern glare. We all have to cope. Dierdre had whispered caution to me about a few of her male co-workers, and I gathered from the furtive glances toward her in *that dress* that she was a hot topic among a few of them. Not that I blamed them a bit.

Eventually, the evening's official events began. We sat toward the front of the massive auditorium, and Dierdre was introduced by network management as a rising star in the business. I smiled and applauded, suitably proud of her. Then the previews of 'major-league, big deal, sure-to-be-a-hit' new and returning series began. I pretty much loathe being told when to laugh by sitcom producers, but I had been warned about that, too. I put on my best fake smile. We were in Hollywood. I fit right in. A new cop show looked interesting but for the improper hairstyles of an LAPD rookie cop and the way-too-cordial banter of his training officer. I leaned into her and suggested that she pass my name on as a consultant for such things. She shushed me, whispering, "Street... It's network television. Get real." Good point.

Three hours of canned laughter, fawning introductions, and masochistic false praise came to a merciful end with the closing address by the network President, wishing all present a great season of stellar entertainment and massive financial windfalls. Finally loosed back into the night, we went to Dierdre's condo and vedged blissfully until morning. I rose early, fixed breakfast for both of us, and served hers to her with a small glass of champagne on an antiqued enamel tray as she awoke. Her day-after work regimen was, as she described, informal. As she bit the corner off a piece of toast, she paused to say, "I assure you, nothing of value will be accomplished there today. Most of them are hung over. You rescued me from that awful fate." She smiled at me. "Twice, as I recall. Anyway, I'll call in if anything of any news value pops up, and I'm officially *on call*, but it is all under control."

We moved the meal to her kitchen table and talked for an hour, mostly about my ongoing involvement in the Carty problem. Her take from my description was that Roberta seemed to be an incidental player, a victim of sorts, going with the flow of her former boss/mentor Bongelli and Carty because the crooked business practices were all she'd ever known. That wouldn't help exonerate her when the hammer fell, but as a clever attorney, she might wiggle free. I was hoping that the situation would take Carty and his son down permanently for their crimes. Though somehow Trey now seemed a *fresher offender* than his dad, Grant's earlier victims still richly deserved redress, including the vehicular homicide of Dierdre's own father.

Carless at Dierdre's place, I asked that she drop me at the LAPD North Hollywood station on her way to spend lots of money at the mall in downtown Burbank. At the cop shop, Adam Fair updated me on the burgeoning plan of attack for the following week. We had lunch at Barney's Beanery in WeHo, and then he dropped me at home. There, I snagged the Tahoe, made good on a promised document and invoice delivery to my attorney ally in Century City, and ran a few errands before catching up with Sarah by phone. Nothing of import was happening at the apartment, but that would soon change.

———

On Wednesday afternoon that week, Roberta received a phone call from an officious LAPD supervisor, a Captain Adam Fair, with news that the stolen dark blue Chrysler 300 had in fact been recovered and could be retrieved at the North Hollywood LAPD substation. He stated, "I believe your son Trey was the last licensed driver of that vehicle. Perhaps he could accompany you to drive it home?"

"Pardon me, Officer Fair. How do you know he's the driver?"

Sharp lady, Fair thought. "Well, we found some personal items that he will need to identify before we can release them."

"That sounds good," she responded. "I have a busy schedule today, and my son is working as well. It will probably be after five this afternoon before I can get there."

"That'll be fine, Ms. Schwinn. Please ask for me, Captain Fair. I'll take care of you myself." Adam Fair added as the call ended,

"Said the spider to the fly..." as he looked at me across his desk and smiled his widest.

Adam said, "We're on for six for the Chrysler." Then he turned to Sarah and smiled. "You, madam, are responsible for the take-down of this guy. You have eleven officers at your disposal, we will deploy them as you see fit. Why don't you go to the meeting room down the hall, and you and Street put your heads together and let me know how we're doing this."

Sarah looked at Adam, then at me. "Got it, Cap. Street? Follow me. Adam, I'll have the plan in a half-hour. Thank you for this."

## 37

Roberta answered the scheduled call from Ross Caviglio on the third ring of her private cell. She had decided early in their arrangement that the new escort driver would need to pull his own weight instantly if she was expected to make good on extending their deal past the first week. So far, it had worked out, though she knew he was padding expenses on his vehicle buys. "Ross, listen to me. A raggedy old Expedition procured from a donation site in Van Nuys does not cost $11,000," she told him, "Regardless of how well it worked. I saw it, remember? That piece of shit probably didn't cost eleven grand brand-new. Do not play me." The replacement, she decreed, a necessity after the Expedition was disposed of after the event in Encino, would not be as expensive. Her employee agreed reluctantly. "Call me tomorrow. I need input on another project that I may need you for."

With that business concluded, Roberta called her son Trey, with no response. She left a voice message and then texted him to meet her at 6 pm at the condo so that they could make the trip to reclaim the stolen Chrysler from the Police station in NoHo.

———

Sarah and I walked twenty feet or so to a room marked *Strategy*, for which she had taken a key from a locker on the wall in the hallway. Opening the door and turning on the light, we entered a room that offered a number of options. "We'll use the streetscape," she said as the door closed. From a glass-doored cabinet, she selected a variety of Matchbox-sized model cars, including a set of five with numbers from one to five on the roofs, three of which were trimmed as LAPD black and whites. Car number *1* was painted appropriately dark blue for the Chrysler, and another sedan in red was number 2, her takedown unit. She set the models on a table laid out with several and chose one layout that simulated an intersection. She wrote in chalk on the road surface, *#1: Vineland* and *Riverside,* and laid out the cars in a variety of positions. She took a photo of the layout, then wiped the *#1* out, moved the cars, and wrote *#2* for the appropriate scenario. As the blue car passed the intersection, the three black-and-whites would bracket themselves around the subject vehicle, and the takedown car would order the stop from the primary position. Sarah took the second image of the layout, then turned and asked me, "Whataya think?"

"Looks good, but I'd restrict traffic a bit back from the intersection, open it back up after he's taken into custody. And definitely separate mommy dearest from the son, lest she try to get in the middle of the situation. You're less than a half-mile from her condo, y'know."

"That'll work. Thanks. And just for giggles, I think I'll suit up in blues to do it as a regular traffic stop. The contraband found in the crime lab is still in the car, so that'll be the PC for the arrest. The APB for the car itself will still be in effect. This won't be *fun,* but it'll feel really good being right smack in the middle of it. You wanna suit up and play along with us?"

"I do feel like I've been a part of it from the start, but I'm not the one with skin in the game. This is your deal. You do the stop. I'll take a ringside seat." I called up a map of the affected area and pointed out a short frontage road leading into the residential area just off Vineland at Aqua Vista. "You do the stop somewhere along here. I'll be parked over here, well-armed if needed, but out of the way. I can't afford to piss you guys off."

"Aw, Street, that'd never happen. You have accumulated about a decade of cred with me and the LAPD. I think Adam wants to hire you."

I looked at her and smiled. "Happy to be of assistance."

I sat quietly for five minutes while Sarah proofed and printed up her concept for the arrest. When she was finished, she let me read it. It made sense. I nodded my approval as she prepared to exit the room. I even got to put the toys back in their proper places on the shelves.

Finally, she said, "Let me take this to Adam. Thanks for your help. I'll meet you in the lobby."

A half-hour later, at four-thirty, Sarah came from the Command offices to the lobby. She looked pleased. "We're a go for six-thirty, Street. Squad members will be lined up and ready to boogie as soon as Trey leaves the station in the Chrysler. We'll have detours set up to funnel him into the right area as he drives here, then *bang!*" I noticed that she looked rather happy about the whole setup. I was glad. "If you would take me to the rental house, I'll change into my blues, and we can come right back here."

As we drove back toward Silver Lake, I called Dierdre. She had invited me to be her escort for a Hollywood Bowl event that would start at eight, and I knew I would be, at best, late. She sounded disappointed at the news but said she'd invite her secretary if she chose to attend at all. We commiserated about work hours and parted friends.

Sarah looked across the car and asked, "Everything okay there?"

I answered, "Yeah, I think so. She gets a bit abrupt when I have to cancel a date, but I think she gets it. She's canceled a couple of times, too."

"Are you two exclusive?"

I glanced at her. "Monogamous? Last I heard, yes, and happily so. We may be coming to a permanent situation soon. I hope so anyway."

"Street, give it some time, let it age, see the good and the bad a couple of times."

As I made the turn-off of Sunset toward the rental house, I said, "Right, mom."

———

Trey had plans for the evening. He had spoken to the growing collection of friends he'd been accumulating while skimming here and there from the weekly production of meth from the apartment house, and he was starting to see a decent profit from it. He was also snorting similar product from friends in his posse. He called the better of the group at five that evening to announce the availability of a fresh ounce of product, and they had agreed to meet him that evening.

He wrapped up the apartment house operation that evening, checking for unlocked doors and bidding Carty a good evening. Carty was still trying to contact the call girl and waved him off when he peeked in. Trey drove his mom's F-150 back to the condo on Aqua Vista. He parked next to the new Infiniti, a handsome thing still, and made his way inside to shower, change clothes and prepare for the jaunt to recover the Chrysler. He secured the small Ziploc bags, salable packages of *his* product, in a backpack that would transfer to and stay in the Chrysler.

Roberta was sitting at the dining room table searching through her attaché case for a certain file and stalling the client with whom she was speaking on the phone. She saw him come down the stairs and called to him, "Wait in the living room. I'll be done here in a minute."

Trey sat on the couch and hit the remote to fire up the TV, finding a cable rebroadcast of an episode of Prison Break. He didn't *get* all the skullduggery of the final season of the show, but he marveled again at Michael Schofield's tattoo work. He'd heard that it really was a big decal the actor wore. That was cool, too.

Roberta came into the living room and sat on the couch opposite her son. He asked her, "So you like the c-car, right M-Mom?"

"Yes, son, I love it. Let's work some stuff out though, you and me, okay? We have to keep you under the radar, so I want you to stay off the streets for as long as possible. There is still an APB out for a car like that, so I don't want you to drive it. If I can get the car cleared by the police this evening, I will do so. I just want you to be prepared for the bad news. Okay?"

"S-sure, Mom."

Now she looked at him squarely, unblinking. "And, just to be clear, I do not want you to smoke herb when you're going to be driving...or doing any other drugs at all. If I find that you are, I will have to have you move your skinny white ass out of here. Is that clear?"

"Yes. I understand. C-completely."

"Okay, then give me a few minutes to make a call, and we'll go get the car. We'll ride up there in mine." She smiled now. "Grant says you picked it out. How did you know what I'd like?"

Trey smiled wide. "Y-you're my mom! I'm supposed to kn-know what you like!"

## 38

I had parked the Mustang at the curb in front of the rental house and sat in the living room scanning cable nets while Sarah went to her bedroom to change into her blue uniform. Any career law enforcement officer is careful about appearances, and it can take a while to assemble a striking state of command presence while wearing city duds. When she emerged, she looked fit for a recruiting poster.

"How do I look, Street?" she asked, turning side to side on her heel, smiling a wide, confident smile. "First time in weeks that I've worn a uniform. It needs a trip to the tailors if I ever decide to wear it again." She looked a bit wistful after the words were spoken.

"Hey, are you kidding? You look great!" I looked at the clock on the wall. "Time to go bust some Trey Thomas, Officer?"

"Let's get this show on the road." She opened the front door before I caught up.

"Sarah, let me move the car to the side. Use the kitchen door. I still don't want you seen out in the open in uniform."

As I backed the Mustang from the curb into the driveway, I stopped for a pedestrian on the sidewalk. Dressed in khaki slacks and a red knit polo shirt, wearing a pair of off-brand running shoes, looking thin but healthy, his face markedly cleaner-looking since the recent surgeries, Carty was out for an afternoon stroll. He looked directly at me and frowned a bit as he walked in front of the idling Mustang. I dipped my head a fraction of an inch in neighborly recognition, and he held my gaze as he passed. I backed further into the driveway, and Sarah took the passenger seat.

———

When we arrived at the police station, I was directed to take part in the surveillance of the subject vehicle in case it made an unplanned exit from the target route. Sarah chose a veteran-marked Crown Vic from the garaged line of *shops* and parked it at the edge of the property. Other marked units would transfer to the surveillance from their normal duty when the takedown started. I could see the Chrysler sitting on the wash rack at the rear of the facility, a cadet officer rinsing fingerprint powder and storage dust from its flanks.

Note: Police departments do not usually provide valet or detail service when returning stolen vehicles. It just never happens. You usually are referred to a scary-looking tow yard, populated by scary-looking people and patrolled by large, hungry, scary-looking dogs. This particular instance was brought about because of the preponderance of evidence against at least one of Sarah's assassins, and department actions were recorded and cleared at every stage by the department's legal counsel. The LAPD watches out for their own, and Sarah was their *cause celebre* for the moment. I was proud to be a sliver of the operation.

The new midnight blue Infiniti arrived at about ten after six. Roberta and Trey walked to the public entrance of the facility and went in to tackle the bureaucracy of reclaiming their stolen property. They had no idea what was in store for them, but I later heard from Adam that all was courteous and calm. Roberta asked a few questions and signed the necessary paperwork. Adam assured her that the APB on the Chrysler would not be focused on her car any longer. Trey walked outside about fifteen minutes later with a pleased look on his face, having run the gauntlet successfully. The plan was for the delivery of the car to be delayed in order to try to separate Roberta from the proceedings. She drove off the lot as soon as the gate opened for the Chrysler to be brought to the front of the station. I saw Adam enter Sarah's Crown Vic behind the closed gate as Trey regained the Chrysler.

Trey smiled. He looked carefully at his Chrysler before he took his driver's seat, fired the car off, and drove to the ramp exiting the facility to the eastbound Burbank Boulevard. He used his turn signal, unlike everyone else in L.A., and made a right into the sparse flow of traffic. I followed two cars behind him, and Sarah took a place a quarter mile back for the moment. She and I commented on the proceedings via cell phones on speaker. Trey stayed eastbound for a mile or more, and from my position, I could see he was using his cell phone, weaving occasionally as his attention strayed. Ticket magnet he.

A mile later, he signaled again and turned into the drive-thru lane of a burger place I'd never heard of. I copied his move. I was relieved to be the next car in line as his order was delivered. I made an order and waited for it to arrive. Trey had pulled the Chrysler into a parking space and proceeded to chow down, staying on his phone. I parked farther back and had a fast meal that I quite enjoyed. Sarah and Adam were parked across Burbank Boulevard in a doctor's office parking lot, their car darkened by shadows in the dusk light.

Nineteen minutes later, Trey started the big sedan, pulled forward to the trash receptacle, made a deposit, and drove off the parking lot, this time heading west on Burbank. I heard Sarah's comment hoping that Trey would hurry the hell up as we followed. I had a hunch about his destination, and two miles later, he made a brief stop to deliver some of his product. I drove past the parking lot, pulled a U-turn, and waited out of his direct view, at the opposite curb, for him to return to the street. I had an idea that might herd him in the desired direction, and Sarah approved the ploy when I suggested it to her.

It took two stoplights to pull it off. He was driving east, back on Burbank Boulevard, when we caught a traffic light at one of the lesser traveled intersections. His driver's window was down, and his elbow rode the windowsill as I stopped beside him. He looked at the Mustang, well-polished and rather stylin' if I say so myself, and I blipped the throttle a couple of times, the worldwide universal invitation to a street race. Trey gave me a thumbs-up. His 300 was a Hemi, and he had a modified exhaust that sounded at least as good as the Mustang, but with a lighter curb weight, equal push, a six-speed stick, and far better driving skills, I felt secure of victory. In the mirror I could see the profile of Sarah's Crownie, hanging back as agreed.

As the light changed to green, we both took off, he with a healthy tire chirp, me with a popped clutch and a little hazed rubber from the rear tires. I had him from jump but feathered the throttle to make it a little more even. By the next intersection, he had a slight lead. He was hunched over the steering wheel with a huge smile on his face. When the next light turned red, I rolled up on his driver's side. I dropped the window, gave him a thumbs up, and called, "Best two of three?" and held up a fifty-dollar bill. He nodded, and we went four blocks before catching another light. I won.

He caught up to me at the light, and again, I called out to him. "Let's do a right on Vineland and head south, it's less crowded." He responded with a thumbs-up and a smile. I was in contact with Sarah, who concluded, "You're having fun with this, aincha, Street?"

"Copy that," I smiled as I responded.

I led Trey to the Vineland/Burbank intersection, and we made the right and stayed in the column. Past the complex Lankershim intersection, I rolled slowly into the inside lane. Trey took the outside, and we did a rolling start from 15 miles per hour. As we took off, I saw Sarah follow, her cruiser blacked out in preparation for the fireworks to come. The race was a brief one, and I drove off and left him in a brief plume of tire smoke. I was really liking the new car by now. As I drove south on Vineland at 65 under the second freeway overpass, in the mirror, I could see Sarah close in on the Chrysler, still dark but for the Ford's daytime running lights. As the Chrysler crossed the Vineland/Moorpark intersection, doing almost 70 miles per hour, Sarah lit him up, now joined by three other cruisers, arrayed for a full-fledge felony stop.

After Trey crossed the underpass for the 101 freeway, he finally slowed to pull to the curb. As the car rolled to a stop, Sarah pulled behind the sedan and lit the pure-white takedown lamps on the roof of the car. Far ahead of the congregation, I had pulled off at Aqua Vista, taking a prime viewing position on the frontage road fifty feet from the production.

I wasn't surprised that the operation began as a full-on felony stop. The car had been on an LAPD All-Points-Bulletin for weeks, so Sarah put some distance between her unit and his car and made the appropriate demands over her cruiser's PA. Adam commanded that he do the whole *walk backward to the sound of my voice, get on your knees with your hands behind your head and your fingers interlaced* drill. Trey was calm through the process, somewhat less so when the product of the personal search was arrayed. He looked downright upset when the satchel, the drugs, and the shells from the hit on Sarah—documented material evidence found earlier in the interior of the car—were stacked atop the nice flat trunk lid.

Finally, he was inserted into the back seat of one of the new LAPD *Watch Your Head edition* Chargers and carried off to the first component of his new future. As the flatbed tow vehicle finished loading the 300, Adam walked smiling to where I was leaning on the fender of my car. We did a fist bump, and he looked genuinely pleased at the events.

"Street, can you give me a ride back to the station? Sarah's going to be busy for a few, and I'm clocked out as of 45 minutes ago. It was worth it though. That was fun."

"No problem. Hop in." I answered.

## 39

Carty sat in a lawn chair at the back of the top-floor walkway at the apartment house, sipping the last Michelob from a nearby cold six-pack. He looked south to the skyline of downtown Los Angeles. The buildings that evening seemed closer than they really were, and he thought they were beautiful though he knew he would never be more than an occasional visitor there. There had been lots of cocaine from his system moving around in those towers in the late 90s and the early years of the decade that followed, and he could recall some of the faces to whom he had sold copious quantities. He had come close to getting busted a time or two, prompting Bongelli to coerce him to leave the sales end of the operation to others. He had stayed close to the ranch north of Vegas after that, a location fraught with its own perils.

As his mental condition had improved in recent months, Grant had been occasionally bothered by trying to place faces that appeared to him. He would sometimes awaken at night wondering where or when he had been in contact with someone with *that face*. It made him nervous. The face he'd seen earlier in that car in the driveway a few doors up, the one that had shown some recognition of him as well, now bothered him. Where? Who? When? He would awaken again for a few more nights before it all came back to him. He was also bothered by the departure of his favorite female play-thing. How do you get dumped by someone you pay $700 an hour?

———

Roberta looked at her watch again and picked up her cell phone. She lowered the volume on the inane sitcom she'd been ignoring anyway and pressed speed dial for her son. The line rang three times and then went to his outgoing message, after which she spoke. "Trey, you were to come back here after we left the police station, remember? What the hell happened? Call me back!"

———

Handcuffed, Trey was taken to the rear entrance of the LAPD station in North Hollywood and placed in a holding cell at the rear of the facility. The cell was all concrete block, had been painted *beige* numerous times, and had an aroma of Lysol, ammonia, urine, and stale sweat. There were strange, deep reddish-brown oval-shaped stains on the floor near his seat- blood? There was a streaked, cloudy Plexiglas window in the front wall through which he could see an occasional officer stop and look in at him. His phone, belt, and watch had been removed upon his arrival, and his pockets turned inside out. The lighting was very bright. He had no real concept of time, but he knew that it was now later in the evening.

His mind wandered. He wondered if the older cat in the Mustang had been nabbed for street racing as well. He knew he'd catch hell from the old lady when he got home. She would prob-ably make him move from the condo, but he also knew she wouldn't abandon him completely. He could get an apartment in one of the rehab projects, maybe she'd even pay for it, set him up, get him started off right. His one regret that evening was that he'd gotten busted in the 300. That was such a sweet car, and he was so glad to have it back!

## 40

Eventually, a middle-aged black LAPD officer appeared at the window, looked in, and called to someone else, "He's in Seven." An electronic lock actuated, and the door opened a few inches.

The officer looked at him and at the paperwork he held and said, not asking, "Your last name is Thomas, your last four of your Social are 6549, correct?"

"Yeah."

"Come here. I need to cuff you. Stand on those dots on the floor and hold your hands out, palms up." The officer clasped the handcuffs on his wrists, took him by the left forearm, and said, "Come with me." Trey was walked through a labyrinth of hallways toward their destination, a more formal paneled office occupied by several senior officers. The black female officer stood opposite him and told him to take a seat at the table. He did so then she locked his cuffs to an appliance on the tabletop. She took the seat opposite him, carrying an accordion file filled with manila folders. I watched from the observation room behind one-way glass.

"Good evening, Mister Carty. Do you recognize me?"

"Sure, you're the c-cop who p-pulled me over?"

Sarah was patient. She smiled thinly, then added, "Yeah. Trey.

That was me. Thank you for being polite out there. I appreciate that. I want to talk with you for a minute, and then these officers will take over. Again, do you remember me? I mean from before. A while back. Think about it." She paused and raised her face a bit. "A few months back? East of Hollywood? Nice quiet residential street off Sunset? You and a buddy out for a ride in that fine Chrysler of yours? Little shotgun action?"

With that, Trey flushed, swallowed, and moved in his chair. He said nothing.

"See, I remember you, Trey. I remember the big green bin I was wheeling to the street for trash day. I remember the big ol' Chrysler driving toward me. I remember trying to duck away after I saw the gun barrels pointing out the passenger side window, and back behind those gun barrels, I remember your shiny young face all squinted up as you fired that pistol. I also remember the feeling of my leg being shot off by the other kid's shotgun blast...and your shots going through just under my ribs. I remember it all as if it was still happening right now!" She slapped the table in front of her for effect, and the kid jumped at the noise.

"But, let's talk about something else. Let's talk about this woman here." She showed the picture of Heather Lynn Loomis. "Remember her?"

Trey looked at the photo, and his eyes darted side to side. "Naw."

"Oh, come on, Trey, try harder. She's smokin' hot! You and your buddy followed her from your dad's place above Sunset to her home a couple of days ago! You forced your way in, then you both raped her a few times. Lucky for you, she's not the most serious situation you're facing." Sarah was laying it on now. Trey was silent, his face ashen. "Hope you had a good time, kid, it might be a while before you get with a woman again."

"Then there's this little fella." She showed the pic of the kid found at her house, Abel Juarez. "Remember him? He came with you the first time you came to my house, when you did the shooting, then after you guys fucked that up—I lived—the gang types killed him and brought him back to my house and dropped him there as some kind of dumbass message." She showed the picture of the dead kid in the KIA. "But hey, you didn't kill him. We know that." She paused, he said nothing. "See, Trey, all that stuff almost makes the drugs we found in your car small potatoes, y'know? I mean, c'mon...a possession for sale, a sale that we witnessed a while ago, a felony amount of what, meth? Crappy, cloudy, weak meth, but still meth. Almost an ounce of coke in your backpack? That wad of cash that was in the console? That's small potatoes next to shooting a cop! And in this town? Court's gonna be rough! Hey dude, you ain't even black!" She smiled. "But y'know, it's not all hopeless. You answer some questions for these officers, tell them the truth, you might just luck out, get twenty years or so instead of a nice juicy LWOP." She leaned closer to him, speaking in a lower tone. "You know what a LWOP is, Trey?" She pronounced it Ell-wop.

The kid shook his head, "No."

Sarah smiled at the response. "That's okay, you'll find out. There's a big pile of shit about to fall on you, but you're lucky. Your daddy might be a drug dealer and a multiple murderer, but you also have a mama who's a..."

Trey spoke the first intelligible word he'd uttered yet. "Lawyer."

Sarah smiled, and rose to leave the room, looking at the bystanders, saying, "She better be a damn good one." She rose and turned to her cohorts. "Guys, do your thing, then get this lil' boy down to Men's Central." She looked at the senior officer. "Sarge? Read him his rights again. I'm gonna limp my ass outta here. Thanks." She smiled as she fist-bumped her cohorts, then she left.

Sarah smiled as she led me into an office down the hall. "I have some paperwork to do before I can book. You wanna take off, feel free. Your name will not appear in this report."

"Thanks for that. I figured I'd hang and we could go to dinner to celebrate. You pulled all of that off in grand style. I am endlessly impressed."

She put her hand on my arm. "Thanks, Street, for everything.

Dinner sounds good. I'll be about an hour. There's a break room three doors down if you want coffee or anything."

"That actually sounds good. You want coffee, right?"

"Black, two sugars."

"Done." I rose and walked up the hall to the well-lit room with a bank of five vending machines on the wall to the right, a pair of microwaves, and a formica countertop under a set of cabinets on the other side of the room. The coffee smelled great though I can't touch the stuff. The pot wasn't quite done brewing. I bought a Sprite from the machine and leaned against the counter, waiting. The room wasn't large, but there were a pair of booth-style seats at the far end. Of the three occupants when I had arrived, one remained, a uniformed officer facing the far wall talking quietly on his cell phone. I couldn't help but hear his quiet end of the discussion, and I paid it little attention until later. "Robbie, he'll be taken to Men's Central within the hour. They're dead serious about this. He shot a cop, a female Gang Task Force officer. They have a bunch of other charges to file on him as well." He paused and listened. "Best idea is to wait till morning and tackle it then."

The coffee was ready, so I snagged a large styrofoam cup from the cabinet and poured the coffee, then looked for the sugar— packets, bowl, wherever cop shop break rooms hid it out here.

The officer concluded his call with, "You're welcome. We'll talk again tomorrow." He rose from the booth, turned, and saw me. He looked a little surprised. As he walked past me, I absently saw his name tag, COMACHO. "Pardon me," he said as he stepped toward the door.

I found the sugar packets in one of the drawers, fittingly, next to the ant bait. I grabbed a couple and returned to Sarah's post. Mulling over the conversation I'd just overheard, I decided to consult with Adam about it at a later time.

## 41

Carty had called Candice's—Heather Lynn Loomis'—cell phone a half dozen times today with no answer, so he turned to another woman for his *comfort*. She looked to be maybe nineteen, an aspiring porn star, and she'd had a recent overlarge boob job. She was convinced that she was hot stuff, he was less certain. She arrived late for their appointment, and she had a *friend* waiting in the car outside. She made a face when she saw his still-extensive body scarring, and she made it rather clear that she was just *in it* for the money. He finished early, having *lost the urge*. He paid the girl and ushered her toward the door as soon as possible.

Something else was bothering him as well. He knew he was regaining memories as time went on, but the one guy he'd seen in the car by the house up the street seemed to be a face he should remember. A cop? Another dealer he'd had contact with at some point? He just couldn't recall clearly. He turned on the TV and caught some cop show he wouldn't remember ten minutes after he turned it off. Criminals on TV were always stupid. He called Roberta and asked her to lunch the next day. He decided he'll try her out after all. Any port in a storm.

———

Trey had been read his rights and placed back in the holding cell at the back of the station, then led to a black Chevy Suburban for his fast trip to the jail in downtown L.A. He knew he'd blown it this time, and he was further depressed because he had sighted his precious, newly recovered Chrysler sitting at the back of the lot awaiting examination by officers. A half-hour later, he was put into a holding cell at Men's Central Jail, another concrete room. This one was colder, though, and smelled foul from a stopped-up toilet and something else. Trey hoisted himself onto the side bench and hugged his knees, rocking a few inches from side to side as he waited for them to come for him.

———

Sarah was done with her paperwork in fifty minutes. She slid the forms and sheets into a manila folder and went into the Watch Commander's office to deliver them. As she returned to the hallway, she sighted me at the other end of the hallway and called out, "Street! Meet me outside. I'll be five minutes."

———

I sat in the Mustang in the staff area of the station's rear lot after I looked at the car and swept a bit of the burned rubber off the paint behind the rear wheels. Destroying evidence? Hope not.

Sarah exited ten minutes later, and we left the station, headed for a great restaurant at Ventura and Laurel Canyon. I had frequented the Daily Grille regularly for a couple of years and had always been treated well there. This would be Sarah's first visit. I parked in the lot, and we walked to the escalator toward the second floor, choosing a table on the open deck in front.

As we were seated, Sarah said again, "Thank you, Street. I really owe you for this last stretch. Thanks for your work...and for saving my life."

"What are friends for? We have an opportunity for some serious strategy now with regard to Carty and Roberta's drug racket. Carty still needs to be herded once and for all. Wanna stay on board and play a while?"

She smiled. "I wouldn't miss it for the world. And before I forget it, I got the insurance payment for the Soul today. I need a car. Can you help me shop for one?"

"Aha! Finally, something I'm good at."

———

Heather Lynn Loomis looked toward the lights of the Century City towers from her beige suede lounge chair on her balcony as the sun went down that evening. As she poured herself another glass of wine, she looked at her phone, which she'd turned off for most of the day. She saw that *Grant* had called twenty-one times in thirty-six hours. She smiled when it reminded her of how she had felt back in her junior year in high school when that geeky senior who had taken her out once became totally fixated on her, following her around like a puppy. He had been pleasant enough in short doses, probably harmless, but she had tired of him and had sicced her current boyfriend on him to warn him to keep his distance. That had handled the issue. She wondered where all of them had ended up. Then she remembered the source of her current hurts, remembered her anger and pain. She speed-dialed the number. It was time to cut this loose once and for all.

Carty's cell phone rang once before he picked it up. She said, "Yes, Grant."

Carty sounded thrilled to hear her voice. "Hey, beautiful! It's been a while. I was afraid something had happened to you. Are you okay, baby?"

Heather wasn't in the mood. She spoke curtly as she laid out the truth. "No, Grant, I'm not okay. Something did *happen to me*. A couple of your boys showed up here after I left your place last time. They worked me over pretty good. They were here for a couple of hours. I'm off work for a while. Scratches and bruises aren't pretty, and I know you expect perfection in your *hired talent*."

Grant was dumbstruck. His voice rose. "Wait. What are you talking about? Did somebody hurt you? You think it's someone I know? That can't happen! Tell me who it is. I'll take care of them. Count on it."

"Oh, you know them. One of them was a Mexican. He has tattoos, some kind of bird—a parrot or something—on his chest. He smelled bad, like cat piss. The other was a skinny white kid. He had a speech impediment and a scratch below his eye. They forced their way into my condo, and they raped me. They took turns. Neither of them was worth a shit, either." Heather stopped her description there, resisting the urge to embellish the event.

Standing in the middle of his living room, Grant was now livid. He knew the two she was talking about. "Did they hurt you bad?"

"It's not the worst anyone's ever suffered. It put me out of action for a while. I'll heal."

Carty stumbled, tears in his eyes, as he said, "Look, baby. I'll get this taken care of on my end. You can count on that. Let's talk again. I'll get you some money to recuperate on. Don't you worry. It's already handled." He followed with, "You pick up when I call you, okay?"

"Sure. Whatever. I gotta go." She ended the call, put the phone on the side table, and sipped her wine. And she smiled.

———

Carty sat in the recliner in his living room, his face knotted in thought. The girl being attacked, the kid involved? That had to be dealt with ASAP. He'd also decided that he needed a car. He couldn't be immobile in case shit went seriously sideways here. He might need an escape route, fast. He just had *that feeling*.

He also kept obsessing about that face he'd seen in the car up the street. He just knew that it was connected to something bad. He put on his walking shoes and hoofed it down the hill that evening, taking a three-block walk along Sunset Boulevard. He crossed the street to check out the little suburban used car lot on the west side of the six lanes. The dealer was based out of a nicely-renovated gas station, stocking mostly late-model imports. He liked the charcoal '08 Ford F-150 sitting on the second row better. Coupla years old, it had a scratch or two, and it would never be all that identifiable in a *stress* situation. There were a million of 'em in L.A. That one would work fine.

He started back toward the side street to go back home. He stepped around the winos stationed outside the shabby, badly-lit, smelly corner Latino market, went inside, and snagged a twelve-pack of cheap beer, a bag of pretzels, and a fifth of bourbon. He had some thinking to do, and that might help.

———

Carty waited in his apartment that next morning for the arrival of the mix crew. He climbed the stairs to the third floor of the apartment building after he knew they'd all be suited up and working and had all three of them gather on the walkway outside the apartment. He cleared his throat and addressed them in a soft, but he thought authoritative, tone. Chino repeated his words in Spanish after he spoke each sentence.

"Guys, we got a change of plans today. Trey won't be coming, maybe not for a while, so we're gonna shut production down at this location for now. I need you guys to take this setup down and clean it really well. Stack the hardware at the back of this floor, back by the storage rooms. Then take down all the plastic sheeting inside the apartment, take it to the dumpster out by the street. Then mop the floors. Do that, and I'll get the reno crew upstairs to come here and paint this unit. You guys can watch them and learn something new. Help them out with getting this unit finished, and we'll try to make room for you on one of the other projects." He pointed at the kid standing in the middle. "Chino? You're in charge today. Get all that done, and come see me. We need to talk about something else." He addressed the men as a whole. "Got all that?"

Chino nodded his head and left the apartment. The other two followed. Carty returned to his apartment one floor down, gathered his billfold and some cash, and walked down the hill to Sunset Boulevard.

———

I was in the den writing checks when the phone rang. Sarah. "Street, something new at the curb in front of the apartment building. I'm sending an image."

"Thank you. I have some stops to make on the way up there. Give me a couple of hours. Your image is coming through now. Thanks."

———

At ten-thirty, Carty received a frantic call from Roberta. Trey had been arrested for street racing or something in North Hollywood the evening before, but he was being held on other, far more serious charges as well. Frantic, she spoke rapidly over the sound of her car. "I have to go to L.A. Men's Central Jail downtown to see him. Do you know anything about that place?"

Carty, a bit hung over and quite annoyed since talking with Candice the previous evening, was curt and loud in his response. "Robbie, how the fuck would I know anything about it? I've never been there. Goddam kid did something bad to someone and got caught, he gets to pay!" He realized as he said the words that it was an odd response coming from him, but he didn't care anymore. The beaner kid would account for his involvement soon as well. "Look, Robbie, just go see the kid and see what the cops say. You've done this shit before. Trey's just another client at this point, right?"

Angry and feeling abandoned, Roberta didn't respond to the remark. She just disconnected and drove on.

## 42

I'd had a feeling about the remnants of Sarah's situation since the night of Trey's takedown, but since she was busy closing the account on her shooting, I decided on another tack. I called Adam and asked him to come to my house for a brief consult. As his big black Crown Vic arrived at four o'clock sharp that next day I was behind the house cleaning the Mustang. He pulled in directly behind me and stepped out.

"So, no police station firehose wash jobs for you, huh, Street?"

"No. I don't even use soap anymore. Everything's soft cloth, detail spray, rinse, and chamois dry now."

"Well, your stuff is always top drawer, I know that. You were a big help with that Thomas kid. It was really imaginative the way you lured him in." He extended his hand in greeting.

"Thanks. I get one right once in a while. Actually, there's something from that night that I want to talk to you about. Let's go inside." I folded the cloths and put the cleaning kit in the shade under the car. Adam followed me onto the patio and then into the office. He took a seat in front of the desk, I sat on the corner. "Adam. What are the chances that you have a mole in that station?

Someone in the know, someone passing info to gangs or drug types regarding Sarah's address first, and more recently, sending info on Trey's arrest to his mom, the attorney. That someone would have access to station dealings and staff info to get that information out to hostile interests in the time frame that it occurred, right?"

"That's not my primary workstation, so I would imagine a lot goes on there that I'm not privy to, but yes, that would be a negative development. What do you know about it?"

I related the information of my trip to the break room the night of Trey's arrest and the phone conversation I had overheard. "Now granted, I only heard one side of the discussion, but I'd see it as a possibility for more problems."

"You saw the officer? Which one of the staff was it?"

"That station has an officer Comacho on staff, right? Hispanic guy, thirtyish, I think he was working Communications that evening."

"Reggie Comacho? Yeah. He's about six years in. Transferred from West Valley patrol after he hurt his knee. He's been a work-able officer since I've known him, but I haven't known him all that long or that well."

"Does he offer to help with communications for your task force? Does he ever want to ride along? Do any of the operations for which he has information ever go sideways?"

"You bring up some good points, Street. I appreciate it. I'll look into the situations you mention and decide what needs to be done. This may go deeper than Comacho." He frowned and let out a deep breath. "Thank you for telling me."

"No problem. I heard it in passing and didn't think about it till later."

"I'm glad you did. We're getting ready for the big drug house takedown. We have surveillance active on all those locations you and Sarah sourced for us. They'll be hit all at once when we do it."

"Okay. Is Officer Comacho involved in the operation?"

"I'll make some calls and find out. If he has been, he won't be for long." He rose from the chair, stood beside me, and put his hand on my shoulder. "You have been a huge help to us through this, Street. I appreciate it. This will all stay between us. I'll keep you posted." We shook hands again, and he left through the patio doors.

**43**

Carty answered the knock at his apartment door at 4:03 that afternoon to find his employee Chino standing on the perimeter porch outside. The wind was stiff that afternoon, and the blue vinyl tarp fluttered in the background. "Mista Grant, we're finished moving the equipment from the apartment and moving it upstairs. You want to come take a look?"

Carty walked onto the porch and closed the door behind him. "Sure thing, Chino. I need to talk to you about something else, too." The pair mounted the north-facing outside staircase to reach the third floor of the building. Walking toward the rear of the building, they stopped at the former cook site apartment. Carty opened the door and looked in, finding bare apartment walls and fixtures, readied for a quick paint treatment that would come next week. He nodded his approval and swung the door shut as Chino stepped aside, grinning with pride.

The pair climbed silently the next stairway to the rear of the top floor, where the disassembled apparatus from the emptied apartment was stacked outside the closet doors at the rear of that floor. "The crew from the other shop will come get this stuff tomorrow morning. We're setting up another site, and they'll use it there."

As they stood at the closet doors at the rear of the exterior walkway, Carty turned to Chino and opened the new subject. "What's this I hear about you and Trey finding that girl the other day? Was she fun or what?"

"The puta?" Chino smiled wide. "She was primo!"

At which point Carty backhanded Chino full force with his right hand. It wasn't the strongest hit ever, but it did knock Chino off balance. He leaned back against the edge of the stucco wall inches from the wrought iron railing that surrounded the external walkway on each floor of the building. Carty struck the smaller man again, and Chino rolled away from him, raising his arms in defense. The third punch, a solid closed-fist right, landed more solidly on Chino's chin.

Chino, already off-balance, was bent backward over the railing. He lost his balance and began his fall past the railing. A quarter-second too late, his arms flailed toward the blue plastic tarp that still wrapped the building, falling short as he did a sort of vertical spiral toward the banked concrete surface below. He landed first with the back of his head. His torso folded back over his head, then beyond thought or concern, he slid in an awkward fold until his body stopped at the junction of the concrete surface and the rear of the building that housed the storefront tailor shop and the Taqueria next door. The concrete slope now wore a deep red vertical streak formed from bodily fluids that Chino would never again require.

Carty, his heart pounding at the sudden exertion and its result, looked down and waited for some sign of notice from the street below. He needn't have bothered.

## 44

Sarah e-mailed me on Friday morning, mentioning that she had seen Carty depart from the apartment house moments ago in the Mercedes town car, a sign that he was destined for another session with his cosmetic surgeon. He would be gone for the weekend, which set my agenda for a couple of steps. I went to the garage and found the electronic tracker I'd kept after Bongelli's PI had tagged the GTO with it. I had run tests on it and decided its future utilization. I packed my *go bag* for a late-night walk through Carty's apartment and a quick check of the drug manufacturing setup. Traffic to and from the structure had lessened in recent days, and I wondered if the operation was winding down.

I ran errands, made phone calls, and had lunch with Dierdre that Friday, and we made plans for our long-delayed Saturday detailing session on her Challenger. I drove home afterward and chilled in the garage for a couple of hours, then I went inside and updated my event board with the week's happenings. I left early for the trip to the rental.

At midnight, I left the rental to make another run through Carty's abode. The night air was clear and crisp as I took the lower stairway of the apartment house. First stop was the power meter at the rear by the laundry room, no signs of active occupancy there. At Carty's apartment, I let myself in and made a quick tour through the rooms. The only new item I saw was a decent new machine-finished Ruger pistol and a box of hollow-point bullets in the desk drawer. The apartment needed a good cleaning. The bedroom and bathroom were dirtier than before, and he needed to do laundry, perhaps due to the cessation of visits from the rental-unit girl-friend. I'd have been depressed at that loss myself. Before I left, I dropped one of my burner cell phones between the cushions of the sofa. I had a plan for its future use.

Upstairs was a different story. The one unit devoted to drug manufacturing was being re-purposed as an actual apartment. The other apartments being re-modeled were near completion, so I decided to take my leave and go home. I rounded the outer walkway to the rear of the structure and sensed an odor, something dead for a full warm day at least. Searching for a few seconds, I used the flashlight and looked down the steep, brightly-muraled concrete slope behind the rear wall of the structure.

The brightly-muraled concrete wall behind the street-level storefronts below was unlit, but I could still see a dark vertical smear running down from the mid-level of the surface. At the bottom was a crumpled male body suited in overalls. One shoe was off, and that leg was bent at an impossible angle to the rest of the body. From my vantage above, I speculated that the victim had been tossed off the back of the building. I wrapped up my visit and went back to the rental to consult with Sarah about the discovery. Sarah called her peeps at the cop shop to explain my role in the drama and gave Adam as a reference for my input.

The patrol cops came to the scene immediately, the murder cops within a half-hour. The scene was cordoned off until about 3 am on Saturday morning before the assemblage broke up. This was seen as just another murder of just another Latino male in L.A., no big deal. I spoke at length with a Detective Roarke, Robbery Homi-cide, giving the massaged details of my discovery of the body from the street above after seeing the dark vertical streak on the concrete slope and recognizing the aroma of a not-quite-stale corpse. The obvious fall of the corpse from above led the investigators to look at the apartment house and take notes, but the early conclusion was an unassisted accidental fall from an obvious construction site.

With those festivities concluded, I walked back up the hill. Carty had taken delivery of his pickup that morning before he went for his weekend session at his plastic surgeon, so this was my best opportunity to get up close and personal with the truck. In the low early am light, I paused at the grey F-150 parked at the curb and slipped the locator inside the rear edge of the right-side frame rail about a foot forward from the bumper. I had installed a new watch battery into the unit so that we could have a dependable feed for weeks. Our finale wouldn't require that much time.

With that task completed, I worked up the darkened curb side of the pickup, used my trusty slim Jim to pop the door lock, and left a second burner phone inside the glove box. I wanted to stay in touch with Carty in the mid-term.

———

Saturday morning Sarah and I drove to the valley to look for a replacement for her bespoiled KIA Soul. Five dealers and a quick lunch later, she closed the deal on another KIA Soul, a red one this time, and drove it home to the rental. The hamsters won that round. I went back home to wait for Dierdre and her new purple hot rod Dodge Challenger to arrive.

That interlude went swimmingly. In a simulated replay of her weekend income producers during her college years after her parents' deaths, she had undertaken a unique entrepreneurial effort by detailing vehicles while dressed in a rather demure one-piece white swimsuit. A lithe young dark-haired woman so dressed is a draw for me anyway, but given my natural attraction to her, the afternoon was fascinating. Her movements gave the swimsuit a very impressive life of its own.

With the car nice and shiny and a brief interlude inside the house completed, we went for a spirited dash through the canyons around Hollywood. Dierdre took to Woodrow Wilson Drive off Mulholland with particular verve and finally left that twisty stretch of asphalt after four energetic laps in each direction. We stopped at the Mulholland overlook above the Hollywood Bowl at sunset, sat at the top of the centerpiece rock, and probably embarrassed a few onlookers with our spirited necking, then laughed all the way back home. The rest of the night was tender, energetic, invigorating, exhausting, and renewing all at once. We awoke Sunday morning smiling, tangled in one another's limbs. Being in love was kinda cool this time around.

The only thing we ever really disagreed about was her station's seeming obsession with televising police chases. I hated them. Dierdre took them as a welcome part of her job as assistant news director, an element that lessened her workload. Whenever Pedro or Freddy decided to rip off a Sentra so he could run from the PoPo for an hour or two, scheduled news programming and script editing went out the window. The boost in the station's viewership meant that all other concerns were cast aside. The public loved 'em. Case closed. Welcome to L.A.

## 45

The doctor came into the recovery suite with his clipboard in hand and approached Carty, who was sitting on the side of the bed. The most recent procedure, dealing with the skin on the patient's throat and chin, had gone well. He pulled the gauze away from the newly modified surface, lifted his penlight, and looked closely at Carty's skin. He then examined the less-recent work, the cheek and forehead areas that had been dealt with earlier. He frowned a bit, then clicked off and lowered his flashlight before dropping it into his smock pocket.

He took a step back and asked, "How did you sleep last night, Mister Grant?"

"Truthfully? Not very well." Carty stood from his bedside perch and started buttoning his shirt. "I'm not comfortable anywhere but my apartment, Doc. Thing I wanted to ask you...is there any way we can pick up the pace on this process? Is there a way I could stay here for a week or ten days, and you just get it all done at once? I'd pay extra if that would make it happen."

The doctor clasped his hands in front of his body and looked at Carty. "I would strongly advise against that, Mister Grant. Your body can handle only so much at one time, and I insist on a high margin in your body's ability to deal with all the work we are doing. Slow and steady is the best path, by far. You're looking far better than you did two months ago, don't you agree?"

"Sure. So, you won't do it for me," He stated it as a fact. "Even for a big payday."

Slightly louder now, the doctor explained, "Mister Grant, it is not about money. For me, it is an ethical concern. I refuse to bend my ethics beyond a certain point for a bigger wad of cash. It would lower the quality of the finished product. I will not willingly agree to do that. If you insist on chasing that end, I can perhaps get you a referral to another practitioner."

Carty looked at the doctor and nodded. "Okay, dude. That's how it'll be then. You done good work here, and I can't question your decisions. We good?"

The doctor smiled at his increasingly annoying patient. "But of course, Mister Grant. You are an excellent patient. I greatly value your cooperation and your patience. Have a good day. Your driver will be downstairs at the top of the hour." The two shook hands, and the doctor left the room.

An hour later, Carty left the big grey Mercedes town car that brought him back from his latest medical session. He returned to his apartment, took a shower and an hour's nap, then rose and started planning his next steps. He snagged his F-150, drove to the nearest Fry's electronics store, and bought a Dell laptop computer that was marked down. To help with the upcoming conversion to his new plans, he'd bought an *Internet for Dummies* book explaining how to make Windows cooperate. He thought he had a handle on it by that evening.

At 11:20 am that Monday, Carty learned that the cops had found the body at the bottom of the concrete slope behind the apartment house. His doorbell sounded twice. He opened the front door to find a pair of LAPD officers—a well-dressed plainclothes female and a cadet uniform of some kind—on the outside walkway, asking about the body that had been found down below. Still gauzed from his surgery, he made quick work of the inquiry.

Standing at the door, he said, "No, ma'am, I haven't been back there. I just left the hospital from having surgery this morning, as you can see." He gestured toward his bandaged throat. "The property owner has workers in and out all day every day. I don't talk to them much." The officer scribbled on her pad and seemed satisfied. She wished Carty a speedy recovery and left him at the door. Carty chuckled when he realized moments later that he had actually told her the truth.

That afternoon after lunch—some fat egg noodles in a hearty seasoned chicken broth from a little place down on Sunset—Carty took a stroll around the neighborhood. As he walked up the short hill past the house where he'd seen the face in the Mustang, he paid particular attention to the front window toward the west side. He could see through the sheer curtains that there were two big screen TVs mounted vertically on the west-facing wall, probably a living room. Odd. The upper screen was playing some show, looked like old cop cars and stuff. He couldn't clearly see what the lower screen showed, but the whole thing made him a little nervous for some reason. He'd think on it for a while.

Then Carty remembered the new cat from Nevada who had been doing the security for the hauls. He called Roberta and asked for the number. The huge man knocked on the door of Carty's apartment three hours later.

Cary answered the door and looked up at the visitor who filled the door frame and blocked most of the daylight in the opening. The large man looked down at the host and said, "I'm Ross Caviglio. Miz Schwinn asked me to pay you a visit." Carty saw that

Ross seemed to have no throat. Below his lower lip, the skin dropped straight to his chest. Odd.

"Come on in, Ross. Damn, you a big one, ain't ya?"

"I am." He walked into the apartment and shook hands with the man.

"Have a seat."

The man walked to the upright chair next to the window. The chair groaned under his weight. "Miz Schwinn says you're an old friend. I've been protectin' her hauls for a coupla weeks. Nice lady."

"Yeah, we been friends for years. She says you're pretty good with a set of wheels. I wanted to ask about your other talents."

"Mostly, I been muscle. I did some transport for an outfit in Vegas. Landed in a DUI stop, car got searched, I did ninety days in Metro Vegas Jail. Met one of the former peeps worked for your man Bongelli. He gave me the reference for over here. I'm glad to be away from Vegas."

"I can relate to that." Carty looked at the man and asked, "How're you with guns?"

"I hold my own. What needs doin'?"

"I ran into a problem a while back, and one guy caused me a shitload of trouble. Turns out the guy may be right up the street from here. I think some kinda shit's goin' down soon. I need you to take a look and see what's up at a house up the street. Robbie says you can handle yourself pretty well. I want to see if this is a threat. If it is a threat, get rid of it. I can't afford to fuck around. I got too much at stake."

"You got money, right? I don't need to play for free."

Carty's voice raised an octave as he said, "Hell, I wouldn't ask you to do that, bro. I pay for risk and effort. Let's take a ride, I'll show you what I need."

"Let's go take a look."

An hour later, the two men returned to the apartment house. Carty parked his newly acquired pickup truck in front and walked Ross to his older grey Explorer. The two shook hands, and Ross departed.

I was waiting in a line of cars on the 405 that Tuesday morning when I answered the cell by tapping a dot on the screen in the center stack of the Mustang. "Zig! What's up?"

The voice came over the sound system. "C-man, check this out. I keep hearing of a guy wanting to stock up on firearms and ammo, dealing on the *down low*. You said you expected that your man Carty would start arming up at some point. I put two and two together and called you."

"I'm glad you did. What do you have?"

"Well...last night, a guy in a nice F-150 wants to meet a guy I know to buy some handguns and an AR15—nice stuff—and a lot of ammo. Out of a car trunk. In a darkened parking lot. Behind an office building on Van Nuys Boulevard. At midnight." He paused, then, "Seems this cat had gauze on his face, on the left side. Skinny white guy."

"Sounds like a definite maybe. Anyone get pictures?"

"Ah, yes. The nether regions of the clandestine side of the illicit firearms trade has been far more careful of late. License plate and face pic on the way to your e-mail."

"I appreciate that, Zig. I'll let you know what turns up."

"Keep me in mind if you ever need a wingman."

"You know it. Thanks."

———

"Street, I got a suspicion about this guy." I had brought Sarah's requested fare for lunch—paper-thin pastrami on long fresh buns, yellow mustard, and pickles—from The Hat, a favorite stop of mine in Pasadena. We had taken the lunch out onto the wide front porch of the rental. We sat in patio chairs in the warm breeze, shielded from street view by the tall wall surrounding the porch. She showed me the facial recognition picture of the large passenger of Carty's pickup.

I swallowed a bite of my sandwich and offered, "I'll take your word for it. What's he good at? You said he had done a little time in Vegas?"

Sarah had plenty of information. "He left their Metro Jail a coupla weeks ago, been arrested for drug possession, but there wasn't enough direct evidence to justify a lot of effort getting him a long sentence. Looks as if he was just a nuisance for them, so they cut him loose early. He may be the escort driver for the drug hauls recently. They have a jammer working the transports to keep them from getting nabbed. That's been working for the last couple of weeks, anyway."

"I put that tracker on Carty's truck. Does it show where they went?"

"Way ahead of you, C. They just drove to the park at Silver Lake, sat for a half-hour, and then drove back."

"Maybe they sat and talked. Makes me wonder if he's suspicious of the security at his apartment." I looked down the hill toward the apartment house. "Or maybe it's just general-purpose paranoia. Since there's a new player on site, let's step up security here. Use the nanny cams that Zig brought."

"Gotcha. Not a problem, Street. You know I'm packin' 24/7."

"I know."

———

That evening at nine pm, we made a fairly big display of leaving the rental house. I had parked the Mustang at the curb out front, and at the appointed time, we walked, smiling, to the car. I opened the passenger door for Sarah, then popped the trunk to put her valise inside—giving the suggestion of an extended absence—then I crossed to my side, and we drove away. I even made a U-turn at the top of the street and slowly drove back past the apartment house at the curve, intent on drawing them out if that was their wish. We drove to our destination, tuned in on the laptop, waited, and watched.

At eleven pm that evening, we got a little action. The image from the camera on the porch showed a large Caucasian man walking up the three steps onto the porch, looking in the front windows, then crouching in front of the front door to pick the lock. We'd made the process an easy one. Then Ross Caviglio entered the living room and drew the solid curtains on the front windows. He prowled around, looking at the electronics package, at one point hitting the remote for the two vertically mounted big-screen TVs on the west-facing wall. There he saw that the lower image was a full-frame view of the apartment house at the end of the street. His worst suspicions realized, he took particular interest in his discovery from then on. He started a cursory examination of the notebooks and records left in the area around the recliners. His suspicions grew as he read on.

We had pulled onto the alley at the back of the house, then entered the house through the back bedroom door. We stood and watched on two interior monitors as ol' Ross rifled through the accumulated paperwork, intermittently looking back at the lower of the two big-screen images. The low electronic hum from the speakers masked any slight noises from within the house.

Sarah and I smiled at one another as the giant unit in the front room became more comfortable with his discoveries and his environment. At one point, about ten minutes into his visit, he sat on the larger of the two recliners and thumbed through Sarah's notes. Sarah made a sign, and we walked silently down the hall from the back bedroom. We emerged from the hallway and approached his recliner from the rear. This lure had been my idea, but the bust was Sarah's alone. A pair of LAPD Crown Vics waited in the alley for our call.

Sarah leaned toward Ross in the recliner and asked, "Ross, have you ever been shot?"

Ross Caviglio first jumped about a foot, and then he launched himself sideways from his perch in the recliner as he reached for his own sidearm. As he did so, he also got a full view of Sarah, holding her LAPD-issue Glock pointed directly at his center mass.

The attached red laser target pointer had its own effect. I played a supporting role with my pistol aimed a foot lower. Ross looked at each of us, wisely reconsidered his next move, relaxed, and raised his hands in surrender. Sarah looked disappointed. Ross dislodged himself from the chair with his hands high to lie on the floor to be searched and cuffed. This was not his first episode under this particular posture.

"Ross Caviglio, you are under arrest." She spoke over her shoulder to me, "Street, cover me while I handcuff this turd." Back to her arrestee, loudly, "Okay, numbnuts! Face down on the floor, hands behind your back." It took two sets of cuffs to properly restrain him because of his sheer bulk.

After he was secured, Sarah turned Ross over and raised him to a sitting position, raised him to upright, then to standing, and spoke to him as she searched him. "Ross, you are one big dummy, but you could've got yourself blown away just now. You and Carty are in waaaay over your heads. Have fun in County. You may be there awhile. I may drop by and say 'hi' sometime." She pushed him toward the patrol officers waiting at the kitchen door. "Guys, *read him* and take him where he needs to go." They assumed control and escorted Ross Caviglio to the rear seat of a black-and-white parked in the alley, departing minutes later.

Sarah looked at me as the cruiser pulled away, then raised her fist for a congratulatory fist bump. "That was fun, Street. I woulda blown his ass up, but I didn't want you to lose your rental deposit."

"Thank you for that," I responded. "Brain matter on the ceiling fan is never a good look. Are we done here? Let's go to the house." We left through the back door, still unseen from the apartment house down the street. We stopped at the end of the alley and looked over at the apartment house. Carty was safely contained inside, with little or no concept of what was being prepared for him in the short term.

Carty wondered about his new friend Ross after the man didn't return from the last assignment. He's been watching from the apartment house, he'd seen the man enter the house, then...nothing. He could only conclude that there had been some kind of issue on site. He called the cell phone number he had for Ross and waited. The phone rang four times before a bored female voice came on. "Hello..."

Carty took the phone away from his face, looked at the screen, then answered, "I'm calling for my friend Ross. Is this the right number?" He looked at the screen again. Yeah, it was notated as Ross's phone...what the hell was going on?

"Yeah, this is his phone, but like I told ya, he ain't here. He just left with some friends of mine a few minutes ago. You got a message I can give him?"

Carty, now thoroughly confused, responded, "Um, No? He'll get back to me, I'm sure."

"Okay, whatever." Sarah disconnected.

————

Adam included Sarah in the next day's 1 pm conference call that established the protocol for the drug factory takedown that would occur at 3 pm that afternoon. LAPD SWAT, Gang Task Force, and Narcotics Trafficking Eradication teams would be involved in the raids, while Traffic would restrict routes in and out for a two-block radius. The Gang Task Force would process the arrests, and the Narcs would examine and verify the product for quality and volume. Four locations, the apartment complexes, would be first.

There would also be attention paid to the law office of Roberta, the apparent ringleader of the operation. I had suggested that, as I knew there would be records and paperwork at that location that would show the path of the income that had initiated the whole process. Since the connection between Roberta and Officer Comacho had been established, Adam had determined that Comacho would be dispatched to an urgent three-day training program in one of the South Bay precincts far away from the take-down as a part of mission security.

A total of eighty officers formed the raiding parties, split between the four primary sites, with the ancillary Traffic operations under separate command. Patrol functions would be stepped up in and around the specific areas of interest, and copters would watch over the proceedings from above. While similar operations had been run dozens of times in the last decades, at significant expense, the drug business in the L.A. metro area was still constantly burgeoning. This effort would make a dent in the volume and reach of the drug trafficking in the valley and would decimate the Thomas/Carty drug operation.

The subsequent raid on Roberta's offices, just starting as the raids were wrapped up, would require eight officers from LAPD, including three from the upper ranks of Adam's team of drug and gang cops, plus representation from the FBI, which was by then finally wrapping up its study of Bongelli's operations.

———

From the four locations, a total of thirty-nine arrests were made. The Balboa apartment complex location netted the biggest results, with eleven gang types, a cache of weapons, plus five stolen vehi-cles, an assortment of stolen building materials, and a pound and a half of *fresh* meth. A further search netted a total of twenty-seven active arrest warrants from only the occupants at that one location.

I had called Dierdre at work and had given her a tip on the take-downs, and her station's helicopter coverage started at three that afternoon, after the raids had begun. I'm not a fan of allowing the media to hassle law enforcement types when the cops are in the middle of their primary tasks. The LAPD was great at post-event information sessions, and that would happen later this same evening in front of the Police HQ in North Hollywood.

With Officer Comacho out of the picture, Roberta had received no advance word of the impending events at her properties. She was preoccupied with trying to locate Trey in the labyrinth of the Petri dish that was the L.A. Men's Central Detention facility. Finally, after three hours of waiting outside the offices of various administrators, she was led to a remote conference room in the administrative wing of the facility.

## 46

Fifteen minutes later, Trey was led into the room in shackles. He wore a ragged, faded orange jumpsuit that was thirty percent too large for him. The attending deputy led him in and sat him in the straight-backed office chair across the table from his mom. He closed and locked the handcuffs around the kid's wrists after running the attaching chain through the fixture atop the table.

As soon as the door closed on the meeting room, Trey started in on his mom. "You g-gotta get me out of here, mom, this p-place is gonna k-kill me!" He held his fists together and rocked back and forth in his chair. His facial expression told of fear and a hopelessness for which he'd been utterly unprepared.

Roberta looked at her son and said in a loud whisper, through clenched teeth. "You listen to me, Trey. They have you charged with a lot of serious offenses, and I won't be able to even get bail for you. You were holding when we retrieved the car from the police station? How could you be so stupid? You shot a police officer? Do you have any idea how seriously that is taken in this city? They want to put you away for life! How did you get mixed up in this crap? And I want the truth! None of your bullshit this time!"

"Ma, I had nothing to d-do with the c-cop shoot. That wasn't m-my idea! They m-made me d-do it!" Roberta looked at her son and shook her head.

Now louder, Roberta asked, "Trey, goddammit, which is it? Either *you had nothing to do with it,* or *they made you do it.* One or the other!" Roberta was enraged. Trey's response was a blank stare, and he was trembling.

She looked at her son with sorrow and, as she would realize later, considerable resentment. This was going to be a tough go, and she didn't have the patience for it right now. She had a migraine headache. Everything was hitting her all at once. She decided her tack with the kid. "Okay, Trey, shut up and listen. I am not going to defend you on this shit. I'll hire another attorney to take care of you. The DA will not set bail on the shooting of an officer. You'll be here till the preliminary hearing. I'll talk to you then." With that, Roberta, completely frustrated, stood from her chair, gathered her materials, and left the room.

As the deputies removed Trey from the interview room, Roberta got the attention of the senior of the two. "Could I ask you something, deputy?"

"Yes, Ma'am."

"Could he be kept in isolation for a few days until I can arrange proper counsel for him? I'm worried about his mental condition."

The deputy frowned at her. "Ma'am, given the gravity of his charges, he'll be under observation, kept in a solo cell next to the duty station. I'm a shift leader, I'll make certain that my staff keeps an eye on him. He is accused of trying to kill an LAPD officer. We take that very seriously. He's not going anywhere anytime soon if we have anything to say about it. I will keep your card and keep you updated on his condition." He took a card from his shirt pocket and handed it to her as he accepted hers. "Here is my contact information. Call me if you think you need to."

As she walked to the exit, she considered the ambivalence of the answer. She shook her head as she reached her car in the parking lot across the street from the jail complex. Still, in something of a fog, she made her usual mental list of things she needed to do at home or at the office. Item one, counsel for Trey. Her head continued to ache as she started the car and left the parking lot to catch the nearby onramp for the 101.

Thirty minutes later, Roberta left the Hollywood freeway at the Universal City exit. At the bottom of the ramp, she caught a green light, a rarity there, and made the left turn under the freeway, then made her way to the right at the top end of Ventura Boulevard. She followed Ventura down the hill past the porn mills on the west side of the six lanes, into the gentle turn to the main westbound run of Ventura. Traffic was a bear that afternoon, and she had her own new concerns to sidetrack her concentration.

As she approached the corner of Ventura and Vineland to turn across the intersection to her office, she noticed the LAPD cruiser parked at the curb. That sight woke her up, then she saw the charcoal cop-spec Crown Vic parked in front of the black-and-white.

Trouble.

She flipped the right turn signal and re-merged into the inner thru-lane. She frowned as she made her way across the busy intersection, thinking as fast as she could. Was her office being raided? What else was happening? She pulled to the parking pad of a 7-11 a block west, filled a space, and let the car idle in Park. She popped her briefcase open and took a quick look at her laptop, finding that she'd missed eleven e-mails from Lucy, her secretary at the law office. Lucy was panicking via e-mail, asking what was happening and where the hell she was. Roberta knew that her preoccupation with her son had taken her eye off the ball. That had to change quickly. Trey would keep...

Roberta called her assistant and listened to three rings before she picked up, whispering, "Just give me a minute, Robbie, I'll call you back." She knew that Lucy was speaking through her Bluetooth headset, and she knew the trained actor was hiding her movements. Roberta used the next seven minutes checking the rest of the e-mails, finding the news of the raids on the apartment buildings. Oh, shit.

I laughed as I looked across the car at Sarah. "You are one cruel woman, you know that?"

Sarah smiled. She looked across the car at me and asked, "So what's our next step, Street? I'm all in to help you if you want. You helped me get my shooter rounded up, what do you want to do next?"

"That depends on Carty. If the drug ring is out of commission and his kid is locked up, the distraction factor will work to our advantage. I'd like to catch him in the act of doing something really evil, but I'd rather not make anyone else a victim. He has so much of that in his background that it shouldn't matter."

———

Carty's phone rang three times as he was returning from the bathroom. He picked up and asked, "So, Robbie, what did you decide?"

Roberta spoke quickly. "Grant, the shit's hit the fan. The apartment complexes have been raided and the crews arrested, and my office is being raided by God knows who right now. We have to get together somewhere and talk, figure out what to do."

"Okay, look. Nobody knows about this place, do they? The cops were here asking about one of the workers, didn't seem like there was any issue at all. Why don't you just come here? We can figure it out."

"God. Okay, give me an hour. I'll go home for a few minutes and tie up some loose ends. I'll be there soon."

"You got it."

**47**

Carty sat on his sofa and poured a shot of his cheap bourbon as he tried to think. If the drug operation was shut down, that also meant his cache of, well, cash may also be gone. He knew the jig was up, though he didn't know where he'd heard that phrase. His *criminal* mind told him to take what he had with him, maybe four million dollars cash plus the firearms he'd bought last week, hop in his truck, and book for parts unknown. He hated to do it, but with the kid in jail and Roberta up to her ass in alligators, there really wasn't anything to keep him here anymore.

Her Infiniti rolled to the curb forty-five minutes later. Instead of inviting her into the apartment, Carty walked to the car and took the passenger seat. He suggested that they take a drive and go somewhere else to talk.

Roberta suggested, "Let's go up to Griffith Park. We can go to the Observatory and walk around. We can figure some of this stuff out. We'll be anonymous there."

The trip took a half-hour into the foothills before Roberta put the car into one of the outlying parking lots near the observatory. It was hot and windy that day, so they just sat in the idling car with the A/C on. "You've never been up here, have you?"

"No. Just saw it on TV and in movies and shit. I'll have to come back here sometime and check it out. So what do you want to do about all of this stuff that's goin' on, Robbie?"

"Well, I have to find Trey a defense attorney. He's really in deep this time. They'll want to try to give him a life sentence. I can't believe all the charges they filed against him." She opened her briefcase and withdrew a copied form with the L.A. County Jail heading at the top. She looked at it for a few seconds, then handed it to Carty. He read it slowly, his lips moving as he went down the page.

Carty handed the paper back to her. "Whoa. That's bad. They got him dead to rights, or is this all just spec?"

"I'm not sure. The cop shooting is the most serious accusation by far, but the possession-for-sale charge does not help. I have calls in to some of the big defense attorneys, we'll hire one in the short term if we can find one that takes the challenge seriously. I'm devoting a half-million to it. We've cleared a lot more than that from the Chandler Avenue sale. I knew we should have cut back on the drug operation. That's a big fail."

"Robbie, how about we just cut out of here completely? Find a buyer for the remaining apartment complexes, cash 'em out on the cheap, get a mouthpiece for the kid, and split from L.A. once and for all. Go somewhere else, re-establish...use a new identity. It's all good from that point. What's wrong with that plan?"

"Grant, I can't. I'm a professional. People depend on me. I can't just up and disappear like you can. I have employees, financial alliances, obligations, clients. It's not all that easy." She looked at him. "I wouldn't blame you for bailing out, though."

"Have the cops gone to your condo yet?"

"No, not yet, but I need to keep an eye on that. If they raided the law office, they may have filed an arrest warrant."

Carty was silent for a few moments, then, "Okay, you got me that new identity, I have those credit cards, I can support us until you make your decisions. Just lean on me for a few days, I'll get you through this." He paused, then, "Find us a place to stay, make a reservation or however you want to do it. Let's keep both of us outta sight for a while. Get this crap with Trey settled. I'll be givin' some thought to what I want to do."

Roberta answered, "Okay, let me have your card, I'll make arrangements." As he handed her one of his VISA cards, she opened her phone and started her hotel search. Carty lowered the visor on his side and checked his image in the vanity mirror, pushing on the new surface of his cheek and chin. Soon Roberta finished her conversations and closed her phone, turning to Carty to say, "Okay, I found our place for the next few days. It's a boutique hotel over in Burbank. I sometimes used it for out-of-town associates. It's nice. You'll like it."

"Awright, fine. Let's go there. I don't feel like lookin' at the sky all that much anyway, do you?"

Within the hour, the pair arrived at the hotel and were ensconced in their suite.

———

From our vantage point, one row back and three spaces north of Roberta's shiny new Infiniti, Sarah and I sat in her shiny new KIA Soul and watched. She had taken a walk past the pair going to the food truck parked by the curb just beyond and had returned with our lunches, an aromatic carne asada combo plate for me, and a couple of chicken tacos for her. We sat in the car and watched and waited for something to happen.

"How's your food, Street?"

"Rather good, and quite un-food-truck-like. Good choice, madam. And yours?"

"Yeah, it's good. So, what do you think of the car? I'm likin' it."

I responded, after swallowing, "Neat little ride. I'd need one for each foot, but it seems perfect for you and the urban landscape."

"Yeah, and it cost about half of what you spent on that Mustang. If I do a lot of work like this, red might not have been the best color choice."

"I dunno. You can get away with red in some cars. Some cars just blend better than others." I looked at the Infiniti. "What do you think they're discussing over there?"

"Probably meth recipes and ways to break her rotten kid out of Men's Central. Her whole world has pretty much collapsed in the last twenty-four hours, hasn't it? The drug raid, her kid getting busted, her office raided. And now she's back hangin' with daddy dearest. There has to be some resentment going on there, don't you think?"

"Between the lot of them, her tolerance for bad boys has to be at record levels. Bongelli really trained her well for this workout."

Sarah looked at me and asked, "How's Bongelli doing, anyway?"

"He's almost done with the Feds. I get updates from Jack Wilkes once a week or so. Seems they've milked Bongelli for all he's worth. The guy has millions of dollars stashed all over Nevada and southern California in safe deposit boxes, and so far, they can't touch any of it. They want him sent away for a long time. If or when he gets out, he can afford to buy his way back into respectability. His only worry would be that some of his incarcerated victims get out too. The ones we spoke with were not pleased with him."

From my position, I saw the other car's stoplights flash. "Okay, it looks like they're leaving. Give her about thirty seconds lead, keep them just within sight, and you'll be fine."

"Toss your food tray in the barrel there, mine, too. Don't need food stinkin' up my new car."

I smiled. "That's the spirit."

We followed the pair down the north side of the park, along routes that had been locations for a thousand TV car chases through the years, finally ending at Magnolia Boulevard in Burbank at a kitschy little upscale hotel hideaway. I would return later that evening to put a tracker on the Infiniti. I figured they'd make a run for it if Carty had any voice in the matter.

———

The next morning, Carty woke to find Roberta sitting at the counter in the suite's kitchenette, working on her laptop. Her bloodshot eyes didn't divert from the screen as he walked past her to the fridge. Roberta said without looking up, "I can call out to room service for breakfast. What would you like?"

Carty answered, "Don't get me anything. I'm not a breakfast kinda guy. Any updates on anything?"

"I think I landed an attorney for Trey. He's based in West L.A., has a good track record for criminal defendants. He's supposed to call me back within the hour."

"Well, Robbie, I think I'm gonna pack up and leave town. I'm not doing you any good here, I'm just in the way. I think you're probably better off without me. I'll make sure the work gets done at my building, and I'll put 'em on my apartment when I leave."

Roberta had realized earlier the night before that she was tiring of Carty, again, as she had in high school. "Well, if that's what you want to do, I understand. Where do you think you'll go?"

Carty pursed his lips, looked at her, and said, "I think I'm gonna go to the ranch for a few days, check it out, see what can be set up there. Looked like the cops had cleared it last time." He wrote on the front of an envelope and handed it to her. "You have my number and my e-mail. Let's stay in touch, okay?"

"Well, stay in touch so that I can get your funds to you when the properties are cleared. I'll do that, at the very least, unless there's a seizure instituted. I don't see your building being a part of that since there were no arrests there." She paused and looked at Carty. "I'm sorry this didn't work out, Grant. I thought we had it knocked."

Carty was dismissive. "Yeah, I know. Gotta try anyway, right? Keep me posted on the kid. Good luck with him." He returned to his bedroom to change clothes before calling a cab to go back to his apartment.

Roberta said, "Hold on, Grant. Let me walk out with you. I need some stuff from the car."

Carty, considering anew the threat that their separation might pose, grabbed his bag, pocketed one thing from it, and followed her out. He'd made a split-second decision.

Roberta led Carty out the back door of the hotel, making small talk the whole way. She said she felt bad about him leaving, but that was his choice. She was busy and had bigger concerns. She smiled as she reached the new midnight blue Infiniti, parked on the third row of the parking lot, and Carty said, "Hit the lock, Robbie, my bag's on the back seat." She hit the button as she opened the door and took the driver's seat as the rear door opened.

Roberta started, "When do you think you'll le—" then she felt the jolt from her upper back, a fraction of a second of blinding pain, followed by a heavy metallic taste as her mouth filled with blood. Her chin sagged to her chest, then there was nothing.

**48**

I had concluded a few days prior that Carty would depart from southern California as the various situations with which he had involved himself all went south at the same time. Roberta was circling the drain, and the kid was in jail. The cosmetic restoration operations he needed would take months to resolve. There was nothing but risk here for him now. I needed to keep an eye on him. The previous evening, I had walked to his parked pickup truck and used a thin metal *Slim Jim* to pop the lock on the passenger side door. As it opened, I reached into the dashboard glove box and dropped one of my burner cell phones inside, then closed the lid, re-locked the door, and walked back to the rental house. Just a late evening stroll with a slight case of *Breaking and Entering, Vehicle* added. My career as a petty B and E artist was progressing nicely.

The next morning, I was having a discussion with Sarah, who had stopped at my house for a confab. Her new mobility fit her quite well. I updated her on my most recent update from Jack Wilkes at the FBI. He had faxed me the semi-final report from their weeks of discussions with Vinnie Bongelli. While Bongelli was still cagey regarding the specifics of his business practices and clientele, the ancillary inquiries had shown positive results. Bongelli's incarcerated clients were not pleased with him at all. The Feds were able to assemble a handsome package of Criminal Conspiracy, Racketeering, and Fraud charges for which he would be held liable in court. The big-deal lawyer would definitely need a better, bigger-deal lawyer.

I spent that morning running errands and making calls in preparation for my own departure to Vegas and, probably, to Carty's ranch. I called my not-quite friend Marshall Quince in the Clark County Sheriff's Department there to warn him about the approaching Carty. He related that his department had at long last filed charges against Carty, and he asked for specifics about the when and where of the expected arrival. I told him I'd keep him in the loop and let them play along in the roundup. He also explained that there was a $250,000 reward for his capture, the whole *multiple murderer* thing having finally gained traction with the legal community in Nevada.

Then I went to Zig's gun shop in Burbank. He and I had lunch, and he talked me into taking him along as backup. In reality, it had been a while since he had seen action, but I knew him to be an exceptional assist in stress events. Additionally, he was a far better shot than I'd ever be. Another advantage to having Zig in the mix was that he would bring his own arsenal. He advised me to gather my troops, so to speak, near the destination and plan a military-style incursion of the ranch. Back at his office, he called up a satellite map of the property. I explained the various topographic elements and methods of approach, and we agreed to work further on the final plan as the event approached.

My periodic check of the cell phone locator indicated that Carty was indeed approaching the ranch, little by little. He had stopped at the State Line commercial complex for an hour, probably for a meal, so the F-150 was stationary for the moment. He had taken a full five hours for his trip to that point, so that gave us plenty of time for our own journey.

I went to the rental house to confer with Sarah. She'd had a meeting with LAPD that afternoon, her standing in the Department finally having been decided. The final choice was hers: take a desk job in the Administrative department for a year in preparation for a Lieutenant's Admin spot at one of the precincts in a year or two, or a straight cash-out retirement with a pension at her current rank. I had my own opinion as to the proper choice, but I kept mum. The decision was hers.

Because I knew the upcoming trek to Vegas to confront Carty would tie me up for a day or three, I went to the massive TV studio complex to spend a few minutes with Dierdre. Her greeting smile was always the high point of my day. I entered her corner office and sat at the chair opposite her, and waited as she held her end of what appeared to be a relatively contentious discussion. After four minutes, she closed the conversation, disconnected, and looked at me.

"Street, honey, let's go to Hawaii for a couple of weeks. I am sooo tired of this place." She smiled that smile. "Please?"

"Sounds good to me. I wish I could leave right now. I have to go to Vegas and cancel the ticket of a really bad guy. After that, I'm in! Unless he cancels my ticket instead." Her smile turned into a frown, "But that," I continued, "will never happen. My reflexes are far better, and I have better hair." I smiled.

"Why don't you take this stuff seriously, Street? I worry about you."

"I know that. And as you once told me, I take my work far more seriously than I take myself. With regard to Grant Carty, I'm taking it all very seriously. And I have some great backup. I expect I'll be back before the weekend, and after the work is done, I will indeed accompany you to Hawaii. Make sure you can get vacation time. I'm there if you are." I rose from my chair as she did, and we held hands as we walked through the hallways and across one of the newscast soundstages, eventually arriving at the parking garage and my Mustang.

As we held each other, she said sternly, "You'll call me when you get there?"

"I will do that."

"And you'll come back as soon as you can?"

"I will indeed. You are someone I always want to return to."

She smiled. "Okay, big guy. Do your thing. Stay in touch. And let me know where to send the news crew when you catch the bad guy." It almost sounded like an ultimatum.

Back at home, I packed the Tahoe for three days *out*, closed up the house, and double-checked the security systems. All was in order, so off I went, first to the rental house for Sarah, then to Zig's in Burbank.

———

Sarah had decided to take a trip to Albuquerque for a few days after the coming events as well and would drive her own car. Zig had a fully-equipped cop-spec Ford Excursion with its own pull-out artillery deck in the rear cargo hold. The thing was equipped like a SWAT truck, and that might come in handy. As an early SWAT-type vehicle for a small town, the preparers had riveted metal step-plate to the external sheet metal, adding weight and a considerable level of intimidation. We agreed that we would meet at the East Side Cannery on Boulder Highway that evening. I called and booked a trio of rooms and set off before the afternoon rush hour started. Two SUVs and a subcompact were not the best nod to efficiency, but hey, we were workin'!

While on the drive, I called Danny Tanner, who had kept his promise about keeping an eye on the ranch. My cell phone locator indicated that Carty had not yet arrived there. Danny verified the truck description but said the place looked deserted otherwise. He also mentioned a feature I hadn't noticed, a mid-sized diesel generator tucked next to the rear wall of the barn. That made sense. The barn had been used as a shop to load the drug courier cars years before, so an independent power source was not unusual.

———

After we arrived at the cannery, we had dinner at the buffet and planned the coming events. Zig and I took a trip out to the ranch, and using the behind-the-foothills approach as I had before, Zig got a look at the layout. Together we formulated an approach for the *landing*. Sarah had asked, "Are you gonna call Carty on that phone you left in his truck? That would really shake him up."

"I'm not planning on it. If he finds the phone and opens it, the only number it calls is mine. If he calls me, I will appeal to his sense of fair play and ask that he surrender and come along peacefully."

"Oh. Right. This is a death penalty state, isn't it? With all the charges he has pending, you think he's just gonna waltz out of there with his hands up?"

"Absolutely not. I'd actually like to get face time with him at some point. I doubt it will happen, but it would probably be a fascinating conversation. I think he's past the point where he knows or cares about the stuff he did, the people he killed, the lives he screwed up. He has almost taken a pass on being human, as the rest of us see it."

Zig asked, "Do you think he'll suicide?"

"I doubt it. His ego would never allow that. His best *out* would be a shot to the base of the skull from the rear, like he did almost every one of his own victims. I do not want that to happen." I thought for a few seconds. "Second alternative, he would probably want to go out in a blaze of glory, fighting for his freedom."

"Are the Nevada authorities going to come for him?"

"Sure, when I call them and tell them we have him."

"So, you want this one yourself." Sarah asked, "Why?"

"I feel like I promised Elizabeth Damarow that he'd go down. He murdered her son, her brother, her brother's wife, and lots of other people along the way. He killed Dierdre's father. We found him, we had him in hand, we did our part right, then he took a walk anyway. I collected the pay for what we did, then it unwound. I want to make that right."

"He'll be ready for you."

"Probably. That's where you and Zig come in. Cover me if needed."

Zig said, "Consider it done, Street."

Sarah's phone rang, she looked at the face and took the call. "Hey, Adam. What's up?"

Adam Fair asked, "Are you with Street? Put me on speaker."

I called across the car, "Adam! How're things?"

"I wanted you two to be the first to hear. Roberta Thomas-Schwinn's body was found in her car in Burbank a half hour ago, shot to death."

I was surprised at the news, but I had my suspicions about the executioner. "Adam, let me guess... One shot? Base of the neck from the rear?"

"Si, signor."

I said, "Grant Carty is the shooter, Adam. It's what he does. There have been a dozen examples of his handiwork in the Clark County morgue in the last year. He's cutting ties with anyone who can hurt him."

Adam paused, then answered, "You know a lot more about the guy than anyone else does, and far more than I would ever want to. Since he's a multiple perp, is there anyone else he would go after?"

"There are two I can think of. First is his cosmetic surgeon. He's an Indian fellow, has a practice based in one of the old medical facilities on Wilshire. I'll find his card image and get it to you."

"That'll work. Who else do you have in mind?"

"He was tight with a high-end call girl. West LA, very pricey. His kid and a co-worker followed her home and attacked her a week or so ago. Carty has already dispatched the other kid, and Trey is in Men's Central. I don't think he'd go after her or hurt her. He's smitten." I looked at Sarah. "I can relate." Sarah smiled.

"Would he hide out with her? Between Burbank and our murder cops, he's a popular guy right now. I'll pass the word and ask for a warrant to be prepared. Everyone here at the cop shop wants to cut this off before it gets worse. The DA agrees." He paused, "Where do you think he'll go now?"

"He's headed for his ranch in Nevada, and we are close behind. I'll get in touch with the call girl and verify that she's above the sod. She'll be warned, I doubt she'll be an issue. If you guys would take a look at the doctor, I'd appreciate it. Let's stay in touch."

"Always. Thank you, Street. Sarah? Keep me posted."

"Copy that, boss."

I found the surgeon's card and reference numbers and sent them to Adam.

Sarah noted, "That's the first murder he's done in California, isn't it, Street? And now he's going back to Nevada where there are multiple warrants out on him?"

I looked at her. "Not the first, just the newest. Odd, isn't it? My money's on him for the guy that was tossed off the back of the apartment house. He and Trey were the attackers at Heather's place. I doubt Carty took kindly to that."

## 49

Carty sat in his truck, parked at the curb near a taqueria on Lankershim Boulevard in North Hollywood, and thought about his alternatives. He needed to cover his tracks in L.A. so that he could be free to go anywhere else. He thought of his alternative targets. Who knew the most about his movements and activities since his re-emergence? That would be Roberta. She was destined to be arrested for all the drug operations any day now. He'd always thought she was sloppy trying to manage all those deals at once. The LAPD had already raided her office, there was a *want* out for her, and the arrest warrants were already written, based on information given by those in her condo crews who had already been arrested. She was toast. She would turn on him in a heartbeat. She'd shown how concerned she was with his fate when she ignored him while he was laid up in the house in the desert. Her real estate development ploys, which he'd always been lukewarm on, had taken a third of his stash of money. Oh well. Her body would be found in her car in the parking lot at that hotel in Burbank sometime today or tomorrow. It was a shame to mess up that new car.

Who else should he go after before he left town? The cosmetic surgeon? Not worth the effort. Trey? In jail where he belonged. The call girl, Candice? Damn, he'd miss her. What about the nurse in the facility in Vegas or her kid? No, that seemed a lifetime ago. No one else had been close enough to him to do any damage. Then he thought about the face in the windshield of that Mustang up the hill from the apartment house. He knew he'd seen that face before, he still couldn't place when or where.

Carty drove the truck back to the apartment house, parked, and went in for the last time. He gathered the cash he had hidden in the apartment—he just needed one tub this time—and collected whatever else he found that might be of value while he was traveling. He reached down between the couch cushions and was surprised to find a cell phone. Probably the kid's. He tossed it onto the pile of stuff in the tub, clamped the lid, then carried it to the truck. It fit fine behind the seat. He filled the second tub with the guns and ammunition he'd bought in Van Nuys that night and stacked that tub on top of the first. He kept one pistol, the one with the silencer, inside the pocket built into the driver's door, just in case.

The drive to Las Vegas was long, hot, and tedious for Carty. He got off the freeway in Barstow, drove up the hill to the Jack In The Box on the main drag, did the drive-thru deal, and got a big chicken sandwich. It had too much lettuce, and the fries were too salty, but otherwise, it was good. He drove across the street to the big gas station and filled the tank. While he was there, a California Highway Patrol car, one of those big Fords, parked in front of the storefront, and the patrolman went inside to take a leak or something. He felt himself tense up, but then his finger touched his repaired face, and he remembered he wasn't *that Grant Carty* anymore. It made him smile. When the patrolman walked back to his car and glanced his way, Carty smiled and nodded his head. The cop returned the gesture. Wow, he thought. This *respectability* thing was kinda cool.

Energized and alert, Carty resumed his trip and made it all the way to the Nevada/California Stateline before he stopped again.

He'd dealt with the I-15 construction zones that added an hour to the trip. When he finally made it to the Stateline, he parked in the lot of that big Outlet Mall thing, under a sickly-looking tree that provided a little shade. He let the truck idle with the air conditioner on *low*, and he fell asleep for a half-hour. In his one dream, he saw Roberta dying again and woke with a start. During his nap, the sun had moved the shade so that the cab of the truck was glaringly bright. He tried to find a radio station, finally settling on an FM station playing '80s *oldies*. Huh? When had that happened?

Carty resumed the I-15 northbound and passed the *flats* approaching Las Vegas. It was odd. You drove around a curve and could see the city in the distance, but it was an optical illusion. You had to drive another half-hour before you actually got there. Cars from the Nevada Highway Patrol were plentiful, so he kept to the right lane and used the cruise control to curb any curiosity or unwanted attention. The truck traffic worsened past the Sahara exit and then eased after the Speedway complex. He rolled off the highway as the Caraway exit appeared and made the short sprint to his ranch—this would be the first time in years that he'd driven himself to his own place.

He parked the truck beside the barn's side door, gathered all the Do Not Enter ribbons from the ground, put them into the trash can, then he went inside the barn and looked around. He had a plan: get the place livable and serviceable and stay there until the situation calmed down. He knew there would be *legal issues*, and he figured his time was coming, probably soon, but he wasn't going out without a fight.

The second tub from the pickup came inside next, positioned near the door for easy access, for whatever reason. He took the lid off the tub, and there, right on top, was the cell phone he'd found in the couch cushion at the apartment. He looked at the screen on his own phone- three bars. Who knew there were cell towers out here? Maybe Shirley had ordered them installed when she was taking care of him. Where was she now?

For comparison, he looked at the other flip phone. He opened it, and sure enough, there were four bars, then the face lit. It was receiving a call. What was that about? He put the phone to his ear and listened.

The voice from the phone said, "How ya doin', Carty?"

## 50

As I'd expected for a while, the face of my phone lit up as I sat with my feet up on a small ottoman in the hotel room that afternoon, chatting with Zig and Sarah. The number matched the phone I'd left in the seat cushion at Carty's apartment on my last visit. I answered after the second ring. "How ya doin', Carty?"

The voice on the other end said, "Um, yeah. Who's this?"

"Grant Carty, my name is Street. I'm a private cop based in L.A. You and I have quite a history."

There were a few seconds of silence, then, "How's that?"

"Well, several months ago, I was hired to find the killer of Ronnie Connors and his wife. In my travels, I found a lot of other dead bodies, and at the end of the rainbow, I found you, right there in that house at the ranch in the desert, getting your beauty sleep."

Carty paused, assembling and re-arranging all of the images that had been wandering around in his mind. "Hmm...is that what you call it?" He paused a second, then asked, "Wait. Are you the guy in the Mustang over by the apartment in L.A.?"

"That's me, babe. A few friends of mine and I talked about it, and after I found you when you busted out of the hospital, we decided to let you have your freedom for a while, keep our eye on you, and see what happened. You led us on quite an adventure. We learned a lot."

Carty's head was swimming. "Yeah, I guess you probably did."

I spoke quietly, calmly. "I have to ask, Carty, why did you kill Roberta? She had done quite a lot for you in a short time. She was your go-to from the time you got out of the hospital in Vegas. Why did she have to be put down that way?"

Carty flared. "Well, she cost me a shitload of money for one thing. And she was so damn sloppy about that drug shit, I figgered she would get arrested in a few days, she'd turn on me, and I'd have to deal with all that shit all over again."

"That might have happened. The warrants for her had already been prepped. Her days of freedom were numbered. It still seems a bit harsh, though." I paused. "What about your kid?"

"Little fucker beat up my girl, raped her. I did away with that fuckin' beaner, too, and I'm not sad the kid got busted. He deserved it."

"Yeah, you guys did seem a bit short on familial warmth. Well, from my vantage, he looked to be headed down the same path you took. Hooked on drugs and using anyone who crossed his path. Yours has been a brutal life, Carty. There are a lot of things you need to answer for. Lotsa dead bodies there in the patch, plus the Connors, that P.I. in Jarupa, the Prosecutor's husband, that car dealer kid, right here at the ranch. Are there any more people you did away with in California?"

"Dropped that one piece o' shit slinger-wannabe from that plane, too. Don't forget him."

"Yeah, Grant, you are one mean mother. One of the meanest I've ever encountered. And we have to come to some final settlement on that. Nevada State cops want me to bring your ass to them on a silver platter. I told 'em I'd give that a hell of a try." I paused. "I'm bettin' you're not gonna make that easy for me, right? You do tend strongly toward self-preservation."

Carty chuckled. "Yeah, I guess I do. You know where I'm at."

"I do indeed. I'll see you soon."

Carty closed the phone and walked across the barn to the raised concrete pad that had served as the staging area when the cars were being packed for the transport of the drugs into California six years before. He grinned at the thought of the successes he'd seen back then and ran his fingers over the surface of his mostly-repaired face as he smiled. He felt good once again, after a long time, years really, when he hadn't felt anything at all. He stepped to the mirror next to the toilet near the side window of the barn and looked at his new face. It made him smile. He walked across the barn, stood next to the workbench, and tried to put his priorities in order.

His internal *to-do* list included getting his Bronco back into running order and figuring out where else to go next in case this pain-in-the-ass private cop decided to take him on. After he checked the fuel level in the big diesel generator behind the barn, he sat on the stool in the barn and considered his options. He sorted the firearms he'd acquired in Van Nuys that evening and positioned them next to doors and windows in case he had to defend the barn.

Carty rubbed the side of his face as he sorted the sockets in the top drawer of his big rolling tool-chest, then he stopped and looked around the barn. He walked over to the big old Bronco, then went to the compressor and hooked up the hoses so he could inflate the flattened off-road tires. Two of the three flats had separated from the bead of the big chrome rims, so that task would have to wait until he could jack the truck up and take the rims off. Everything there was covered with a half-inch of pale-beige dust and grit.

Halfway through the tasks, he stopped, walked back to the stool, and sat. It had been a long time since he'd done anything constructive. Suddenly he was tired, and the side of his face itched.

We had the plan mapped out, so Sarah, Zig, and I left the hotel at 4 am to make the trip to the ranch in the desert. I drove my Tahoe, Zig had his big cop-spec Excursion, and Sarah brought up the rear in her little red box thing. We used my previous staging area as a storage spot for the vehicles and climbed to the top of the abrupt foothills to reach my former camera perch, where we sat in the darkness and watched the barn. Carty's pickup was parked next to the side entrance door. There were signs of activity from inside the structure, and the big clear glass globe lamp above the side door burned brightly. Light seeped around the floor and panel openings from inside, and in the stark silence of the desert, I could hear the low hum of the diesel generator behind the barn. I gathered that Carty was busy preparing for our eventual meeting.

Our final plan was decided as we crouched at the top of the foothill in the darkness. The desert sky was its usual bright black, and the stars appeared to have been planted just out of reach. A few puffy clouds wandered across the western horizon. It was a beautiful night, and a stunning dawn approached. After an hour at the perch, we ascended back to the trucks to set the plan in motion. Zig packed a satchel from the back of his Excursion, slung a sighted rifle over his shoulder, and climbed back up to the camera perch, where he would remain as a ready observer of my interaction with Carty and provide intervention if needed. I would approach the barn at dawn in the big armored Ford and would attempt to charm Carty out of his secure hiding place. Sarah would be the ground back-up, parked at the road outside the driveway, ready to make her own tactical move when the time was right. She carried the arrest warrants from California, but I hoped the situation would be rectified before the possibility of that involvement presented itself. Nevada was holding warrants as well and was a capital punishment state that occasionally followed through.

I had wanted my approach to be a surprise to Carty, so I pulled the Excursion across the ditch alongside the driveway at its junction with the road, avoiding the electronic gate sentry built into the metal cattle guard. It wasn't a silent approach, the truck's big diesel engine thrumming away through twin 3-inch exhaust pipes as I crept down the driveway headed for the barn. Our team was joined by radio. Each of us wore earpieces with mics, so communication was not an issue.

As the driveway curved toward the ranch buildings at the crest of the mild slope toward the barn and house, I cut the engine and let the truck coast the hundred-plus feet to its stop in the middle of the driveway near the outer edge of the barn structure. I left the parking lights on and sat in the truck as the sun started its launch from the eastern horizon a little after six-thirty am. There was no hint of movement from within the house, but I suspected Carty was holed up in the barn, perhaps pulling an all-nighter.

At six thirty-five, Danny Tanner's copter began its oval circuit above, and he buzzed in to say "Hi." I always considered the distant background noise from his copter a comforting element.

At 6:44, my earpiece lit, and I heard Zig say, "One male exiting from the barn, C."

"Copy, Zig. Thanks."

I focused on the face of the structure as Grant Carty, dressed in khakis and a red sweatshirt, walked a few paces from the barn. I could not see any firearms on his person, but I knew that he was clever in the use of the property for hiding places. I heard Zig in my ear, "If he pulls a gun, Street, I have a shot."

"Copy, Z." I opened the door of the truck and climbed down to stand behind the sheet metal of the door. "Carty? How are things? We talked earlier. I'm Street. It's good to put a face to a name. You need to come with me. Let's get this over with, okay? It's gonna happen sooner or later, man. Let's get an early start."

"I have a better idea, Mister Street. Just inside the door of the barn is a big blue plastic bin with two million dollars in it. Turn around, walk away with that tub full of cash in the back of your truck. You forget me, I forget you, ever'body goes away happy. How 'bout it?"

"I appreciate you thinking of me, Carty, but I already collected two mill for finding you the first time. You do slippery rather well.

No, you need to keep that money and use it to pay for your legal defense."

"No defense necessary, Street. All that shit they say I did? I did it all and a lot more. And I have no intention of leavin' here vertical with you or anyone else. Take your best shot, dude. Come on and get me."

Carty stood a few feet in front of the side door to the barn. Above the door frame was a large clear antique light globe, probably original to the structure. Into my mic, I whispered, "Zig? Give him a pop and wake him up. Aim for that big clear light bulb, top of the door behind him."

"Copy, C." Five seconds later, a distant shot rang out, and the large clear glass lightbulb just above and behind Carty's head exploded. Carty jumped at the noise of the explosion that showered him with sparks and tiny glass shards. He re-opened the door and rushed inside. The door slapped closed, and the window next to it opened. The barrel of an AR-15 poked out and fired, a dozen bullets striking the side of the truck but going no further. I crouched against the front fender of the far side of the truck, shielded by the tire and the engine compartment. Zig fired twice more, taking out the left edge of the window frame. I looked over the hood of the truck at the window frame and called, "Carty? You're seriously outgunned, pard. You don't get to shoot anyone in the back this time. Let's wrap this up. Give yourself a break, come on out, hands over your—"

My modest proposal was answered with another burst from his '15. Zig popped off a couple of closely-targeted shots that widened the opening of the dried-out wooden barn wall that carried the frame of the window by about a foot. I heard a cry of pain from inside the barn. I took the opportunity to run across the space between the truck and the barn. I crouched next to Carty's F-150 beside the hinge side of the walk-in door, standing among the glass shards from the light bulb, waiting for Carty to come back out. I spoke into my mic, "Sarah, can you cut the power from the generator?"

"Copy, Street." From a distance, I heard the low ambient hum of the generator cease, followed by shuffling noises from inside the barn. There were five minutes of utter silence from within the barn.

I called, "Carty? Give it up, pard. You don't want to get hurt again. Come on out, man, hands above your head. It'll be easy."

After a minute, Zig said, "Street, I think I may have hit him. I see no motion from inside the barn. Let me come down to you, we can enter together."

"Copy, Zig. Sarah? Want to join us?

"That'll work. I'm on the east side of the barn." I looked at the sky to see the tiny, distant, slowly circling shape of Danny Tanner's copter. "Danny? You with us?"

With the accompanying hum of the copter, I heard, "Ready when you are, Street. Keep me posted." Sarah approached from my end of the barn and took a position behind me.

I called toward the door again. "Last chance, Carty! Give it up, man. Let's not drag this out any longer." There was no response. At the other end of the barn Zig—in desert camo and carrying his sniper rifle in a sling, his right hand carrying a machine-finished .40 caliber semi-auto pistol—walked the length of the barn, stopping at the other side of the window opening. From the far side of the opening, he quickly poked his head up to look inside. He looked back at me and made a finger slice across his throat, then closed his left eye for a minute to adapt his eyesight to the inner darkness of the barn. I did the same. At the minute mark, he held up three fingers and pointed at the door. Two fingers up, then one, then we rushed the door, crouching, crossing one another, firearms at the ready, heads on a swivel.

In the dark interior of the barn, I had to look around for a few seconds before I saw Carty's form below the open window, trembling, bleeding from the *new* side of his face, a variety of wood splinters and glass shards protruding from his scattered facial wounds. His gaze was fixed on his image in the dusty mirror near the casement window.

After discovering the figure and clearing the rest of the barn,

Zig opened the entrance door to allow some light into the interior. After I cuffed Carty, I went to the door and called up to Danny, "DT? Call the State guys and an ambulance. Carty is down, wounded, not life-threatening."

"Copy, Street."

---

So it really wasn't the boffo ending I had expected. It almost seemed anti-climactic. Carty was taken away by the Clark County Sheriff's deputies and Nevada Bureau of Investigation officers a couple of hours after the wrap of the semi-confrontation. I called and alerted Dierdre of the impending caravan exiting the ranch. Her station hired one of Tanner's birds to carry a local stringer, and Danny got face time on L.A. television acting as a *local authority*. Ah, show biz.

Zig, Sarah, and I finally left the Carty ranch a little after noon that day. The Clark County Sheriff's deputies, under the direction of newly promoted Senior Deputy Marshal Quince, had interviewed each of us separately, and we had passed muster with ease. A search of the barn showed Carty's cash reserves to be a little over four million bucks, untaxed. His facial wounds from the exploding light bulb and window frame would be pretty ugly but less than critical. He did have an eye injury from the exploding lamp. The glass shards and wood splinters had punctured his recently-completed cosmetic surgery areas in about two dozen places. The new side of his face now looked a bit edgy. The med crew cleaned the wounds, wrapped his face in gauze, and turned him over to the Clark County officers. It was a relief to me that a new crew was, at last, taking the security of the detainee very seriously. There would be no escape by Carty this time.

I walked over to Zig as he was examining his ex-MPAC Excursion for the bullet pocks that Carty had inflicted on it. The step plate exterior panels, fabricated by the L.A. County Sheriff's shop well over a decade ago, had lost a bit of paint, but there were no perceptible dents. Zig smiled and said, "Gives it some character, don't you think?"

In the end, Carty's defeat was a lot easier than I'd thought it would be. I'd expected fireworks in the desert, but it took only a couple of well-aimed *warning shots* to bring it all to a close. Thank God for small favors.

After we left the ranch, the three of us went for a late lunch at the cannery and talked about it. Sarah opined that Carty's spur-of-the-moment murder of Roberta had been a surprise even to him. Maybe he'd regretted it after all. One can hope.

# EPILOGUE

Back home in L.A. that next week, I spent two solid days giving statements and video depositions regarding the actions we had taken in the apprehension of multiple murderer Grant Carty. Some of our actions were considered sketchy by the desk-bound minions of officialdom, but all is well that does not end in indictments.

California and Nevada decided to engage in a tussle over custody of the eee-ville Carty. He had done many worse things in Nevada, but California felt that the prominence of the victims in the Golden State was higher, so they deserved to have him. My only comment was to remind everyone that Nevada was a death-penalty state and the place that actually had arrested and convicted O.J. Simpson, so they deserved precedence as much as Carty richly deserved the needle. The counterpoint was that in California, the victims had been prominent people—the Connors—famous, the Damarow kid—wealthy, and Roberta Thomas-Schwinn—attorney. We can't have people killin' lawyers, can we? In the end, he took a place on Nevada's Death Row. Yay team.

A month later, I received a check from the Attorney General's office in Nevada, the $250k reward that had eventually been posted for the capture of Grant Carty. By then, I had done the accounting of my expenses in the matter. I'd dropped a lot of money in the pursuit of Carty, but I didn't really mind the expenditure. Helping Sarah and ridding society of a few of its more negative aspects were pluses. The LAPD did help a bit, covering some of the direct expenses for Sarah, and I did adopt the electronics that Zig had sold me in the effort. The shop/apartment out in the backyard now has vertically-mounted tandem big screens.

Sarah spent a week at a resort in New Mexico and returned to L.A. to resume her new administrative duties. I'm happy that she's happy.

The rental house was emptied two months after Sarah returned from her vacation. Her house was cleaned, restored, de-corpsed, and sold within a month. She replaced it with a nice-but-kinda-cramped-place just off Griffith Park Boulevard. The driveway almost has enough room for her KIA.

Adam Fair remains a good friend though he did take a bit of heat for the method of takedown in the Trey Thomas capture. Word of the street racing ploy got out. We won't be doing that again right away.

Adam Fair and the gang squad detectives arranged a sting of Officer Comacho for his part in informing the gangs of sensitive information regarding LAPD staff. He was fired and arrested on the same afternoon in a ten-minute period. The media carried news of a *former LAPD officer* being arrested. There was a lot more to the story.

Trey was afforded a Public Defender after his mother was found murdered in the hotel parking lot in Burbank. Roberta had not returned the calls from the expensive West L.A. defense attorney with whom she had inquired, so no financial arrangements had been made. Bereft of potential remuneration, the high-powered defense attorney had lost interest in a nanosecond. High-end L.A. law is coin-operated. Sarah and I both testified at his trial. His eventual conviction for the attempted murder of a law enforcement officer, along with the drug charges, landed him a forty-year sentence. He got off easy.

Dierdre King and I took a thirteen-day vacation in Hawaii starting a week after the Carty arrest. We still disagree about televised car chases, and now she wants to hire Danny Tanner as the copter pilot for the coverage thereof. We may have gotten engaged. The jury's still out.

———————————

I leaned against the passenger side of the Tahoe that breezy day in mid-December as I waited for Dierdre to walk out of the elevator doors at the TV station. She smiled as she saw me. I always looked forward to that smile. She took the passenger seat and leaned across the console to kiss my cheek. I snicked the truck into gear, and we left the garage through the staff exit.

She looked stressed as we walked to the small, quaint café on Melrose. I asked her the problem as we waited in the foyer.

"The programmer for the station just plopped a task in my lap. The current evening weather girl just quit. No notice at all. I have a stack of resumes of potential candidates to examine before Friday. They all look like friggin' sorority girls, and their speaking voices are awful. Using the term *like* five times in a thirty-second conversation? Accchhh!"

"What are you looking for? Physical appearance, speaking voice, screen presence?"

"Yes! All of that, combined."

"Do you have any leading candidates?"

"No. They all look alike to me. Is that a sexist comment of some kind? Sorry." She frowned.

I thought of an acquaintance. "Are you taking any interviews? I may have a possible candidate for you. I could make a call and see if she's available."

"What's her background? You know what these women look like. Would she fit in?"

"Oh, she's a looker. Pretty girl from a small town in Tennessee. Teaching degree, so some speaking experience there. She came out here after she and a fiancé broke up. She's twenty-five or so, I think. She's, um, on leave from her public relations gig that wasn't working out all that well for her. Sweet kid. She deserves a break."

"Sounds good. How do you know her?"

I didn't lie. "I encountered her in the course of the Carty takedown."

Dierdre frowned. "You dated her?'

"Absolutely not! I only have eyes for you."

She smiled. "Do you like her?" We followed the hostess to our table and took our seats.

"That's a loaded question, isn't it?" Dierdre grinned and nodded. "Okay. I do. She looks great, she's poised. I think she'd be an excellent screen presence. This would be a good bridge for her, and I think she'd knock it out of the park, meteorologically speaking. Her southern accent would work well, too. It's cute. She's no Dierdre King, of course, but she's very good in her own way." I paused, frowned, then added, "Am I talking myself out of this situation adequately?"

She looked at me and grinned. "Yes. You are. Do you have her number?"

"I do." The waiter led us to our table, and we took our seats. Dierdre looked at me.

"Well...okay. You win. Call her and have her get in touch with me. Fresh faces would be a welcome change. I like the idea,"

"I'll do that. Whew! That was work! What are we having for lunch?"

# ACKNOWLEDGMENTS

Many thanks to longtime friend Gary Schmidt for getting me started, Rob Lund—California Highway Patrol—for keeping me going, Attorneys Dave Beuoy and Bill Barrett for moral support and encouragement, and the late Mike Connors—Joe Mannix to the rest of us—for the inspiration.

# A LOOK AT BOOK THREE:
## WHERE THERE'S A WILL

**A DETECTIVE BEFORE HIS TIME.**

In this prequel to the first two C Street Mystery books, L.A. Private Investigator Street's assignment is simple—locate an estranged sister for a midwestern man who wants to grant her a share of their late parents' sizable estate.

But when Street discovers that the sister changed her name almost twenty years ago and became a famous actress, his strait-laced case becomes more arduous. Even more so after a lethal attempt is made on the movie star's life.

Surrounded by an actress with secrets of her own and a man looking more suspicious than at-first glance, Street is stuck in a race against time to solve his investigation before someone gets hurt beyond repair...

*AVAILABLE AUGUST 2023*

# ABOUT THE AUTHOR

Tennessee native Rick Rothermel grew up in Huntsville, Alabama and lived in Southern California after a decade split between Alaska and Oregon. He was a columnist and freelance contributor for automotive magazines for twenty years and worked in the TV and movie production industry, specializing in automotive subjects. Classic TV and literature of the detective genre are hobbies that led to the creation of the C STREET MYSTERY series.